Haunted Worlds

riaH gnoL

Haunted Worlds

Jeffrey Thomas

Introduction by Ian Rogers

Hippocampus Press

New York

Published by Hippocampus Press
P.O. Box 641, New York, NY 10156.
http://www.hippocampuspress.com

Cover painting "Nightmare Sentinels–the Nightmare Grove"
© 2017 by Kim Bo Yung. Courtesy of the Stephen Romano Gallery.
Frontispiece "riaH gnoL" © 2017 by Kim Bo Yung. Cover design
by Kevin I. Slaughter.

Hippocampus Press logo designed by Anastasia Damianakos.

First Edition
1 3 5 7 9 8 6 4 2

ISBN 978-1-61498-197-8

Contents

Introduction

Jeffrey Thomas haunts me.

Most of the time I'm okay with that. Sometimes I even think it's a good thing. I've been a fan of Thomas's work for years, from his standalone works of horror to the stories set in his sprawling monstropolis of Punktown. As a reader, I am an ardent fan. As a writer, I am in a perpetual state of awe.

The title of this new collection is appropriate for several reasons. Thomas has established himself as a creator of worlds, a dark architect not just of cities but of lives. Whether it's Punktown, Hades, or Boneland, his worlds come alive because of the people he creates to live in them. Punktown is revisited here, but Thomas has upped his already considerable game by exploring inner landscapes of the human soul that are no less dark and unsettling.

We live in a world of doubles: our waking lives and our sleeping lives; our work lives and our home lives; day and night; love and hate. No matter how bad things may get, we're told that it's always darkest before the dawn, that tomorrow is another day. But what if the day never comes? What if our lives are left to the darkness of a never-ending night? Or what if the day comes but nothing changes, nothing is better? Can the sun shine in the sky and still leave us drowning in darkness?

We may not want to consider such things, but Jeffrey Thomas does. I don't know if that makes him foolish or brave. I suspect it's a bit of both. As an author you could say it's an occupational hazard. I'm torn between wanting to pull him back from the brink of this dark gulf and letting him go on so he can report back on what he finds. If he comes back.

The theme of duality in *Haunted Worlds* is present at the outset, in the table of contents, which groups the stories into two sections, "Our

World" and "Other Worlds." But this is more than a categorization. In fact, the worlds presented in these stories have a great deal in common. In some cases, so much so that it suggests there is really only one world, a haunted landscape with no delineated borders. Such things may not seem possible, or are they? It would seem so to the protagonist of "Spider Gates," who says: "a thing can exist in two places, and in two forms, at one time."

One would do well to remember that upon entering the bifurcated realm of Thomas's imagination. We are not readers; we are travelers, pioneers. Moving through lands of dark and light, love and hate, looking for the path, like the road between the two bodies of water in "The Left-Hand Pool"—one teeming with life, the other a stagnant quagmire of decay.

People can be haunted, too. Not just by ghosts, but by feelings, memories, regrets. The things they lack or, like the protagonist in "Carrion," the things they've lost. These stories are populated by broken people, broken hearts, and broken lives. Thomas doesn't truck in anything so banal as good or evil. Despite his penchant for opposing forces, there is no black and white to be found here. There is only gray—the color of ash, the color of the past.

Thomas has learned, as we all must learn, that life is a series of shades. Through his work we come to understand that there are those who welcome the dark, who welcome the end with open arms. The thought of pain may be feared, but its arrival can be seen as a gift, a mercy. Pain is simply another type of haunting. For the scarred protagonist in "Saigon Dep Lam" pain is loneliness, the thought of never making a connection with a man she sees wandering the streets. She follows him, she *haunts* him, and becomes the ghost.

One of Thomas's strengths as a writer (and he has many) is his ability to create realistic characters who exist whole and breathing in fantastical settings. This is perhaps best displayed in the dual-novella "The Green Hands," beating at the center of the book like a black, double-chambered heart. In addition to providing the connective tissue between Thomas's haunted worlds—a feat of literary bilocation that caused me more than one sleepless night—the story also presents an idea that is horrifying both in its implications and its believability:

that there is no escape from the numinous, that every world is haunted in some way, that we carry our ghosts with us wherever we go.

Perhaps that is the most frightening aspects of Thomas's work: the realization that there is no protection from the forces that haunt our lives, no succor even in death. The truth that comes with such knowledge is that these haunted worlds are not only connected, but may in fact be shades of a single world—a frail, broken reality where everything is gray.

But there is hope in Thomas's *Haunted Worlds*. It is perhaps fitting that the story that closes the collection is titled "Redemption Express." I do not think this was an accident. For all the darkness that fills these stories, there is a promise of light at the end of the tunnel. But is it a promise or is it merely something else that will elude us in the end?

As I said: Jeffrey Thomas haunts me.

He will do the same to you.

You can thank me for it later.

—IAN ROGERS

Peterborough, Ontario

PART ONE: OUR WORLD

Carrion

Lambert had never in his fifty-five years lived in a rural area, but he did now. Back roads carved through woods that just seemed too dense for central Massachusetts, unaccountably curvy as if they twisted up mountainsides. At night on some of these wooded stretches there was no light from houses—indeed, there were no houses—and there were no streetlights, so that sometimes he couldn't see anything beyond the reach of his headlights, feebly pushing back all that blackness like the beams of a bathysphere. Just unbroken double yellow lines unspooling before him, seemingly unto infinity. As a boy, riding in his father's car at night, he would imagine the broken white line of the road was a stream of energy beams being fired ahead of their fighter spacecraft. Back then he could trick his eyes to perceive the white segments as flying away from the moving car, rather than toward it. It had only been an illusion, though. In truth, the white dashes didn't carry a rider forward with them, but trailed away behind to vanish.

Lambert felt somewhat exiled out here. His wife, an attractive Filipina fifteen years younger than himself, had met a man four years younger than herself, and now Lambert's house was gone along with his marriage. He had stayed on in the city, paying too much for too little in his one-bedroom flat. Last month he'd finally roused himself to move from the city where he'd spent nearly his entire life, having found that apartments tended to be less expensive out here, in a region he had always derided as "the sticks." One of the young men who had moved him into his new place—a second-floor apartment in a large house divided into four units—had confided, "You'll like it in this town . . . there aren't any blacks or Asians." Lambert had wanted to say there would have been one Asian, if she hadn't divorced him.

Today on his drive to work he noticed a dead animal on the right side of the road, where it had been thrown by impact or crawled to die.

It was curled away from him, head and limbs and tail—if it had one—tucked out of sight from his viewpoint, leaving just a rounded shape. Almost ball-like. It was maybe the size of a cat, but too plump, and he could tell it was not a cat or small dog by its coloration. It didn't have fur that was black, or white, or brown, but actually a kind of equal mix of all those colors; the coloration of a wild thing that needed to blend into shadows and leaf litter. This grainy color gave the fur the coarse appearance of an animal that had not been bred for petting.

But if Lambert had been pushed to describe the carcass as being of a single color, he would have settled on gray.

*

Lambert didn't know her name, but from her dark complexion and general aspect he assumed she was Indian, though she had no detectable accent that he had discerned when he saw her in the cafeteria at first break or at lunch, exchanging small talk with coworkers or the cashier. He also presumed, since she worked somewhere upstairs, that she was part of the company's extensive human resources branch, while he himself worked on the ground floor helping manage the data storage company's inventory, which for him meant mostly disk drives. (Sometimes he would bring to the shipping dock, on a hand truck, a pallet of boxed disk drives exceeding the value of the house he had lost in his divorce.) He often thought of these human resources people upstairs as Eloi and the downstairs people like himself as Morlocks—or, as his friends put it, inhuman resources.

Sometimes when he and this woman made eye contact in the cafeteria—and he often, probably too often, stared at her from his table until she did make eye contact—she would smile at him, her white teeth and dark eyes shining as brightly as when she smiled at her sharply dressed coworkers. Then other times she'd avert her eyes quickly, looking uncomfortable or even, he worried, perturbed. What was he to make of this?

She was very short, and very cute, with shoulder-length black hair. Late twenties, early thirties? While there was a good number of attractive female employees of all ages and ethnicities working in the company, he found himself watching for the Indian woman in particular at each break. His taste had always run toward more, dare he say, *exotic* manifestations of beauty, as his ex-wife might demonstrate. His two immediate coworkers—seated with him at their usual table like judges at a beauty contest—avidly followed the strutting appearance of taller, blonder women. Lambert would whisper appreciatively along with his friends, never telling them that it was only the unnamed Indian woman whose appearance he was truly enthusiastic about.

God, he would wonder, why did he still feel this way at his age? Was it that he still possessed a healthy sexual appetite, or was it simply (*simply?*) that he was lonely? Either way, he was fifty-five; he would have thought that he'd be past such concerns. He supposed it had a lot to do with having something, *anything* to look forward to each day, to help break up his stultifying work routine. After all, he'd had better jobs—more rewarding financially, and in every other way. But those jobs had gone the way of, well, everything else that he'd lost.

He kept an eye out for her today as always, while he ate his breakfast of cereal, which he brought in with him to save money and to help regulate his weight. (In the past, every morning he'd had the cook behind the counter make him an omelet or egg sandwich.) He was always careful not to drink the remaining milk from his bowl while she was around, lest she think he was crude. Ah . . . and here she came now.

But as fate would have it, in fate's typically sadistic way, he felt an irritating tickle in his left eye just as he saw her enter the cafeteria. It had to be a detached or bent eyelash. He rubbed at his eye, but that only seemed to make the itchiness worse. The tickle turned into something more insistent, and though he was afraid to scratch his cornea, he kept rubbing at it. Finally he pinched his eyelid and pulled it away from his eye, hoping to dislodge the lash or bit of grit that was harassing him.

When his eye finally felt clear again, she had already passed his table. Leaning around one of his friends, he saw her standing at the counter, ordering something from the cook. She always requested eggs, or pancakes, or something else substantial. Her body was compact, meaty, humanly imperfect, and he liked that. It made her—seemingly, at least—more accessible.

Today, when she crossed the room again to carry her tray of food back to her own work area—rather than dine with the Morlocks—it was the quickly averted gaze and the perhaps disapproving little frown.

Lambert's eye felt burned and sore from all his rubbing. He felt burned and sore inside as well.

*

When next he spotted the dead animal, it looked the same: a plump ball of coarse black/white/brown grayness, almost as serene as if it were merely taking a nap. Peacefully hibernating in plain view, as it were. It was September, after all, the air becoming cool, and maybe the ants and flies were feeling too sluggish to set to work on it. But in any case, there it was in the same spot, like a stone set down as a mile marker, a kind of landmark, placed precisely at the border where the road met the edge of the woods. Straddling worlds.

*

Because she was curvy, Lambert didn't notice right away that the perhaps-Indian woman's belly was becoming rounder, until one day it was simply unmistakable—as if she had leapt into her second trimester overnight. He'd considered that she might be married, and yet it was a disappointment to realize her condition. Seeing her pregnant was like seeing her strut into the cafeteria wearing a T-shirt that proclaimed "I HAVE FUCKED." It made him irrationally jealous, irrationally hurt, as if scorned. As if he had been cheated on, cuckolded all over again.

Previously, Lambert had mostly just fantasized about kissing her, holding hands with her while they walked through a mall or museum, basking in her avowals of love. Now, as if for the first time, he imagined what she looked like when she was making love . . . the expression on her face. Did she smile dreamily, as some women did? Or contort her face as if physically pained, as some women did? Did she cry out? Did she stifle all sound?

Her husband must be so much younger than him . . . like the man his wife had left him for. Recently, noticing in his new bathroom mirror with its row of harsh light bulbs the way his lips had become thinner in recent years and the flesh around his chin had begun to sag, he had started growing a mustache and goatee so as to mask these changes. But the coarse facial hair grew in stark white, whereas the hair on his head was a salt-and-pepper mix of black and white. Though if he had to use only one word to describe the color of his hair, it would be gray.

Because it only made him look older, he had shaved off his white mustache and goatee.

He watched the woman cross the cafeteria with her tray of food. He could smell it as she passed, taunting him as he hunched over his cardboard cereal. Eating for two; now he understood. She didn't smile at him, nor did she glance at him and look away. She didn't acknowledge him at all. And yet, despite that, and despite her pregnant state, he was attracted to her all the more.

She was bearing new life. What could be more vital, more sensual, than that?

*

When he'd first moved in here, the glossy wood floors had been gritty with dirt, as if the college student who'd been the previous occupant had never once swept them. Lambert had spent hours sweeping, vacuuming, then washing the golden boards prior to the move, and in the course of that he'd found dead bugs on the floor: large moths, and even an alarmingly sizable spider stuck to the wood as if it had been there for a very long time, preserved in amber. Had the boy propped the door open while he'd moved his furniture out? It seemed too much even for that scenario.

Furthermore, even after his eight-hour cleaning session and the move, one night in his first week of occupancy Lambert had found a dead cricket in his bed. He had never heard a single chirp in his apartment. Had he rolled over and crushed the poor thing before it could sing a note? And then, several days later, he found a second cricket under his quilt. But when he picked this one up, it seemed lighter, a mere hollow husk. Did crickets molt their old skins? Was this a couple that had mated and then died together, under his unconscious godlike body, or two halves of the same creature? A self and a shadow self?

*

The roadkill was finally starting to look a bit less plump, more deflated, like a pregnancy in reverse. What processes, what *creatures,* were at work inside it? he wondered. Only microscopic entities, or a stubborn autumnal swarm of bugs? Idle thoughts to pass the time as he drove toward his latest bout of monotony.

His ear itched deep inside, the way it had tickled years ago when his wife would tease him by inserting one of the long black hairs growing from her head into his ear when he was almost asleep. He reached up to dig a finger in his ear, and he thought he felt a whispery touch brush across his knuckle when he did so . . . but the sensation withdrew, and he returned his hand to the wheel.

*

Today she wore a tight black top under her open blouse. The black top made her belly—again, seemingly swollen much larger overnight— look taut and hard like a ripe fruit. Munching his cereal, Lambert wondered if the orb of her stretched skin was just as smooth and perfect as that epidermis of black fabric. Never having had children with his wife, he wondered what sex with his coworker would be like. He wouldn't want to lie directly on top of her and press down on the fetus. Maybe they would lie on their sides, then, in a V, with just their legs entangled, like twins conjoined at the lower body.

With his organ separated from the child only by thin membranes, as he rhythmically churned its mother's insides right in front of its tiny face, would it smile smugly and speak to his mind telepathically? "You know this is only a dream. *My father* fucks her. Not you, old man."

In her constricting top, Lambert thought her ball-like belly resembled a giant black egg. And he pictured that egg stuffed full, stuffed hard, with countless black insects with jaws like stag beetles . . . fresh life just waiting to burst upon the world as if from Pandora's box. To feed upon the rotting carrion of all that had gone before them.

*

The body of the dead, unknown animal was finally just a sack, a collapsed hollow hide like that molted cricket he had discovered in his bed. But this morning, just as his car was swooshing past it, from inside the carcass two long feelers emerged, whip-like and twitching, maybe probing the air for vibrations. As if they somehow sensed that Lambert was aware of them, they were yanked back down into the diminished remains in a flash.

Lambert snapped his head around to look back over his shoulder, but his vehicle drifted over the double yellow lines, and a car traveling in the opposite lane honked at him. He faced forward again, startled, and continued on his way to work.

*

One night he was awakened, though not entirely, by a tickling sensation in his anus. He tried to dismiss it—probably one of his own hairs, or maybe an errant thread of his boxer shorts—but it was as niggling as if someone playing a half-mischievous, half-sadistic prank were tickling him with a feather. It was like something his wife might have done, but of course he lay alone in the darkness.

Finally, coming a little bit further awake, he reached his hand down inside his boxer shorts to itch himself there, though he was as reluctant as if it were another man's body he was being compelled to touch. As his fingers found the area, the tickling sensation passed over his thumb. He made an instinctive grab for whatever it was, a horrible image bursting into his imagination as if lit by a camera's flash. In his mind's eye, he saw a long intestinal parasite—a roundworm or tapeworm—sneaking a look out of him when it thought he was asleep. His hand closed around something, string-thin and all but insubstantial, but it was sucked through his fist and then gone. Seemingly sucked back inside him.

Lambert scrambled out of bed, into the bathroom, slapped on the light, and felt at his nether region. He spread himself open with his fingers, twisting his upper body around awkwardly to try to get a look at his lower half in the mirror. He might have laughed at that man in the mirror . . . if it hadn't been himself.

He found no trace, no evidence, of what he had experienced, and in the stark light of the bathroom, with his adrenaline-flushed body fully alert, he asked himself if it had only been a hair or thread or purely his half-dreaming imagination after all.

He glanced at the time. It was still pitch-dark outside, but it was already five-thirty in the morning. He'd have to be up and getting ready for work in another half hour anyway.

With a heavy, soul-shuddering sigh, he trudged into his kitchen to make coffee.

*

He still took first break in the caf, but at lunch break—instead of sitting with his friends and waiting for the appearance of the Indian woman, trying to make eye contact with her without being too overt about it, and hoping she might follow that up with conversation even though it was entirely irrational to think she would want to do that— he had taken to napping in his car.

He was exhausted from sleeping poorly recently. Sometimes those stealthy, tentative appendages seemed to emerge from his ear, his nostril, or even from his tear ducts, probing at his face. He had snapped awake one night to feel a thread being withdrawn quickly down the back of his throat. He had bounded out of bed, rushed to the bathroom, and gargled with mouthwash as if to chase the retreating invader with vengeful pesticide.

He then stared at his shirtless body in the mirror. His saggy breasts, his rumpled flesh. His hairy belly seemed to be swelling by the day, as if he were expecting, too. Could his guts be full of round-worms?

He considered making a doctor's appointment, but in his heart of hearts he knew essentially what his doctor would tell him. That the only thing that infested him was mortality.

*

One day, the Indian/Eloi woman stopped coming to work. Was it that time already? It had all seemed to go so fast. Maybe she'd found another job, Lambert considered, but that was unlikely in her gravid state. No ... time simply had its way of speeding along, as the earth hurtled and spun at unthinkable velocities.

He gazed at other women, hoping someone else in particular would fire his fancy, someone who would make it just that little bit more bearable facing the daily commute, the crawling hours at his computer and boxing up disk drives. He watched, but so far no one else seemed an especially promising contender. Again, there were plenty of attractive women of all types at his company, but no one who inspired him in the same inexplicable way. Maybe he was just becoming too tired, in every sense, to rouse himself once more to such extremes of yearning.

Sleep hadn't gotten much better. The tickling, probing sensation persisted. Maybe because he expected it now. Perhaps it was psychosomatic, he told himself, the way one becomes itchy with imaginary bugs after finding a real specimen on one's body. A spectral giant tick seemed to be sucking away his life essence, a little bit more each night, each morning leaving him that much more shriveled and gray.

*

Somehow the dead animal's carcass still lingered at the roadside, but then it must only be the equivalent of an empty fur glove by now. If it had seemed a mixed sort of gray before, it was absolutely gray now, and nothing more . . . a washed-out anti-color, as if not only the flesh and juices but the very pigments of the animal had been consumed by the insects and much smaller organisms that had feasted on it.

As Lambert came up on the animal—he was actually watching for its appearance—he tightened his grip on the steering wheel involuntarily, as if he had a foreshadowing that this time he would witness something more. And sure enough, there they were: those two wavering feelers he had seen that other time, wire-thin but rigid, rising up from inside the tattered skin like twin curious periscopes. But it didn't end there. Following these feelers, these antennae, an entire body pulled itself out of the carcass as if it were shedding an exoskeleton it had outgrown.

It was an immense beetle, maybe bigger even than the furry animal had been in life. The monstrous insect was entirely a smoky, ghostly gray. Its barbed front mandibles were spread wide, like a bear trap waiting to be sprung.

Lambert's fists, squeezing the wheel, made another involuntary movement. This time, they turned the wheel sharply to the right. His instinctive reaction was to kill that creature before it could harm someone. Before it could breed more life like itself. He meant to crush it under his tires.

As if he'd been jarred out of a nightmare, only at the last moment was he able to jerk the wheel the other way and stamp down on his brake. The nose of the car narrowly missed scraping across the trunk of one of the many trees that lined the wooded back road. With a jolt that rocked him forward against his seatbelt, his vehicle came to a stop.

The car that had been riding behind him honked long and loudly at him, in alarm or irritation, as it whooshed past.

Lambert sat there for several minutes, as more cars passed him obliviously. He wanted to get out to see if he had succeeded in running over the monstrous beetle, but he was afraid to leave the safety of his vehicle. What if he hadn't struck it, or it was only superficially injured and was waiting to come scuttling at him? What if even now it was climbing up onto his idling car or hiding in the undercarriage, waiting to be borne along as a parasite?

He got his car moving forward again, toward his workplace. He glanced nervously into his rearview mirror, raising himself from his seat to do so, but he saw nothing behind him . . . not even the leeched scrap of dead animal.

He kept moving, faster than he normally drove, even though he knew there was no running away from this creature.

Not for him. Not for anyone.

Not when its kind was already at work inside him.

Spider Gates

This all happened when I was a teenager. That may be significant. It's an in-between time—between the worlds of children and adults. As if those are physical locations: the neighborhoods of childhood and adulthood. Sorry, that was a joke. But it's true, and we all know that time is a place.

I was fifteen, specifically. This was, God, twenty-five years ago. So my brother Christopher was ten.

We lived in Spencer, in that thick band called Worcester County right in the middle of Massachusetts. Every Labor Day weekend we had—and they still have—the Spencer Fair, a county fair that demonstrates that rednecks don't just live out west. That was a joke, too. I loved Spencer and I'd still live there if I didn't live here, but I can never go back again. It's not because of any bad memories, just the directions that our lives take us, sometimes too far to retrace. To me Spencer is bound with my teenage years and my childhood, too. As I said: a time and place that are far behind me.

My father was chief of security at a big abrasives company in Worcester, and my mom worked for Mass Electric, so we lived comfortably in a big house on a pretty back road. We had a sizable back yard and a deck looking out on it, so there was many a summer cookout . . . and my mom being Italian, there were relatives visiting every Sunday after church. Right up into fall they'd sit out on the deck: Mom and her parents and some aunts and cousins having coffee and *pizelles* that my grandmother had made. They'd watch over Christopher as he played with all his *Star Wars* action figures and the like in the yard.

Christopher was autistic. Well, he still is, of course, and he still lives with my mom and dad, but my parents left behind that time and place themselves. After my grandfather passed away and my father developed health issues and had to stop working, they sold the house in

Spencer and moved into my grandmother's smaller house in Worcester. There is only a postage stamp of a yard there, so the parties are all indoors. Christopher has a nice room of his own, and these days he likes to spend most his time in there on his computer, laughing at the same handful of videos on YouTube over and over. But he does have a job, bagging groceries at Price Chopper.

When my folks can no longer care for him, I'll take Christopher in myself. I know my husband John isn't crazy about that idea, but he knows that's just the way it is. It's not that he doesn't care about Christopher, and I understand how he feels, but why should my brother live in an adult-care situation when he has blood family? And I want my son, who's fifteen now himself, to always keep his uncle's welfare in mind when he's an adult. That is to say, if anything ever happens to me so that I can't care for my brother myself any longer. That doesn't mean my son has to have Christopher live with him . . . I just want him to be certain that his uncle is doing okay, wherever he is. And I'm sure he will, because my son has always known how important my kid brother is to me.

To Christopher, I don't think time is as much a concrete place as it is for me. There isn't that neat boundary between childhood and adulthood. There isn't even a distinct barrier, in his mind, between reality and fantasy. It's more like a low stone wall, overgrown with leaves and half tumbled down, that you can step over quite easily.

*

I wasn't a wild teenager, in the smoking pot and drinking kind of way—I never even smoked a cigarette—but I made up for all that with being boy crazy. I lost my virginity at fourteen. Don't tell my mom because she doesn't know that, and she'd still give me an earful even though I'm now forty.

My fifteenth birthday party was of course held out on the beautiful deck my dad and grandfather had built themselves, but we left the adults up there to chatter while we played horseshoes in the yard. For girls, there was my cousin Angela, my new friend Tracey, my best friend Megan, and our friend Beth, who was so pretty I wished looked like her—so pretty that my envy was more like a crush. She was that "every girl wants to be her, every boy wants to have her" girl. I would have hated her if she hadn't been so nice to me.

The boys at my party were my cousin Tony, Megan's boyfriend Brad, and Derek, who I *did* have a mad crush on, though Derek clearly liked Beth. Beth was definitely lucky I didn't hate her.

At fifteen boys act like absolute asses to impress the girls, loud and boisterous, and Brad and Derek were going all out. Wrestling around with each other and even with us girls seemed to be a major tool in their skill set for winning females' favor. The wrestling got a bit out of hand and my mom quelled that by yelling at us from the deck, so our boy-girl interactions grew more subdued: giggling at suggestive comments, and mock insults to replace the physical stuff. Teasing aggression, still, to mask the romantic impulse.

Part of that aggressive flirtation took the form of trying to scare each other, and that was when Derek started telling us about Spider Gates.

"Ooh, I've heard of that place," Megan said.

"Yeah," Tracey concurred, nodding with sudden solemnity.

I hadn't though, and I asked, "What is it?"

"You haven't heard of Spider Gates?" Megan bugged her eyes at me, aghast, as if I'd just confessed I didn't know how babies were made. Huh—and she was the virgin, not me.

"No, bitch, so tell me!"

Derek, seemingly the expert, said, "Oh, man, I'm surprised you don't know." He turned to point into the thick woods that bordered the rear of my yard, a contrast to the grass my dad kept as neat as Astroturf. The pine trees there seemed to form a wall. There was, in fact, a very old stone wall bordering our property at that point—one of the countless stone walls that trace through Massachusetts like corpse veins, marking out old properties that don't exist anymore, yards and farmlands where the invisible ghosts of dead houses might still stand.

Derek went on, "If you walked right into these woods, you'd eventually come to Spider Gates."

"I forget," Megan asked. "Is it in Spencer?"

"Leicester," Derek told her. Leicester lay against Spencer the way the thick woods lay against my back yard. Then facing me again: "You've never gone into your own woods back here?"

"Not very far. Why would I?"

"Looking for Bigfoot," my cousin Tony suggested.

"So what the hell is Spider Gates?" Brad demanded, punching Derek in the arm to keep him focused.

"Spider Gates is an old cemetery," Megan told her boyfriend, cutting in. "Like, from the seventeen-hundreds. Those people made it . . . you know, on the oatmeal box?"

"What?" Angela laughed.

"Quakers," Beth said quietly.

She was the shy one, besides being so pretty. Megan had told me, in whispers, that Beth wasn't happy at home. Her mother had divorced and remarried, and she apparently didn't care for her stepfather. Beth had struck me as being sad a lot—if not always sad, in her reserved way—and maybe that was part of why she seemed so beautiful to me: sadness can make people appear poetic or wistful, when in reality what they're feeling is pain.

"Yeah," Derek resumed, taking back the conversation. "Anyway, this cemetery is way back in the woods there. It's hard to find, but my brother and his friends found it once and told me all about it."

"So you've never been there yourself?" Brad laughed.

"Shut up and listen, man. The place has eight gates, metal gates that look like spiderwebs. If you go through every gate, one after another, when you go through the last gate you'll disappear into hell. That's why Satan-worshippers hold rituals in there all the time."

"Come *on,*" Brad said.

"Listen, lots of people know about this stuff! There's this little hill, an altar right in the middle of the place, where they do their sacrifices. People say when you're in Spider Gates you can hear these loud rumbling roars, from demons in the woods. And this weird white crap comes seeping up right out of the ground. That whole place is evil."

"Yeah . . . those devil-worshipping Quakers," Brad said, "with their damn oatmeal! That must be what's seeping out of the ground."

Everyone laughed, but Derek was doggedly determined to freak us out. "I'm not kidding. We should go there sometime, all of us. All kinds of things happen in that area. One kid hanged himself from a tree in the graveyard, and another time not far away they found a girl who was murdered and shoved into an old root cellar. And then down this old dirt road nearby there's an abandoned house with a rusty old car out front with no wheels, and sometimes when you see the house the car isn't there, and then the next time you see it the car will be back again."

Megan jumped back in: "There're these rocks in the ground all around the outside of the graveyard, and if you flip them over you'll find magic symbols carved in them . . . maybe to summon evil into the graveyard. Or maybe to keep evil forces trapped inside, so they can't get out."

The rest of us had gradually grown more quiet. Derek was achieving the desired effect at last, and our imaginations were joining in his efforts.

At some point ten-year-old Christopher had wandered close to us, from where he had been playing alone in another part of the yard. He stood quietly behind me positioning and repositioning the limbs of the action figure he was holding, seemingly preoccupied—in that world of his own I could never quite imagine—but I felt he was also listening to Derek and Megan with the rest of us.

Derek said, "There's one grave, for this guy named Marmaduke . . ."

"Marmaduke is a dog," Christopher said behind me.

"Shh," I told him.

". . . and if you walk in a circle around Marmaduke's grave ten times at midnight, then you kneel down and put your ear to the gravestone, Marmaduke's ghost will talk to you."

"Christ," Tracey said, hugging herself with a shudder.

"And how did someone discover that?" Brad laughed. "Did Marmaduke tell them? But how could he tell them, if you didn't do the ritual first to get him to talk?"

Megan slapped his arm and said, "Listen, there's more! Near Spider Gates, deeper in the woods, is another cemetery—a smaller one—and maybe you'll find it once, but if you do you'll never find it a second time."

"That's it—I've got to see this Spider Gates," Tony said.

"Are you crazy?" his sister Angela said. "I wouldn't go near a place like that."

"Come on," Tony insisted, "we all need to go."

"Christopher can go to Spider Gates," my brother said behind me. Back then he always referred to himself by name, instead of saying "I" or "me."

"You aren't going, silly," I shushed him. I always felt guilty for it later, but I was often afraid he was going to embarrass me in front of my friends. "Go play on the deck now, okay?"

Dutifully, Christopher turned away and trudged off toward the deck where the adults were having their coffee.

"I don't believe any of it," I finally said.

"You're just *afraid* to believe it, bitch!" Megan said. Best-friend talk—got to love it.

"Okay, so let's go right now," Brad said, turning toward the woods at the back of my property.

"Hang on," I said. "If it's such a long walk and we'll be gone a while, my folks will get pissed."

"Afraid!" Megan pronounced.

Tony asked Derek, "Just how far into the woods is it?"

"Hey, I don't know exactly. I just know it's in the woods."

"You sure it's *these* woods?"

"Okay, look, I'll talk to my brother about it again to be sure where it is. Then when we know more, we'll plan a trip someday and we'll all go explore there together—all right?"

"Yeah, ask him," Tony said, "because I really need to see this crazy place."

My cousin Angela tapped her brother on the side of his head. "The crazy place is right here."

Beth looked over at me then and smiled—that sad, pretty smile of hers that I envied so much, and which I can still see to this day, like a white stone set in the flowing brook of time.

*

The day of my party was actually quite cool for September, a prelude to autumn, and my father had used this as an excuse to light up our wood-burning stove for the first time since last winter. We could smell its smoke outside as the party broke up. The last of my friends to leave was Beth, waiting for her mother to pick her up, but she was late. The adults had all moved inside, and so Beth and I sat alone on the deck as the sun lowered behind the tops of the trees massed beyond the edge of our property. Christopher still played behind me in the yard.

"I've been to Spider Gates one time," Beth confessed to me.

"What—you have? When?"

"My father took me once. He heard about it, too, so he thought we should check it out. My dad's cool like that. My *real* dad," she stressed. "It's in Leicester, like Derek says, but like on the opposite side of Spencer from here . . . there's no way you could reach it from these woods." She pointed past me toward the rear of the yard. "It's not too far from Worcester Airport. You know how Derek said people hear demons roaring in the forest? It's probably just planes taking off from the airport. You know how people like to let their imaginations go wild."

"Why didn't you say anything when the others were here?" I asked her.

She shrugged and smiled. "I didn't want to spoil the fun."

"But is it really scary like Derek and Megan say?"

"Well, I guess any cemetery is scary. Especially deep in the woods—and it *is* in the woods. But all those stories . . . wow. Like, it doesn't really have eight gates—it only has one."

"But is it really a spiderweb gate?"

"The designs looked more like metal wagon wheels to me." She wiggled her fingers. "Though the spokes *are* kind of wavy, like spider legs I guess."

Despite having become nervous by the end of Derek's story, I felt disappointed at Beth's description. Of course all that creepiness had been too good to be true. "So I wonder what's really back there in our woods, if you go in far enough."

Beth shrugged again. "Same as any woods if you go in deep enough. You come out the other side, where there are just more people." She said it as if that was the greatest disappointment of all. More people. Well, they say hell is other people.

Beth looked beyond me again, and her gaze seemed to latch onto something. "Hey . . ." she began.

I twisted around in my seat and sighted Christopher in the purplish gloom, looking distant and indistinct at the edge of the grass where it met the trees. He was peering into the woods as if he intended to step over the bordering wall. "Christopher!" I shouted to him. "Get back over here right now! I'll tell Mom if you go in those trees!"

He turned around—his small pale face seeming to float—and started crossing the grass slowly toward the deck.

Facing Beth again, I explained, "One morning we all saw a deer come out of the woods, and Christopher was all excited about it. So he always talks about deer in the woods back there. But you know, he kind of mixes real stuff with stuff he sees in movies or dreams up. He does what they call 'scripting' . . . a lot of the stuff he says is lines from movies he's memorized. He can memorize every word and even the sound effects from a Disney movie or whatever. When he watches them he'll say the dialogue before the characters do. But anyway, he always tells us he sees a white deer back there in the trees."

"Like an albino?"

"I guess."

"Was the deer you all saw an albino?"

"That time? No, it was a regular deer. Anyway, sometimes Christopher takes part of a sandwich or crackers or something and brings it back in the yard because he says he's going to 'feed the white deer.'"

"That's cute. He's just playing. It's make-believe."

"Yeah," I said, as Christopher was still making his way toward the deck, "but he gets a little carried away with it. He says the white deer talks to him." I chuckled, embarrassed by my own admission, but Beth only listened without scoffing or a wiseass comment, as one of my other friends might make.

She even asked, "What does it say to him?"

"He's never told me that. He just says it whispers to him, and it's a girl. I think it must be from something he saw in a movie—*Bambi* or something." I thought about that. "Well, *Bambi* isn't white, but you know . . ."

"Well, I did think I saw him looking at something back there a second ago."

"Huh? You saw what?"

"That's why I said 'hey,'" Beth said. "It caught my eye. But it wasn't a deer. It looked like a person."

"A person?"

"A girl, I guess. I thought he was talking to someone in your family."

I twisted around in my chair again. I saw only Christopher, close to mounting the steps to the deck. No one in the far shadows of the yard.

"Where did she go?" I asked.

"I think I must have imagined it," Beth said meekly, sounding as if she was sorry she had mentioned it.

I gave her a look, trying to gauge if she were messing with me, but she appeared sincere and I couldn't imagine her pulling a joke like that. I heard my brother's sneakers clomping up the wooden steps.

"Hey, Christopher," I asked, "who were you talking to back there by the stone wall?"

"Christopher gives birthday cake to the white deer," he mumbled, walking past me and letting himself through the sliding glass door into our house.

*

In October, Beth disappeared.

Her mother reported her missing to the police. Her father drove down from Maine, where he'd moved a few years earlier. And Beth's stepfather shot himself under the chin with a shotgun in the basement of their home.

I guess we all put two and two together after that.

But the police never found Beth. Her mother held out the hope that Beth had just run away after what had apparently happened with her stepfather, off to California or someplace, too ashamed and hurt to face anyone who knew her. But I think her mother was the only one who believed that. The rest of us felt we knew better.

My father was an EMT then in addition to the security job, and he volunteered for one of the search parties. He and some other men even ventured into the woods behind our own property. I asked if I could go along to help, but he said no. "I know you're worried about your friend," he said gently.

So I sat out on the deck waiting for my dad to return, watching the trees that stood like drawn theater curtains at the end of my yard, and remembered sitting out there with Beth only a few weeks earlier. I hugged myself against the chilly air, but my mother couldn't get me to come inside. At some point, though, I dozed off in my chair, because when a hand touched my shoulder I awoke with a gasp to see my father leaning over me, his cheeks ruddy red.

I was startled, but glad he'd awakened me. I'd been having a strange dream ... of pushing open a wrought-iron gate, its rusted hinges squealing.

My dad told me he and the others hadn't found a thing.

As I stood up to go inside where it was warm, my father's arm around my shoulders, I asked him, "Dad, what's in the woods back there? I heard there's an old cemetery."

"Old cemetery?"

I felt stupid for it, but nevertheless I said, "Spider Gates?"

"Oh," he said, "you mean the Friends Cemetery? That's what it's really called. No, honey, that place is in Leicester. There's no cemetery in the woods behind our house."

But I now know that a thing can exist in two places, and in two forms, at the same time. In what we consider its true form, and in a dream version we build in our minds. And sometimes, that fantasy construct draws so much power from our imaginations that it becomes real in a different way.

*

One year later—again in October—Christopher disappeared, too.

My mother was hysterical, all the more so because she blamed herself. She had let him play in the back yard without close supervision while she cooked spaghetti in the kitchen. It was a Saturday afternoon and my father was filling in for someone at the abrasives company, but she called him home from work. She called the police, too.

Megan was at my house—we had been in my room talking about the latest boys we liked, not keeping an eye on Christopher either— and we rushed out onto the deck. My father hadn't arrived home yet, and the police were still on the way. But I knew I had to start searching, and I knew where to start: that stone wall bordering our back yard. My friend and I thumped down the deck's steps and raced toward the far edge of the property.

"Oh my God, look," Megan said when we reached it, kneeling down and picking something up from where it rested atop one of the mossy stones in the wall. She held out her open palm to show me. It was a chocolate chip cookie.

"He went into the woods," I said, my voice edging toward hysteria, too. "He must have seen that deer again . . . or he dreamed he did." I stepped over the wall then, into dense bushes growing in the almost unbroken shadows of the pine trees. "Come on, Megan, we've got to start looking for him."

But she reached out to me, as if afraid to follow me over the wall, and tried to take my arm. "Wait until the police get here! They'll know what to do."

"No!" I cried, tears flowing now. "We can't wait for that! He might be scared! He might be hurt!"

"They'll be here any minute!"

"No!" I screeched. "What if it's a serial killer, Megan? What if Beth's stepfather didn't really kill her?"

"You're just talking crazy now. Stop it!"

But I was beyond listening to reason. I whirled around and plunged straight into the woods, yelling my brother's name.

*

I crashed through low-hanging branches that slashed at my cheeks. Once, racing across the slippery bed of rusty red pine needles, my feet went out from under me and I fell heavily onto my back, thumping my head. I cried all the harder, but more from the mounting fear than the pain. My sense of loss was like a chasm that had opened beneath my feet, into which I plummeted with arms and legs flailing. But my arms and legs were only flailing as I ran, screaming Christopher's name until the back of my throat tasted like blood.

Then I thought I heard a voice call out, either another searcher shouting Christopher's name or an echo of my own voice. I stopped to listen for more, keeping perfectly still, and that was when I sensed movement between the trees off to my right. Just a peripheral glimpse, gone as soon as I had turned my head fully to look, but it had appeared to be a large animal. A pale *something* against the shadowy murk.

"Christopher!" I sobbed. "Please!"

"Christopher is here," a familiar voice behind me intoned, surprisingly close.

I spun around, startled, and there he was. Christopher, with a bag of chocolate chip cookies in one hand. He did not look scratched or dirty like me, with pine needles in my hair. He didn't look scared as I had imagined. If he looked a little nervous at all, it was probably due to my own frenzied state.

Sobbing uncontrollably, I dropped to my knees and hugged him tight. Confused, he patted my back awkwardly to comfort me. "Don't do that again," I scolded him. "Don't you ever go off alone into the woods again! Why did you do that?"

I expected him to say then that he had seen his whispering white deer and had tried feeding it cookies. Had followed it. But instead, when I held him away to look into his face, he told me, "Christopher goes with Beth."

"What?" I said. "Beth? You *saw* Beth?"

He nodded.

A chaos of thoughts swirled in my head. Crazy thoughts—like Beth having spent the past year lost in a dense maze of trees, unable to find her way back over the stone wall in my yard. And more realistic thoughts, too, such as Christopher merely spinning fantasies from things he remembered—a person he remembered.

"Honey, are you making this up or what?"

He shook his head no. And he said, "Beth can take Christopher to Spider Gates."

I wiped the tears from my eyes on the back of my hand, to stare into my brother's eyes more deeply. "You saw Beth in the woods . . . and she wanted to take you to Spider Gates?"

He nodded again.

"And did she? Did she show you Spider Gates?"

Now he shook his head. "Beth hears you."

"She—she heard me calling?"

Nodding.

"And then she went away?"

Nodding.

I stood up and took Christopher's hand. "Come on, honey."

"Christopher goes to Spider Gates?" he asked.

"No!" I said. "I'm not taking you there. We don't want to go there, Christopher. You understand me? We never need to go to Spider Gates."

*

One day that November, when my parents were out to the Solomon Pond Mall with Christopher to begin some Christmas shopping, and I stayed home waiting for Megan to come over, I took the opportunity to go out into my back yard alone, to the ancient wall that hid in the bushes like a row of moldering teeth in the mouth of a giant, gaping wide and ready to snap shut.

I stood at the very edge of the wall, gazing into the gray woods. Then I spoke aloud.

"Beth," I said, "I know you're lonely. I know you're sad. But don't talk to my brother again . . . please. You know he can see things. You know he can see you. But he needs to be with his family. He needs to be with me." My voice broke then, and I said, "I'm sorry, okay?" I started to openly weep. "I'm so sorry."

*

Last month, my parents threw a party for my fortieth birthday at their small home in Worcester. My husband and son came with me, of course. My grandmother—still alive, God bless her—even made a ton of *pizelles* for the occasion.

Christopher is thirty-five now, a little overweight and balding. He's very sweet and funny, so he's well liked at the Price Chopper. He spends most of his money on Xbox games and video game manuals, sometimes for games he doesn't even own. He still buys the occasional *Star Wars* figure.

When I arrived at my parents' house, I didn't immediately see Christopher, but it was easy enough to find him—hunched avidly in front of the computer in his bedroom. He was watching a video on YouTube. I could see over his shoulder that it wasn't one of his usual humorous favorites, from questionable YouTube personalities like the "Tourettes Guy" or the "Angry German Kid." It was a video shot in a forest somewhere, by a shaky handheld camera.

My smile of greeting froze on my lips, a sudden frost coating the inside of my chest. I moved around to my brother's side for a closer look, however afraid I was of what I'd see. I expected to view a secluded spot in the middle of a pine forest. There would be a wrought-iron gate with wheel-like designs, wavy arms inside them like tentacles.

But instead—like the person who had shot this video—I caught a glimpse of something crashing off into the underbrush, startled. A pale fleeting shape.

Though I quickly realized what it was the video's creator had spotted, Christopher looked up at me to explain it. He was smiling.

"A white deer," he said.

Feeding Oblivion

A craggy-featured man with a nicotine-yellowed beard stood on a wedge of traffic island close to where Kent had stopped at a red light, on his way to visit his mother. The man wore a filthy gray hoodie with the hood pulled up over his head, shadowing his eyes. In his hands he held a cardboard sign that read: HOMELESS VET. NEED HELP. HUNGRY. GOD BLESS.

Kent avoided looking at the panhandler directly, but he still sensed the man's eyes in the shadow of his hood, certain they were locked directly on him through the driver's side window. Kent groaned inwardly and was just about to lower the window and offer the change he kept for tolls, when the light turned green. With relief, he continued onward.

*

The lobby always smelled to Kent of boiled chicken, no doubt from the kitchen somewhere close by. He signed the log at the reception counter, then turned toward the elevator, where a pleasant Nigerian woman he had spoken with in the past was offloading the elevator's passengers: two elderly women and one man in wheelchairs. Beaming up at Kent as she was wheeled past him, one of the women asked hopefully, "Are you my nephew?"

He wanted to apologize that he was not, but the Nigerian attendant was already pushing the woman's wheelchair away. Kent saw her look back over her shoulder at him, longingly he thought, before he continued on into the elevator.

Because his mother had been living with his younger brother, when it had come time to put her into a "rehabilitation center" due to poor health (as if one could be rehabilitated from old age), the nursing home chosen was close to his brother's apartment. It made sense, of course, and Kent's brother—gay and unmarried—visited her almost every day. But for Kent it was nearly an hour's drive. Well, he'd had to drive that far to see her anyway, when she'd been living in his brother's apartment. So it wasn't the distance that depressed him whenever he set out to visit her, but the sad fact that he would step into her room to find her lying there in that narrow hospital bed. Where once she'd had a whole house to herself, and multiple cats—and later, when they'd had to sell the house and give away the cats, at least a room of her own in his brother's place—now his mother's living space was reduced to half a room, shared with another woman. And here his mother had always been such a shy and private person.

Sometimes Kent planned ahead with his mother on the phone, to let her know he was coming, but other times he liked to drop in unexpectedly to surprise her, to make his visits a little more special. Anything to give her some respite from monotony (though to the rehabilitation center's credit, they did take the patients out on various excursions, organized bingo and trivia games for them, and brought in live musicians). Whenever he came, Kent would always speak politely with her roommate, but only briefly, since his time would be limited. The roommate she had started out with, Carol, had recovered sufficiently from whatever ailment she had suffered and her doctors had allowed her to return home. Kent hoped that wouldn't give his mother false hope, because her condition was different. They couldn't risk another episode like her most recent fall, when she'd lain on the bathroom floor until Kent's brother had come home from work to find her there, waiting for him, too weak to rise.

She was on her second roommate now: Ruth, a woman of ninety—five years older than his mother—and Kent had only met her once before. Much more quiet than the garrulous Carol, when Kent now entered the room she only looked up at him smiling from her chair, where she'd been sitting watching TV. Sure enough, his mother was lying back in her bed to watch her own little TV, too weak to sit up comfortably in a chair for long. This time he had let her know he was coming, and she smiled up at him warmly, toothlessly, as he stepped nearer to the bed and leaned down to give her a kiss.

After his mother had asked him how the traffic had been, how his wife was, how his daughter was doing in college, Kent finally turned to wave across the room to Ruth, who had continued watching him and smiling all this time. "Hello, Ruth," he said loudly, knowing she was a bit hard of hearing.

The snowy-haired woman nodded at him and wiggled the fingers of one hand in turn. She said, "Your mother is a wonderful woman."

"Yes, she is, thank you."

"She's lucky she has two loving sons. I never had any children. I couldn't."

"Oh ... I'm sorry to hear that," Kent said sincerely. His mother had already confided that to him over the phone. She said no one had come to visit Ruth except, one time, a niece. Both Ruth and his mother had lost their husbands over a decade ago.

He had brought his mother a decaf coffee and several doughnuts, and after elevating her bed so she could enjoy this treat, he offered one of the doughnuts to Ruth. She tried to decline, but he persisted until she finally accepted. As Kent stepped to her side of the room to hand her the doughnut, he noticed her TV was playing a nature program with the sound muted. On the screen, time-lapse photography showed the body of a dead mouse being reduced to a skeleton by a seething mass of maggots.

"You're so kind," Ruth told him as she accepted the doughnut. "You and your brother and your mother. It's because of you people that those things haven't gotten me yet."

"What things, Ruth?" Kent asked.

"Those big centipedes that come out of there." She pointed behind him.

Kent turned and saw only a drab, institutional white wall with a cork bulletin board, bearing a single birthday or get-well card, presumably from her niece. He looked back to her. "You've seen centipedes in here?" They appeared in his own house sometimes, the fast kind with long hairy legs. Once, all lathered up in the shower, he'd realized there was one on the tiled wall only inches away from him, and he'd nearly slipped and broken his neck jumping out of the shower to find something to kill it with.

"Yes," the old woman replied, looking sad, as if with fatalism. "Big black centipedes. At least, I guess that's what they are. They're afraid of other people, though. If I was alone they'd come for me, but because your dear mother is always with me they only sneak out a little to have a look. Then they duck back inside again."

"Inside . . . the wall?" He glanced over at his mother. Though she was physically very weak, his mother's mind was still sharp, and he could see the pity in her eyes that told him Ruth was only delusional. The "centipedes" were not real.

"Yes," Ruth answered again. "They pull back into the wall. I don't know what's on the other side, but it must not be good. It must be full of those things. Can you imagine? A place that's nothing but centipedes? Millions and billions of them, pushing all against you? Pushing against your eyes, getting in your mouth . . . in your lungs? Who'd ever want to go there? Not me."

"Huh," Kent said, at a loss. "Yeah, well . . . I'll talk to the nurses' station about the problem, Ruth, okay? Maybe somebody can . . . spray or something."

"Oh, I've already told them," she sighed, sitting back in her chair and breaking off a piece of doughnut. "Again and again."

"I'm sorry," he said, wanting this conversation to be over, "but I'm sure it'll be all right. Like you said, my mother's always here to protect you, right?"

"Mm-hm," Ruth mumbled around the doughnut she chewed, but her eyes remained sad behind the lenses of her glasses.

*

It was three weeks before Kent returned to see his mother. He made excuses to himself that work was tiring, and he needed to spend time with his wife, tend to matters around the house, but he knew he was simply avoiding it. At least he'd been calling her once a week. The last time they'd spoken on the phone, a few days ago, he'd asked his mother, "So how's poor Ruth doing?"

"Oh," said his mother, and he knew that miserable tone of hers, knew that what she was going to relate wasn't good. "It isn't easy."

"Is she awake?"

"Yes," his mother said, lowering her voice to a whisper, "but she can't hear me. Her hearing isn't good, and so she plays her TV so *loud.*"

"Yeah, I can hear it now." Though he remembered it had been muted during his last visit.

"But it's worse than that. At night she has these nightmares . . . night terrors, I guess."

"Yeah? What does she do, freak out?"

"Yes . . . and then the nurses come in. I'm so *tired.* I haven't been able to get a decent night's sleep in days."

"Oh, wow, Mom. Well, that's not fair to you. Did you tell Greg about this?" Greg was his younger brother.

"Yes. He's going to see if they can find another room for me. Or her. I hate to be like that, but—"

"Hey, no, don't feel badly—you have to think of yourself. How is it good for you to have to put up with that? If they don't listen to Greg I'll give them my two cents' on it too. We'll take care of it for you, Mom."

"All right," she sighed, still sounding guilty for having complained about the other woman.

"Anyway, I'm going to come see you on Saturday."

"You don't have to, Kent. I know you're busy."

"Quiet," he admonished her, "I'm coming, okay?" He *did* have to, after all. How much longer could he realistically expect his mother to remain on this earth? He felt terrible enough already for neglecting her as much as he did. This was the mother whom he had loved so much as a boy that on his first day of school in the first and even the second grade he had wept in despair when she'd dropped him off and returned home, as if she might be abandoning him at an orphanage. This was the mother whose auburn hair he would twirl around his fingers while he sat on her lap as they watched movies together on their black-and-white TV. She was still that same person, still here, not just a collection of memories like photographs bundled with rubber bands—as his father had become—stored in the attic of his mind.

How would he feel when *he* was elderly, in some nursing home, and his daughter was too busy to come visit him? He was already in his early fifties . . . it was not so far-flung a consideration. Already he felt sad and a little resentful that his daughter came home so infrequently to see her parents. How could he expect her to act any differently when he set so poor an example?

He was determined to grab his daughter next time she was in town and drag her out to visit her poor grandmother. But in the meantime, he was determined to drag himself to see her this Saturday. No more excuses.

As bad as it was for his mother, though, at least she had two sons, one of whom saw her diligently, and a grandchild. How much worse was it for Ruth, facing her last days alone?

With his mother's roommate having once more risen to his thoughts, Kent asked his mother, "So what does Ruth do when she has these night terrors?"

"Oh," his mother moaned in that tone again, "she starts crying and screaming about the centipedes coming out of the wall. It's always the centipedes. She begs me to wake up and look at them, so they'll be afraid and go away."

"Oh, wow. Poor thing. So you don't think you really have centipedes in there, huh?"

"No," his mother sighed. "It can't be. They're big black centipedes, she says—a foot long."

*

His wife, Veronica, had made excuses of her own for not coming with him to visit his mother today. They'd had a fight about it, and a half hour into his ride Kent was still steaming. He strongly suspected Ronnie looked forward to his trips to see his mother, for then she was free to visit whoever it was he was certain *she* was seeing. Most likely that friend of hers from work, chubby boyish Matt, whom he had caught her texting on her cell phone several times like an overgrown teenager—ostensibly about work matters. During some of their fights, over the past few years, one or the other of them had even evoked the fearsome D-word.

Beneath his steaming anger, what Kent really felt was a despair so great it left him scooped hollow inside. All those yearly trips to Acadia National Park in Maine, first just the two of them and then later with their daughter—until she became a teenager and the company of friends became more desirable than the company of parents. He recalled the joy he and Ronnie had experienced on the day their daughter was born—the joy of bringing her home from the hospital. Remembering these things and more, Kent felt something akin to the sadness of remembering himself sitting on his mother's lap, watching TV and playing with her auburn hair, which glittered with coppery highlights in the mellow light of afternoon. It was as though he stood on the edge of a deep well—a well that was the void inside himself—into which all the things he loved were fluttering away like photographs released from the flimsy rubber bands that had bound them.

Churning with these thoughts, he slowed his car to a stop at a red light, and out of the corner of his eye he recognized that same shabby castaway on the traffic island, holding a new sign that read: NO HOME. PLEASE HELP. NEED TO EAT. GOD BLESS. Kent fought the urge to look at the homeless man more directly, but the imp of the perverse compelled him to steal one quick peek. In that instant, he thought he saw a long dark shape go slithering across the man's face, up into the shadow cast by his hood—as if a sinuous ribbon of blackness had fled out of sight into one of the man's shadowed eye sockets.

The light changed to green, and Kent depressed the gas pedal perhaps a little more than necessary. Just his agitated state of mind, he told himself. The blackness in his own brain.

*

When he entered his mother's room, Kent's eyes were first drawn to Ruth, as if she were the one he had come to see. He saw her lying back in her bed asleep, with her TV still running loudly. He bent over his mother to kiss her and asked, "You want me to turn her sound down?"

"No," his mother said in a hush, "I'm afraid it might wake her up. She told me today the centipedes are afraid of the sound . . . they think it's people talking to her. Poor woman."

"Yes," said Kent. He was glad the blaring TV covered their conversation, but he didn't know how his mother could enjoy her own TV this way, let alone sleep. "Greg and I exchanged a few emails this week. He said he pushed the center about getting you a new room. They told him they'd consider moving Ruth to a room of her own instead, if she's being disruptive. It's a shame that she'll have to go without company, but if she just gets moved in with a different person then that's not fair to them either. It seems like the only resolution."

"I know," his mother sighed, "but . . . I feel sorry for her. I don't want her to be lonely. She doesn't have anyone."

"Like I told you, Mom, you have to worry about yourself. We can't worry about everyone else, can we?" No, he thought. Worrying about everyone else wasn't the way of people. It was enough of a stretch, too often, to get them to worry about those closest to them.

He sat on a chair by the side of his mother's hospital bed, chatting with her as they watched a rerun of an old western program, *The Big Valley,* that they had both liked decades ago—long before he'd had a wife or a daughter. But finally he looked over at his mother and saw she had fallen asleep, her once lively auburn hair now like a gray and decaying halo around her pillowed head. He was tempted to wake her up to let her know he was leaving, but didn't want to disturb her after she'd complained lately of not getting a good night's rest, so he wrote a note for her instead and placed it on her rolling bedside table. In the note he promised he'd call her tomorrow.

As he rose to turn and leave the room, he realized that Ruth had sat up in her own bed at some point, eyes staring wide. It wasn't him she was staring at, however, but the wall opposite her bed, with its nearly empty cork bulletin board.

"They started to come out," the old woman said, without taking her gaze from the wall, "but they saw you here and crawled back inside. They thought it was safe, with your mother asleep, but you scared them."

"You should go back to sleep, Ruth," Kent told her, taking a few steps closer to her bed to be sure she could hear him. "You just need to get some more rest."

She cranked her head around to look up at him mournfully. "That's what they're waiting for. They want me to let my guard down."

"Now, now, Ruth," he told her, "you'll be fine, don't worry. The staff won't let anything happen to you."

"It will happen to them, too, someday," she told him. "Those crawly things come for us all when we're alone and forgotten. Once we get close enough to that black place behind the wall, they get hungry." She dropped her voice to a more confidential tone and warned, "When you start to see them, you'll know you're too close to the wall."

*

Monday evening, after they had both got home from their respective jobs, Kent and his younger brother spoke on the phone. Kent had arrived to find his house empty, with no note from his wife to explain where she might be. Maybe shopping, or maybe in bed with her scandalously younger—at forty-five—coworker Matt. Did it really matter anymore?

Greg had been the one to call Kent, and he reported, "They moved Ruth into a private room today. Mom said she had a really rough night last night, the worst yet. Ruth was really flipping out."

"About those centipede things that live in the wall?"

"Yup. Very delusional. Mom feels badly about it, but—"

"Yeah, I know," Kent replied. "I told her she needs to think of numero uno."

"'Fraid so."

"They going to get Mom another roommate?"

"Probably. The center doesn't make money off empty beds."

"You got that right. Old age is big business." As was the funeral business. Before they had placed their mother into the nursing home, the brothers had met with a funeral director to make advance arrangements for their mother, in an effort to allocate her money before the state sucked up what little she had.

Greg said, "I just hope the next roommate isn't so difficult. I really wish Mom could have a room to herself. She's never been the buddy-buddy type."

"Well," Kent said doubtfully. Once he would have agreed with his brother, but with Ruth in his thoughts he said, "I know that, but sometimes it isn't good to be so alone."

*

Where in the past Kent might have waited weeks to visit his mother again, he did so the following Saturday, without calling first in order to surprise her.

On his way, he lucked out and caught a green light, but he spotted the homeless man stranded on that narrow traffic island as he drove past. The man had set his sign down on the ground and seemed to be slapping at his own body and staggering about wildly. Delirium tremens, Kent thought, with an uncomfortable mixture of sympathy and dread.

*

His mother was indeed surprised, and of course happy to see him, but he was alarmed at her appearance. She had stopped wearing her dentures decades ago, but her face looked more sunken than ever, her haunted eyes in dark hollows. Worried, he asked her, "Mom, aren't you sleeping better now that Ruth's gone?"

It was quite plain that Ruth was gone: the other side of the room was vacant. The bed stood empty. Ruth's TV and even the single greeting card that had been tacked to the bulletin board were missing. He felt a strange stab of guilt, as if he had forcibly ejected the woman from the room himself.

He was surprised they hadn't moved another patient in here yet, and more than a tad concerned about it. What was the holdup?

"*Well* . . ." his mother replied to his question, in a helpless tone that sounded self-pitying and childlike. "Some nights I still hear Ruth screaming somewhere . . . wherever they took her. At least it's not as loud as before."

"Oh, wow. I wonder if they should sedate her or something. Maybe someone should call her niece, so she can come visit her. She should see someone."

"I know," his mother said, still in that self-pitying and childish tone. "It gets so lonely here."

That went straight to Kent's heart. "I'm sorry about that, Mom. You know Greg and I would never want you in a place like this, but you're just so weak. Look what happened when you fell the last time. You can't be left alone while Greg's at work."

"I know," she sighed. "It's just . . . it gets scary at night here sometimes. I know Ruth was noisy with her nightmares and all, but I almost wish they hadn't moved her."

"Oh, Mom, come on now. And why should it be scary here? There're attendants on this floor all the time—you only need to buzz for somebody."

"I *know*," his mother said. He realized she had been staring past him for several moments. He pivoted in his chair to follow her gaze and saw the blank institutional wall with the empty cork bulletin board.

"What is it, Mom?" he asked, facing her again.

"Well, it's just . . . I'm sure I was dreaming . . ."

"What?" he pressed.

"Last night I woke up . . . I heard Ruth screaming again . . . it came from the next room, I think. Maybe that's where they took her." His mother pointed at the wall with the bulletin board. "And when I looked over there, well, it was dark, but I thought I saw something moving around on the wall. A big black crawling thing."

"Oh, Mom," Kent said.

She looked sheepish. "I told you I was probably still dreaming."

"You just heard Ruth carrying on and it made you remember her hallucinations. Try not to think of all that stuff again, okay? You know it isn't true." He stood up from his chair with fresh determination. "Listen, I'm going to go talk to the nurses' station to see if they'll let me take you out for a couple hours, so we can have lunch at that seafood place you like, and then we'll go sit in the park and have some coffee. How's that?"

His mother's eyes looked less haunted already. "Are you sure?"

"Of course I'm sure. I'll go arrange it right now." He wagged a finger at her. "Don't you go anywhere—I'll be right back."

At the nurses' station at the end of the corridor, Kent told the attending nurse of his intentions. The tight-faced woman with her platinum-dyed hair said they'd help him get his mother ready, but rather stiffly advised him that next time he should do as his brother always did, and give them advance warning before taking his mother outside the center. He promised that he would.

Leaning on the counter, he said, "When do you think my mother can have a new roommate? I thought she'd have one already."

The nurse replied with thinly veiled sarcasm, "I thought you and your brother wanted your mother to be alone so she could sleep better."

"Not alone, necessarily. We were just worried that Ruth was keeping her up with all her nightmares."

"Well, your mother won't have to worry about Ruth anymore. She passed away two days ago, in her sleep."

"What?" Kent said.

"Heart failure, poor woman."

"But—but my mother said she heard Ruth just last night, having her nightmares again in the next room."

"The next room?" said the nurse. "Ruth was moved to the third floor." She pointed above their heads. "Your mother herself must have been dreaming."

*

The next day, Sunday, Kent's wife told him she was moving out of their house and in with Matt.

In the kitchen of the house that had once been a dream come true—a proud achievement fulfilled, the place where they had raised their daughter, whose living room had known a long succession of Christmas trees and whose bedroom had known countless nights of comfortable intimacy—the two of them now paced around each other restlessly, agitated and on the verge of ferocity or tears or both.

"Ronnie," he said, "I don't know if you're going through a midlife crisis or menopausal episode or what, but—"

"I already went through menopause!" she shouted. "Do you think this is only some kind of temporary insanity?"

"I just don't think you're thinking this through."

"Kent, I've been thinking this through for the past few *years*."

"What about our daughter? Aren't you thinking about how this is going to hurt her?"

Veronica stopped pacing to bug her eyes at him wildly. "Amy is a woman now. She wouldn't want to see you and me stay together if we weren't happy. She's not selfish like that."

"Selfish—what an interesting word."

"Isn't it, though, Kent? And you're accusing *me* of selfishness? But you're not selfish, wanting me to stay even though I'm not happy? Well, if I am being selfish, I'm sorry, but so be it." Now her pent-up tears were liberated, and she thumped her chest for emphasis. Somehow the gesture reminded Kent of that homeless man beating at his own body. "I'm only fifty years old! My life isn't over yet! I'm still here!"

"For now," Kent murmured, turning away from her and gazing out through the little window over the sink, at the back yard where the three of them had shared cookouts. Where he had built a swing set for his daughter, and where his wife had used to keep a tomato garden, both of which were now gone. Just bare neglected grass, in need of cutting, overcast with the deep blue shadows of encroaching evening. He said to himself, "We're still here for now."

*

Kent called the nursing home from work on Monday, and again on Tuesday, and emailed his brother to pester them about getting his mother a new roommate. Increasingly nervous about the situation, Kent even considered taking his mother to come live with him, now that Ronnie had moved out of the house. Maybe he could use his vacation weeks now, or even request a leave of absence from work. But finally on Tuesday night, when he arrived home, Greg called to tell him the good news.

"They did it," he related. "They got Mom a new roommate. I don't know if it's going to work out, so let's keep our fingers crossed. I'm leaving to visit Mom in a couple of minutes, so I'll get to meet her myself, but on the phone Mom said she's Italian, and she met the lady's daughter and son-in-law, and said they all seem very nice."

"That's great to hear. I'm relieved."

"I agree: I do think it's good for Mom to have company."

"And I need to thank you, Greg, for going over there as often as you do. You're a good son."

"Thanks . . . but you are, too."

"Yeah, well, not like you. But I'm going to try to be a better son. I'm trying."

Greg could sense his mood and asked, "How's it going? With Ronnie and all?"

"She moved over there Sunday night, after we had a big fight about it. She still hasn't taken much of her stuff yet."

"Do you think she'll go all the way with this, or do you think she'll have a change of heart?"

"Who knows?" Kent said. His cell phone held to his ear, he paced alone through his house, from the kitchen into the living room. He found himself staring into the empty corner where they had always put their Christmas trees. Live trees in the early years, but they found the needles turned brown and dropped off too soon, so later on they had switched to a tree of dead plastic. It currently lay hidden in the basement, in its coffin-like box.

"You ought to ask Amy to come home this weekend and spend some time with you," Greg suggested. "She should give her Dad a little company."

"I won't push her about that," Kent said. "She'll see me if she wants to. Anyway, I'm going to go visit Mom again this weekend. Then I can get to meet her new roommate, too."

"Really?" Greg said. "Great. Hey, why don't I arrange for you and me to take Mom out for lunch on Saturday?"

"Sounds nice," Kent said. He realized then how much he loved his brother, and how much he missed him. "I'm looking forward to it."

They said their goodbyes, and Kent pocketed his phone. Evening had descended, and he had yet to switch on any of the lights in the living room. As he turned to head back toward the kitchen and microwave something easy for supper, his eyes trailed again past that corner where they used to set up the Christmas tree.

Peripherally, he had caught a glimpse of movement—a glimpse of something like a living shadow, with a long obsidian body and probing feelers, slithering across the wall. But when his gaze locked directly on the spot, the crawling thing was gone, as if it had burrowed swiftly back into the wall, to some place behind the wall, where it and its ilk would continue to wait patiently.

*

On Saturday, as Kent drove out to meet his mother and brother for lunch, he pulled to a stop at the signal near that familiar scrap of traffic island. The homeless man was not to be found, but before the light turned green and Kent moved forward again, he spotted something lying in the island's mangy grass. It was a crudely scrawled cardboard sign, and its words nibbled at Kent's mind as he continued on.

ALONE. THEY'RE EATING ME. GOD HELP ME.

Mr. Faun

When she'd been a young girl—before city leash laws, when one could still let their dog run around the neighborhood freely—once Jeannie's dog had come home grinning and reeking of an animal carcass it had been rolling around in. The smell that announced the approach of the man behind her flashed that childhood incident back into her mind.

She was standing in front of two large paintings, nearly spanning the space from ceiling to floor, by the acclaimed young artist Jorge Nada. They were portraits done in a primitive style, with huge flat eyes, painted in murky dirty colors and splashed and streaked with more mud brown and rust red on top of that. When she turned toward the odor, startled and suppressing her gag reflex, it was to be greeted by a face that might have been painted by Jorge Nada, though this visage more realistically approximated that of a human being . . . if not by much.

The face of the man who had come up behind Jeannie—in this particular gallery of the Contemporary Art wing of the city's Fine Arts Museum—was caked in dirt and grease, as if he too had been rolling around in an animal carcass, or at least sleeping in a dumpster. His shoulder-length hair and thick beard were impossibly matted, with bits of food or garbage snagged in their knotty weave. His clothes were so layered in stains that their original colors were impossible to guess. Guessing his age was a trick, too: thirties or forties? or fifties?

"Sparafhudullahs?" the man croaked.

Under other circumstances Jeannie would have asked the man politely, "Excuse me?" Instead, drawing back in revulsion so abruptly that she almost bumped up against one of Jorge Nada's looming faces, she blurted, "What?"

"Spare a few dollars?" the man repeated. This time she made out the words, which like his face seemed glued together with dirt. His blue eyes blazed at her like the flames of butane torches jetting through his mask of filth. They didn't blink.

Jeannie held her breath and turned to one side as she dug in her pocketbook in case the man made a grab for it. Meanwhile she was asking herself in a wild inner voice, "How did this guy get past the front desk?" Had he found another way into the museum—some maintenance access door or such?

She held out a five-dollar bill to him, pinched by its end so their fingers wouldn't touch. If her hand had closed on a twenty before the five, she would have given him that just as readily, to be rid of him.

"Thankoo," the grimy man mumbled, turning away, still never having once blinked his vivid blue eyes . . . as weirdly unsettling as those of certain dogs.

A guard had drifted into the gallery, trying to look inconspicuous as he hovered at the far end of the spacious room with his arms folded, but he was tall and imposing in his black business suit. Jeannie met his eyes as the derelict shuffled out through the same doorway the guard had just come in through. She was amazed the guard didn't even turn his head to follow the other man's passage.

Jeannie found herself walking toward the guard, her shoes clicking loudly against the glossy floor. The man arched a brow inquisitively as she approached.

"Can I help you?"

"Well," Jeannie said haltingly, in a lowered voice. She motioned with her head toward the doorway. "That man . . . I mean, I have a lot of sympathy for the homeless, I do, but . . . you know, to come up to people in a museum . . ." She let her words trail away, feeling too guilty to continue.

The tall guard smiled. "That's not a homeless man—that's Mr. Faun. He's one of the exhibits."

*

Jeannie had been married for twelve years, and she still called her husband Bobert, as she had in college. Back then she hadn't known whether to call him Bob or Robert, so she'd settled on both and stuck with it—probably because his own sweet sense of fun hadn't diminished over the past dozen years. One Sunday morning recently, while shaving, he had suddenly and loudly proclaimed, "I am Lord Maldomor!" Throughout the entire day he had remained in character, speaking in the same booming stilted tone. "Lord Maldomor demands eggs!" That night, after making love, he had announced, "Another wench quenched by Lord Maldomor!" The next morning as they quietly prepared for work, Jeannie had remembered the day before and asked, "Hey, what happened to Lord Maldomor?" Bobert had simply glanced over at her innocently and said, "Hm?"

Jeannie had an alternating work schedule at the nursing home, and today had been her day off—hence her trip to the Fine Arts Museum. When Bobert had come home from the data storage company where he worked as an engineer, and as they stood at the kitchen counter preparing dinner together, she told him about her encounter with Mr. Faun in the Contemporary Art wing.

He laughed. "That's so cool!"

"When I came home I looked on FAM's website to read about him, but there's nothing about him."

"And you don't subscribe to their magazine anymore."

"No, though there might be back issues at the library. Assuming they did a feature on him. I couldn't find anything about him on the Web at all, even outside the FAM site."

"Maybe he's a brand new exhibit." Bobert chuckled. "I like that: he's an exhibit, not an artist."

"I guess he's both."

"Maybe FAM doesn't want to discuss him to avoid breaking the sense of verisimilitude."

"Talk about verisimilitude," Jeannie said, "you should have smelled him."

"Oh, I want to! I want the full experience. Next day off that coincides for us, I want us to go there together. I hope he'll still be there." Bobert swept a handful of chopped scallions off the cutting board into his palm. "So you didn't see him again after you gave him the money?"

"No. To tell you the truth, he kind of freaked me out, so I left shortly after that."

"Huh. Sounds like a fun gig. Not only does he get to play a bum all day, but he makes a little cash while doing it. He reminds me of those fake beggars who drive home in a nice car at the end of the day."

"Fake is the word. He's one of those bogus artists I hate so much." Jeannie muttered this more to herself than to Bobert, as she poured some oil into a frying pan.

"I know what you mean, honey," Bobert said.

Jeannie was an artist herself, having attended the Rhode Island School of Design while Bobert had focused on literature under the school's Department of Literary Arts and Studies. She painted, but rather preferred drawing in pencil. Her style was an almost photographic realism, and she was just as adept at portraying animals as she was at human faces. She had participated in a few art shows over the years, and one of these had been sponsored by and housed within the Fine Arts Museum itself, an event that she'd been immensely proud to be part of . . . until she met the museum's director, Diane Segler-Frost. Segler-Frost had briefly passed her gaze over Jeannie's framed series of drawings, smiled thinly, and said, "Pretty." She had then turned away to take in another artist's work, a young woman with hair dyed candy pink. This artist drank from jugs of milk dyed a variety of bright colors and forced herself to vomit it up onto large canvases.

Diane Segler-Frost had rhapsodized over the vomit paintings. "A more visceral Jackson Pollock!" she had cried, gesturing exuberantly. "Your *body* is your brush!"

Later, one of the other artists in the show, a friend of Jeannie's, had reluctantly shared more of Segler-Frost's impressions of Jeannie's drawings, from an overheard conversation. Segler-Frost had said, "Despite their obsessive surface detail, they lack *life*."

Lack life, Jeannie thought, remembering Segler-Frost's comments now . . . as she had countless times in the years since the show. Which had been the last art show she had cared to participate in. But Jorge Nada's gigantic faces, as crudely drawn as anything Jeannie's five-year-old nephew might render, were no doubt overflowing with life. And all the muddy brown streaks across those enormous flat faces, to give them an appropriately gritty and edgy look . . . Jeannie's dog that had once rolled in an animal carcass had had a habit of dragging its rear across the living room carpet when inconvenienced by a cling-on, leaving nasty brown smears. She could imagine Nada slapping paint on his own dog's posterior and encouraging it to go to work on his giant faces, in a human/canine collaboration.

She hadn't drawn anything new for a few years after the show, and Bobert hadn't fared much better with his writing, receiving rejection slips that were the equivalent of Segler-Frost's dismissal. Both of them had concentrated mainly on their day jobs. But eventually Bobert started selling his short stories—horror tales as subtly shaded as those of the masters he admired: M. R. James, E. F. Benson, and their ilk—to small-press publications, and he gently goaded Jeannie into illustrating several of these. The editors of the publications were impressed with her work, which encouraged her, so that when Bobert finally sold his first collection he convinced the small-press publisher to allow Jeannie to provide the color cover art as well as illustrations to accompany each of the stories within. Because Bobert worked the natural world into so many of his stories—taking his cue from another master he worshipped, Thomas Hardy—Jeannie's cover art and interiors were both lovely and spooky at the same time.

The book hadn't sold an abundance of copies, which surprised neither of them, but both author and artist had received numerous favorable comments from the horror fiction community Bobert was active in. They were currently at work on his second book, to be released from the same publisher next year. But of course, quitting their day jobs wasn't even a step closer. They held no more youthful illusions about such things. Only *professional* artists achieved those heights.

Work on the new book was coming along slowly. Jeannie's hands were too occupied wiping aged bottoms to spend much time holding a pencil.

She didn't tell her husband—and they went on to discuss other matters when they sat down to eat—but since tomorrow was also her day off and Bobert would be working, she had already decided to return to the Fine Arts Museum.

*

Entering the Contemporary Art wing, Jeannie wondered if Mr. Faun would find her again, so to speak, before she could locate him. She imagined she could do that simply by following his scent. Before she had a chance to really begin the hunt, she chanced upon that same guard in the black suit of a Secret Service agent she had spoken with yesterday, and once again approached him. Once again his expectantly raised eyebrow.

"Mr. Faun," she began.

"You're intrigued, huh?"

"I guess that's the word."

"Word's begun to get around. You're not the only one who's intrigued."

"So is he a new 'exhibit'?" She might as well have made the quotation marks in the air with her fingers.

"He's been living here a few weeks."

"He *lives* here?"

"Like I say, he's an exhibit." The guard half turned to point toward the doorway at the far end of the gallery they were in. "He usually sets up in Gallery C."

Jeannie glanced that way. "So he's like a performance artist?"

"I honestly don't know that much about him," the guard said. "And we're really not supposed to talk about it anyway."

"Why is that?"

He shrugged his sharply angled shoulders. "Not to spoil the effect, I guess."

"Wouldn't want to do that," Jeannie mumbled, starting toward the doorway to Gallery C. "Thanks," she said over her shoulder.

In Gallery C, huge comic book exclamations were painted directly upon various areas of the white walls, in garish primary colors. There was: AARRGGHH!! And: RATATATATAT! And: SCREEEE!! These were the work of artist Charles Stokley, who had recently entered a daring new phase, which was also represented on the gallery's walls: exclamations reproduced from Japanese manga.

In one corner of the room, humped on the floor like an art display in itself, stood a camouflage pop-up tent such as a camper or hunter might use. Its positioning blocked closer inspection of a piece hanging on the wall behind it: a giant smiley face, framed under glass, composed of another artist's used sanitary pads.

The man's shoes stood outside the tent opening, accounting for a considerable portion of the reek in themselves. Beside them lay an empty potato chip bag, an empty soda can, and several balled-up tissues.

A cluster of people formed a crescent around the tent, some of them bending a little lower in an attempt to peek through the crack between its hanging entrance flaps. They kept at a bit of distance, either out of deference toward the tent's owner or revulsion for the stench emanating from it. One woman had her hand clamped over her nose and mouth. Jeannie heard another woman whisper to her male companion, "So is he in there or not?"

A man standing beside them said quietly, "I saw him in the men's room earlier; he had his shirt off and was washing up at the sink."

A sudden phlegmy coughing erupted inside the tent, sounding as if someone was trying to start up an infirm car in there. Startled, the ring of people closest to the tent jerked back a little in unison. Behind them, Jeannie snorted in amusement. What were they waiting for this performance artist to do next—vomit up a bellyful of cheap wine? Would they then applaud? Maybe he could vomit on a canvas, and Diane Segler-Frost could frame it.

Disgusted as much with these spectators—*more* with them—as the artist himself, not to mention the foul air, Jeannie turned away. She needed the fresh air to be found in great abundance in the museum's galleries of older art, where she had never failed to find inspiration for her own work. She started winding her way out of the Contemporary Art wing, though she did pause here and there to revisit some of the works she admired, which to her mind displayed the true ability that so much of their neighboring pieces lacked.

She was gazing at one such painting when she heard a scuffed footstep behind her and perceived a wafting cloud of stink. A wet and raspy voice croaked, "Sparafhudullahs?"

Hardly surprised at what she'd find, Jeannie whirled around sharply. "I gave you five dollars yesterday!" she snapped.

The man they were calling Mr. Faun stood before her, his grubby hand extended, palm up, its creases like lines drawn in black marker. Those unblinking blue eyes again burned as if through eyeholes in a mask fashioned from grime and hair.

"You like to scare people by sneaking up on them, huh?" Jeannie went on. "When all else fails, go for the easy shock value, right?"

Mr. Faun's hand wavered, as if he were uncertain, and he weaved a little in place. But he still stood expectantly.

"I'm not giving you any more money," Jeannie said. "I'm sure you're already making plenty with this gig, one way or another. Congratulations, Rembrandt—I wish I could be as talented as you." And with that, she stormed away, leaving Mr. Faun standing there watching after her, his hand still extended.

*

Jeannie didn't return to the Fine Arts Museum until the end of the following week, when her day off fell on a Saturday and Bobert could go with her. By that time he seemed to have lost interest, but Jeannie insisted. "I want you to see this travesty for yourself."

However, when they arrived at the entrance to Gallery C (which Bobert joked stood for "Christo"), in the Contemporary Art wing, they found the sizable room so filled with people it was almost difficult to enter. Bobert said, "Huh . . . is there some new show opening today?"

"It's *him*," Jeannie said, seeing how the people in the room faced toward the corner where she had seen the pop-up tent last time, though at the moment all those bodies blocked it from view. "As the guard told me, word has gotten around. Everybody wants to see the brilliant Mr. Faun: artist and artwork in one."

"Come on, honey," Bobert said, gently taking her arm. "Too crowded in there. I really don't care to see this clown anyway. If I want to see method acting, I'll stay home and watch an old Robert DeNiro movie—with no stink involved."

"But you should *see* this fake!" Jeannie was craning her neck in an attempt to peer over the tops of the other people's heads, or between their milling bodies. What was Mr. Faun currently up to that had them so riveted? Making a campfire out of a Renoir canvas, so he could cook a hot dog on a stick?

"Come on, honey, don't let yourself get obsessed over this poser. Let's go have some lunch, huh? This is our day off—let's enjoy it."

Reluctantly, Jeannie allowed her husband to steer her away.

The museum featured a café in an atrium-like courtyard, the atmosphere exceedingly pleasant. The prices were a bit steep for the couple, but they treated themselves. They'd been coming here on dates since before they were married. Bobert ordered a glass of beer, Jeannie some wine. They began talking about Bobert's unfinished second book, an idea he had for one of the stories that would complete it, and Jeannie forgot her sour mood, began suggesting concepts for the illustration that would complement her husband's ghost story. Her ideas in turn caused Bobert to build upon his own, and it went back and forth this way while they dug into their lunch.

With her love of drawing both animals and faces, she was describing a picture that Bobert's proposed story had conjured in her mind—the image of a sparrow standing atop the head of a beautiful ghost child—when she noticed Bobert wasn't looking directly at her anymore, nor apparently listening to her enthusiastic description. He had the look of a man stealing a peek at an attractive woman behind his wife's back ... when the man forgets himself and the peek drags out into something more. Jeannie started turning around in her chair to follow his gaze. This motion caused Bobert to come out of his trance, and he said, "That's him, isn't it?"

"Oh, God," she said. "Yes, that's him."

Mr. Faun stood over the table of a couple on the far side of the courtyard, with all the splendor of a freshly exhumed, but far from fresh, corpse. Was he waiting for money?

"How can they stand the smell while they're eating?" Jeannie exclaimed. "I swear, if he comes over to our table I am going to stab him to death with my fork."

Bobert chuckled, shaking his head. "He is pretty convincing, I'll give him that."

Jeannie realized that it was food Mr. Faun was waiting for. He held out a plastic bag from the museum's gift shop, and the couple at the table placed a few items into it, wrapped in napkins. All the while they were grinning, as delighted as adults placing candy into the sack of a clever trick-or-treater.

"Let's finish up and get out of here before I lose my lunch," Jeannie grumbled.

"I thought he's the reason we came, so you could show me."

"Now you've seen him. I've had enough of this place."

"Honey, calm down," Bobert said, touching her arm. "Come on, ignore him. I have another beer coming. Don't let this joker spoil our date."

Even then the young waitress approached with Bobert's second beer, and Jeannie shifted in her seat to face her. "Excuse me, can I ask you: do you know anything about that guy over there? That Mr. Faun?"

"Oh, him," the waitress laughed. "He's something, huh? He's become like the museum's biggest draw."

"Biggest freak, you mean," Jeannie said. "When does the supposedly starving artist bite the head off a chicken?"

"Well, I feel sorry for him, myself," the waitress said, pouting cutely. "Why?"

"Well," the young woman said, as if hesitant to elaborate, "I really shouldn't be saying this, but I've heard a few things ... not that I know for sure they're true. Maybe just talk that gets passed along, you know?"

"Please," Jeannie encouraged her.

"Well," she said again, glancing over her shoulder guiltily as Mr. Faun planted himself in front of another couple's table, holding out his gift bag. A hacking cough came over him again, but the grins of the couple didn't falter. "What I heard is that ... um, do you remember that bad snow storm we had last month? Right. So that morning Mrs. Segler-Frost was coming into the museum early and she found this homeless guy huddled by the front doors, with just this ratty blanket over him, all shaking and blue. So she felt sorry for him and let him in, and she took him to the employees' cafeteria and bought some coffee and snacks for him until she could figure out what to do—you know, call around for a shelter that could come pick him up or something. But I guess she took a call on her cell phone and then she had to do something in her office, and she told the guy—he said his name was something Faun—that she'd be back to see to him. But you know, she got distracted by a couple things and forgot all about him, until like two hours later it suddenly hit her. Then she got nervous and went looking for him, but he wasn't in the cafeteria anymore. Finally she found him in the Contemporary Art wing. He was lying curled up on the floor under his blanket, asleep, pretty much where his tent is now. By this time the museum was open, and a few people were standing around Mr. Faun, staring at him. And Mrs. Segler-Frost heard them talking about him. See, they thought he was some kind of new art installation—and they liked it. They said he looked so real. I don't know ... maybe they thought he was a realistic sculpture. Or maybe they just meant he looked like a real homeless person." The waitress shrugged. She added in a conspiratorial whisper, leaning in closer, "Either way, I think the gears in Mrs. Segler-Frost's head started to turn."

"So Mr. Faun isn't his own piece of artwork after all," Jeannie said, her expression one of awe. "He's really Segler-Frost's artwork."

"I guess so—in a sense. Yeah, I suppose you could say that, huh?" The waitress straightened, ready to return to her duties. She held a finger to her lips. "Shh, okay? Just stories I've heard." Then she was moving toward the next table.

"Oh my God," Jeannie whispered to her husband, while glancing around for Mr. Faun—but he had stolen away at some point. Gone back to his camp with his spoils? "Bobert, could that really be true? Would Diane Segler-Frost really exploit some poor homeless guy like that?"

Bobert chuckled again. "Honey, come on! Don't you get it? They probably coached her to say all that stuff—to keep up with the illusion that the guy's for real. I have to say, though, I'm starting to admire this whole Mr. Faun thing. You have to admit it is kind of clever."

"I don't know, Bobert," Jeannie said, still twisting this way and that in her chair to cast about the café for Mr. Faun. "I don't know."

*

Jeannie was too self-conscious to tell Bobert of her intention to visit the Fine Arts Museum again so soon after her three recent trips, but on the following week when her days off once more fell on weekdays, she embarked in her car as soon as she knew the museum would be open.

She bypassed the other wings and floors, for so long her favorite sections of the museum, as if they didn't exist, heading straight for the Contemporary Art wing like a woman rushing on a clandestine mission to meet a lover.

What she wanted most to do was confront Diane Segler-Frost and demand that she admit to the truth, but Jeannie didn't know if the woman would see her, or if she'd even have the courage to go through with it if she had Segler-Frost in front of her. Who was she, after all? A woman who worked in a nursing home, whose only gig as an artist was as the illustrator of her husband's stories for an obscure publisher. She knew Bobert hadn't given her this work out of pity, and she didn't mean to think of his stories in belittling terms, but it was simply that she knew she was in too humble a position to expect Segler-Frost to owe her any answers.

So what she had decided to do, instead, was ask for answers from Mr. Faun himself. Maybe the offer of a little extra money would engage him. Maybe all it would take was someone who sincerely wanted to talk to him as a human being, instead of simply gawking at him as a half-willing objet d'art. And Jeannie wanted to apologize to him for the way she had talked to him before—before she had known.

She wondered, though, if he were capable of holding a coherent conversation. In hindsight, he gave the impression of being addled; maybe on drugs. Maybe, Jeannie thought with growing outrage, Segler-Frost even *supplied* him drugs to keep him under her thumb. Jeannie now viewed their two brief interactions in another light. Mr. Faun was no longer a charlatan to her, but something almost pure, like the proverbial noble savage. A mythical Wildman, perhaps, or the feral Nebuchadnezzar, driven mad by God.

All these thoughts, twirling faster and faster like brittle leaves in a whirlwind, settled to earth when Jeannie approached Gallery C and saw even before she entered it that the room was just as full as it had been during her visit with Bobert. But that had been a Saturday afternoon; this was a weekday morning. Mr. Faun had obviously proved an even larger draw in a week's time.

Jeannie noticed something else as she strode with purpose toward the entrance to Gallery C. It was hard not to notice it: a smell so potent that most of the people gathered in the room had a hand or both hands pressed over the lower part of their faces. The reek was far worse than what she had experienced in Mr. Faun's vicinity before. Once she had cooked a whole chicken for herself and Bobert, and left the carcass in the oven until later when she could pick through the bones for scraps of meat to use in a soup. She'd entirely forgotten the carcass until a week later, when she needed to use the oven again. Bending over to open it, she was struck full in the face with an odor of decomposition so profound that it was all she could do to swallow back the bile rushing instantly to the top of her throat.

She edged through the packed bodies, a bit more roughly than she would have expected from herself, until she came to the front of the ring of spectators, who stood back a few paces from the camouflaged pop-up tent.

Mr. Faun's empty shoes stood outside the tent again, and his upper body protruded from between the front flaps like that of a half-born infant. One arm was flung ahead of him, as if he'd been reaching for something to grab onto, to pull himself the rest of the way out. His eyes were open, bulging, the bright blue gone milky gray. The O of his lips had bloated even more than the rest of his face, which had turned purplish. From his nostrils and open mouth leaked blackish streams of what pathologists called purge fluid, while his beard was caked thickly with dried vomit.

"Oh my God," Jeannie gasped, clapping a hand over her own mouth and stifling a retch.

She had not only seen the bodies of dead clients at the nursing home, but on one occasion had been the first to discover one of them, an elderly man who had passed away during the night. So, although she was no pathologist herself, she had enough experience with death to know that Mr. Faun had been lying here dead for more than a day. More than several days—since, she guessed, shortly after her visit with Bobert.

Now she recalled the terrible cough that had come from down in his lungs. As someone who worked with people who often battled against pneumonia, she was ashamed of herself for not recognizing that cough before.

"Has anyone called the police?" she cried, her words muffled behind her hand. "Isn't anyone coming?"

A woman turned to face her slowly, looking surprised by Jeannie's attitude. "It's Mr. Faun," the woman said.

"I know it's him! Someone . . . someone needs to call somebody!"

"It's part of the *exhibit*," the woman replied, spacing out her words with wide gaps as if talking to a child. "It's *Mr. Faun*."

He looked artificial, like some kind of lurid horror movie prop. He no longer looked like a real person. That was how they could all stare, Jeannie thought; he wasn't a human being to them. The leap of empathy was too great. But he was close enough to human, like a chimpanzee in a zoo, to entertain them.

She whipped this way and that helplessly, as if appealing to those who had overheard her agitation and had turned to look at her. "If you won't do it, I will!" she exclaimed, scrabbling blindly inside her pocketbook for her cell phone.

A hand reached out from behind and took hold of her wrist, but not forcibly. Jeannie spun around to find herself looking into the face of the woman who years ago had dismissed her artwork as "pretty." Diane Segler-Frost.

"They're already on their way," the Fine Arts Museum's director told her. "I called them a little while ago. Please . . . don't make a scene. Let these people appreciate the installation until they get here."

Jeannie tore her hand out of the other woman's fingers. She backed away, wagging her head. She wanted to flee and never come back to this once beloved museum again. Before she did so, she scorched Diane Segler-Frost with her glare. The museum director looked unhappily resigned. Not guilty . . . just regretful that the exhibition was at its end.

"Your installation," Jeannie hissed at her, "lacks *life*."

The Left-Hand Pool

How many times had he driven this road . . . back and forth, forth and back? How many drives to work, dreading each mile—each *inch*—his car covered, to get to that place where he didn't want to be? How many rides home again, relieved that he was returning to his sanctuary? But a sanctuary within which there was only himself for company.

It was a rural road branching off from the highway. A long stretch through a tunnel of trees, trees crowding in from either side, as if they pressed forward to swallow up and unmake this manmade divide that kept them separated from their brethren across the way.

And then suddenly the trees opened up and there were two bodies of water, one to either side flanking the road, which crossed what was essentially an earthen bridge. But of course it had originally been one body of water until, again, humans had intervened to divide it into two estranged entities.

He didn't know if this was technically a pond or a lake; he didn't know the name by which it was called, if it had one. Or two. He thought of the bodies of water as the right-hand and left-hand pools. He had designated them thus based on the fact that the right-hand pool bordered the right-hand side of the road on his way to work. The left-hand pool was on the opposite side. On his ride home every evening, the left-hand pool bordered the right-hand side of the road. Come to think of it, he could easily have reversed their designations, but that was what he had decided on.

The right-hand pool was much more sizable: either a large pond or a small lake fringed by trees, with houses built close to its edge here and there, and little wharves and docked boats. But the water had to be fairly shallow, since big rocks broke the surface in places. The water here was a mirror of the sky, bright as a sheet of metal hammered into myriad fluid creases.

The left-hand pool, cut off like a severed limb and apparently ill-nourished, if not outright polluted, was an entirely different story. It was much smaller, with no houses peeking through the trees that thickly bordered it. Rocks broke the surface here, too, but in greater profusion; could the water level be a little lower on this side? The rocks looked slimy, like the humped backs of large animals. Large dead animals, rotting in the shallows. Close to shore the water was covered with fallen autumn leaves, like lily pads, and maybe their decomposition was the cause of the grayish scum that marred most of the pool's surface, except for broken patches of darker clarity.

It was November. The clocks had been set back an hour, and so it was now darker on his ride home from work. The sky would be purplish, tinged with streaks of orange-pink like the last dregs of blood leaking from a sliced wrist, and the left-hand pool lay in gloom.

*

How many times had he driven to work thinking today would be the day he would ask out his coworker? Even as he resented heading toward that building, that soulless box of despair, containing his cubicle like a box within a box, he would at the same time be filled with excitement—sickeningly alive in his belly like knotted eels—at the prospect of seeing her again. *Desperate* to see her again, but also weirdly dreading it, because of the tremor she inspired in him, a tremor like that which his car experienced if he drove it too fast on the highway. A tremor that threatened to shake him apart.

How many times had he driven home in the evening loathing himself because, once again, he hadn't been able to summon the courage? Despising himself for his shyness and weakness. He would feel as powerless to interact with his surroundings as a ghost, helplessly observing mortals day after day after day.

She was an African-American woman who worked in another department. She was usually chewing gum when he saw her; maybe she had been a smoker or was concerned about her breath. She often said hi to him and had occasionally exchanged small talk, speaking as she chewed her gum, which he found endearing. Despite these exchanges she never addressed him by his name, so he didn't think she knew it.

She was as tall as he was, and he had never seen her in anything but a smart black suit, which varied only in that sometimes she wore black slacks with her black jacket, other times a black skirt. Her hair was shoulder length and straight, and she had the most wonderful smile he thought he had ever seen: toothy and bright. A warm smile that made her eyes crinkle.

His other coworkers were less warm. Though no one had ever mocked or derided him to his face in the year he had worked this job, he had sensed their amusement and derision. He frequently heard whispers behind cubicle partitions, snickers and giggles, and his intuition told him these sounds pertained to him. He wondered if the woman's friendly attitude toward him was because she was the only African-American in their office, someone different, who maybe felt like an outsider though she kept up a brave face, and she sensed something in him that made her relate to him.

Imagining her lovely face and sunny smile, he stood at the right-hand side of his bed where he always laid out his clothes, knotting his tie, almost ready to set out for work again. As he stood there, a picture came to him of something that lay in the darkness under his bed like a child's coffin in a crypt. This image briefly eclipsed his coworker's face. But then he shut out the bedroom light and locked up his apartment.

As he left the house in which he had been renting the second floor for the same length of time he had worked at the office, he again determined that today would be the day he had long anticipated. Yes, it would be today.

*

He drove his car through the tunnel of trees again. This past year had been the first time since his childhood that he had lived in such a woodsy area, and it made him uncomfortable. It was too quiet out here, too isolated, the houses too far apart. Civilization seemed too tenuous, too fragile; this was mankind's brittle edge.

When he was a boy, his father had taken him several times out into the woods hunting. On the last occasion they had gone out together, when he was twelve, his father had shot a four-point deer—a beautiful animal that had caused the boy to experience both fear and awe. The rifle bullet entered the deer's shoulder on the right side, and in coming out the left tore off the deer's left leg. The deer managed to rise and continue loping painfully away from them. They followed it deeper into the woods for over half an hour, until finally it fell exhausted from blood loss but still alive. His father had ordered him to stay back, and then had crept up on the deer carefully so as not to be kicked. He had unsheathed a long knife and stabbed the deer deeply to puncture its lungs. It had then struggled with greater urgency, kicking in the leaves and dirt, but not for very long.

He had cried, watching it die, and when he told his mother of the experience she ordered her husband never to take their son hunting again. To this day he recalled the hot, silent look his father had then turned on him. A disgusted kind of look, as if his child had failed some vital test and would never develop into the man he should be.

To this day, he disliked the woods.

*

The tunnel of dying November leaves opened up, and there was the earthen bridge that split the two pools. As he drove, he happened to glance toward the right-hand pool, perhaps because he caught a glimpse of peripheral movement. And there, basking on a large rock that broke the mirror surface of the pond a little ways off from shore, rested some kind of animal.

He saw it for only a second or two, and though he felt the impulse to stop his car abruptly and look more closely, he was traveling at a fair rate of speed with other work-bound vehicles proceeding close behind him. Therefore, he was left with only a quick and unsatisfying impression.

What struck him most was the animal's size. It had a long body and short legs, like an otter, but it was too large to be an otter, and its sleek wet fur was black. Also, its head was not at all otter-like. To tell the truth, the head's shape was more like that of a deer, but without antlers. A doe, then? But a doe with such short legs? With a solid black hide? Some freak doe resting on a rock out there in a pond?

In the brief instant he saw it, the creature plunged headfirst off the rock, slipping into the water smoothly and disappearing.

He tried to look back over his shoulder, yet already his car had taken him too far along and he was afraid to ram into the tail of the vehicle ahead of him.

He knew one thing, anyway. The animal had looked beautiful, graceful and peaceful, in profile showing a placid black eye.

*

He had memorized her routine. Her gum-chewing and wearing of black told him she was a creature of habit. He came up on her as she was making a cup of coffee in the little office kitchenette. The kitchenette divided her work area from his own. He began brewing his own cup while she added cream and sugar to hers. She started talking first, as she always did, for which he was grateful. He tried not to stammer. Because they had superficially discussed movies several times before and found they were both movie buffs, their conversation turned to a popular new film. He took this as a signal, an invitation from her. Finally—*finally*—he did it. Since neither of them had seen this new film, he asked her if she'd like to go see it with him this weekend.

She had been beaming that warm, white smile, but in the instant he asked her out he saw the smile falter and crumble. It was like watching something beautiful, say the Taj Mahal, vaporized in a nuclear blast.

She regained the smile quickly, but it wasn't as wide, and it looked uneasy and maybe even wary. Her eyes no longer crinkled. The woman apologized for having to decline, informing him she had a boyfriend. But she appreciated his offer.

He smiled and told her it was no problem, and they parted for their respective work areas carrying their respective coffees.

He sank down into his cubicle, reflecting on how his months of anticipation had culminated in an ending lasting mere moments. Like a car plunging off a bridge into cold drowning water.

On the other side of his cubicle's partition, he heard soft tittering. Had the person on that side overheard him ask out his coworker? Yes, they must have.

He stared at the partition for a long time.

*

On the drive home that evening, he turned his head to look toward the left-hand pool, with the intuition that he would see that odd black animal again. He was correct and yet wrong at the same time. It was apparently the same animal, but not as it had been when he had seen it that morning in the larger pool flanking the other side of the road.

It was crawling up out of the water onto the jagged, rocky shore, with dead leaves plastered wetly to its black body. He wondered now if that morning its four legs hadn't truly been short, but instead folded up tightly or telescoped somehow, because now the black creature had very *long* arms, very *long* legs, unnaturally long and slender and multiply jointed. Furthermore, the creature walked upright like a human being. The rest of the body and head were the same as this morning, but the eyes in the deer-like head no longer struck him as being placid. They rolled wildly, showing the rim of white sclera around them, as if the animal were terrified or maddened with rabies. This time the animal didn't strike him as beautiful, but rather as something demonic.

As he slowed his car to a crawl to watch, unmindful of the other cars behind him—the drivers of which apparently didn't see the creature themselves, too busy honking their horns at him impatiently—the bipedal creature stalked up through the underbrush that grew along the edge of the left-hand pool, stepped into the murky woods, and disappeared from view.

*

The next morning, as he knotted his tie, in a break of routine he stood at the left-hand side of his bed. And when he had finished he crouched down to drag something out from under the bed into view. It was a long box, looking like a child's coffin, and it contained an object that had once belonged to his late father.

Lifting the lid off the box, he determined that today would be the day he had long anticipated. Yes, it would be today.

riaH gnoL

Nanette's nametag reads *Nan* and she works at the Magicade arcade, on the mall's ground floor. She is required to substitute for her coworker Janet sometimes at the customer services counter, where children redeem their tickets for the colorful but small and cheap toys that fill the glass bins, which might as well represent the reward for all of life's strivings. Mostly, though, she goes to various stations where people require assistance. (Not the mini bobsled ride; she hasn't learned that one yet. She suspects her boss doesn't trust her to operate it.) She's a backup for the snack bar, though there is a person dedicated to that area. The two attractions she herself is the dedicated worker for are miniature golf and laser tag.

When players pass their Magicade membership card through the reader at the miniature golf station, a ball of their preferred color drops from a chute and this is presented to Nan, who gives the player a golf club, determining its length by the child's height. The mini-golf area has an aquatic theme, on its walls phantasmal octopi and eels glowing purple and green under the black lights.

For laser tag, if they need assistance with it Nan helps the players don and buckle their vests (with chest and back plates flashing either red or blue, depending on the chosen team), then runs the short video of instructions and rules if this is the player's first time. She activates the ten-minute game program, then sends the players into the dark maze to hunt one another down, firing spots of red light from the guns they clasp. She is supposed to watch the players on four CCTV monitors above the computer, the action on the screens in black and white and the darting figures glowing as if through military night-vision goggles. She barely glances up at the screens, though; everyone else she saw tend to the game before she became the primary laser tag attendant did the same, even walking away to tend to another function

71

or to chat with a coworker until an electronic horn blast and a recorded voice announced the ten-minute battle was over.

After staring into space for a while, she looks up at a middle-aged
man standing a few steps from her, on the other side of the security
tape she's pulled across as if to cordon off a crime scene. This man, at
least, is following the action on the monitors as best he can make it
out. He's smiling; his two young sons are inside, pursuing each other
through the labyrinth, fighting a miniature Civil War of brother against
brother. Nan's formerly distant gaze locks onto the father's chest. He's
wearing a T-shirt with artwork—it looks like a Victorian steel engraving—that portrays a skeleton bartender offering a variety of poisons,
skull and crossbones on their labels.

Nan asks the man, "What's that on your shirt?"

The man glances down at himself as if he's forgotten what he put
on today, then looks up at Nan and smiles with blooming interest; like
all men, he thinks that if a strange woman instigates a conversation
with him she must be attracted to him. Nan is not particularly pretty
but she's young. She wears glasses with thick dark frames and a black
beanie pulled down over her ears and almost to her eyebrows.

He says, "Oh, I bought this in a liquor store—I thought it was
cool—but I'm sure originally it was like a cartoon meant to warn people about the dangers of alcohol."

"I'm going to bartending school," Nan tells him in her flat tone,
her face expressionless. This is her customary manner.

"Oh, really? You seem young to be handling alcohol," the father
says, sort of kidding her. "That's great, though."

"Do you know what they call a bartender? A mixologist. A really
good mixologist is called a professor of mixology. That's what I'm going to be."

"That's awesome. I'll, ah, I'll have to come to whatever bar you
end up working in and order a dirty martini from you. That's my favorite drink."

He waits for her to ask him whether he favors gin or vodka, a portion of vermouth or just "a quick glance at a bottle of vermouth" as
Alfred Hitchcock preferred, but she only stares at his shirt and the
horn blares that the game has come to its end. They both turn and the

two young boys slip out through the hanging strips that cover the maze's entrance.

"Well . . . thanks," the man says, looking back at her as he starts after his kids, who have already slung off their vests and hung them up and are now rushing in search of another activity. He looks regretful, as if he imagines he's lost the opportunity to sleep with her now that they've bonded over mixology. "Good luck to you with school."

A short time later, when the father approaches the customer services counter so his sons can exchange the tickets they've won for gaudy trinkets, Janet leans toward him over the counter and says in a lowered voice, "Excuse me, I saw you talking to Nanette. She tells some pretty weird stories. What was she saying to you?"

"Ah, well . . ." The man peers over toward Nan, an indistinct figure in the dark of the laser tag antechamber as she straightens the illuminated blue and red vests on their holders. "All she said was she's studying to be a bartender."

Janet, a young woman of Nan's exact age, chuckles and shakes her head and says, "Nanette is *not* studying to be a bartender."

*

A group of boys in their early teens has emerged from laser tag and loudly departed, but without sniggering at Nan or making any little comments half behind her back, for which she is relieved. In their place, she admits through the strips into the labyrinth two young girls, maybe friends, but she prefers to think they're sisters. After starting the timed program, she looks to the woman who stands waiting for them. She figures that this attractive, brown-skinned woman with her long matte-black hair must be from India.

She says to the mother in her monotone, "You have beautiful hair."

"Oh, thank you," the woman says, turning toward Nan, her surprised smile bright against her dark skin.

"I had a twin sister," Nan says. "Named Annette. Ever since we were kids we always had long red hair, down to here." She reaches around to touch her lower back. "We had the same black mole here, too." She pulls her collar down a little to point to a black dot at her clavicle. "Mine is on the left, but hers was on the right. Annette said our mole was the period on the sentence of our face, where boys had to stop looking. They couldn't go below that."

The maybe-Indian woman smiles again and says, "Oh . . . that's clever."

Nan's face remains expressionless. Today her beanie, covering her ears and pulled down almost to her eyebrows, is purple, but she wears her usual glasses with their dark frames. She says, "Annette was diagnosed with breast cancer when she was only twenty. It's uncommon but it happens."

"Oh my," says the mother with long coal-black hair. "That's terrible."

"She had to have a mastectomy. So between the two of us we only had three breasts. I told her because we were twins she could pretend she had two breasts and I had only one. We could share one breast. Sometimes I joked we were the two-and-a-half-Fates."

"I'm so sorry," says the maybe-Indian woman, her eyes intense with empathy.

Nan goes on, without a twitch in her blank face, "When Annette was in chemotherapy, it was really hard for me. Like I say, we both had this long red hair, and hers all fell out. It was like we weren't the same anymore, and I couldn't deal with that because we were always identical. I didn't do it consciously, but I started pulling my hair out, yanking it out strand by strand all day long. That's called trichotillomania. I would eat my hairs, too. That's called trichophagia. It got so bad that I finally had to have a ball of hair—they call it a trichobezoar—removed from my stomach. It weighed five pounds . . . same as a bag of sugar."

"Oh!" was all the woman she was talking to could exclaim, appearing too thrown off center to say more.

"My head ended up looking all bald, like Annette's, with just patches of stubble. It looks like another planet, with these strange continents. So that's why I wear this." Nan gestures to her purple beanie. "Because even though Annette died a year ago, I haven't been able to stop pulling my hair out and eating it."

"Ohhh." The mother of the two girls inside the maze makes a wincing expression. "I have a sister, myself . . . she's two years younger than me. I can imagine how you must feel."

Nan nods, face impassive. "It's hard. Now she's gone and it's just me, so it's not natural."

The electronic horn blasts and the maybe-Indian woman flinches.

The recorded male voice announces the session is over.

Later, when the two young girls have emerged from the maze, they go with the woman to the customer services counter to redeem the tickets they've earned. Janet leans toward the mother and says in a conspiratorial tone, "Excuse me, I saw you talking to Nanette. She tells some pretty crazy stories. I saw her pointing to her head. What did she say to you?"

The mother replies, "Oh . . . she was telling me about her twin sister, who died from cancer."

"And?"

"Well . . . how she's lost all her own hair, too. From pulling it out."

Janet chuckles and shakes her head and says, "Nanette has *not* pulled out all her hair. It's all tucked up inside her beanie. She has long hair, just like mine."

*

"It's good that your kids are in there alone," says Nan, gazing up at the CCTV monitors above the laser tag computer. Ghostly white figures dart furtively through the maze, with its partitions highlighted in paint that fluoresces under the ultraviolet lights. UFOs and alien planets in Day-Glo paint seem to float in the black void of the walls. She knows that teeth glow in there, too.

"Yeah—they have the place to themselves," says the mother who stands outside the security tape waiting for the boy and girl who went inside, looking up from the phone she's been playing with. She just texted her husband to let him know they'll be home soon. It's 8:30 and the mall closes at 9:00.

"Well," Nan says, "what I mean is, a couple times when I was looking at the monitors I saw some strange things in there. One time I let two teenage sisters go in to play, but I saw a third girl in there, too. She didn't have a vest or a gun . . . she was just kind of creeping around, hiding so the two sisters wouldn't see her."

The mother lowers her phone, her face rumpling in confusion. "Really? Was it someone who sneaked in with them?"

"No. I was here, I would have seen. And it wasn't someone who stayed from the last game . . . I would have known they didn't come out."

"Are there other ways in?"

"There's a fire exit in there, but if it opens it sets off an alarm."

"So . . . when the game was over, how many people came out?"

"Just the two sisters," says Nan. "After they left I turned the lights up and went in there looking, but I didn't find anybody."

"Oh wow . . . how weird is that? But is it possible you just misinterpreted it?" The mother gestures up at the monitors. "There are, like, multiple camera angles and all. Maybe it was just two angles of the same person."

"This person wasn't wearing a vest like the two sisters," Nan reminds the woman. "And anyway, I saw her again on another occasion."

"What? Really?"

"Yeah. One time there was no one playing laser tag and I was just standing around out here, waiting for my shift to end. It was just about this time. And I happened to look up at the monitors and I saw, like, a girl or a young woman just standing there inside, right out in the open. I couldn't make out her face because, well"—she nods toward the monitors—"you can see that it isn't easy to make out the details of the people inside. But I could tell she had long hair, down to here." Nan reaches around to touch the small of her back. "That's when I realized who it was. It was my twin sister, Annette."

"Ohhh," the woman says, and laughs as if with relief. "So she was playing a prank on you both times."

"No," Nan says in her monotone. "My sister died a year ago."

The electronic horn blasts, and the voice announces that the session is finished, but the mother holds Nan's gaze for several seconds more while the two children work their way to and through the hanging strips. Nan doesn't blink. She never seems to blink. But then she turns away and helps the girls hang up their vests and she clips the laser guns to the vests' fronts.

The mother hustles her children away, glancing back at Nan.

At the customer services counter, Janet says to the woman, "Excuse me, I saw you talking to Nanette a few minutes ago. She tells some pretty wild stories, but I think she really believes them. What was she saying?"

"Oh jeez," the woman replies, speaking in a low voice so her chil-

dren won't hear and be frightened, but they're too busy anyway looking into the glass bins at all the prizes. "She told me she's seen the
ghost of her twin sister inside the laser tag room a couple of times."

Janet smirks, shakes her head, and says, "Nanette never even *had* a
twin sister."

*

A husband and wife stand outside the cave-like laser tag entrance,
like the family members of trapped miners waiting for some word.
Three boys have gone inside: brothers or friends. The couple have
been talking, but during a lull in their conversation the man notices
Nan is staring at him and when he turns to her she says, "When people
go inside I always think I should be like Ariadne and give them a ball
of red thread to find their way out again, like she gave to Theseus. You
know, in the Greek myth about the maze with the minotaur in it."

"Oh yeah," the man says. "The minotaur . . . right. Heh. Well, it's
not *that* much of a maze in there, is it?"

As if she hasn't heard him, Nan says, "Every hair on our head
could be Ariadne's thread, you know? Every one of them a thread to
another possible path in our life."

Nan has been twisting a long coppery hair around her finger, in
three loops, tightly as if she means to cut off the circulation. She notices the man looking down at this, and she says, "Oh, this isn't mine. I
don't have any hair left, really, just stubble." Today the beanie she
wears is gray. "This is one of Janet's hairs."

"Janet?" the man says, sort of gaping at her. His wife is looking
back and forth between him and Nan.

"My coworker at the customer services counter. Can you see her?"

The man looks over that way, but his view is partly blocked by a
claw crane game. "Ahh . . ." he says.

"Janet's always making fun of me. She thinks I don't know it, but I
do. I wouldn't believe anything she says, if I were you. She thinks something's wrong with me, but I think there's something wrong with *her.*"

She pulls the hair too tightly around her finger, and it snaps, and
the horn sounds and the recorded male voice says that the game is
over.

The three boys emerge. Nan wants to ask them if they saw anyone else with them inside the labyrinth—a young woman with long red hair—but she always resists this urge. The brothers or friends wear different clothing and different haircuts and aren't even the same height, but she thinks of them as a kind of trebled image, one boy shimmering unfocused into multiple parts.

She watches unblinkingly as the boys lead the parents toward the customer services counter. As she does this, Nan walks slowly backward into the murk of the laser tag antechamber, where the red and blue lights on the hanging vests glow like the lights of police cars lined up alongside the scene of some terrible accident. A moment later, and a person looking toward the laser tag game now would not even see her.

At the customer services counter, the three boys hunch down to contemplate their choice of prizes from the glass showcases. No decision they will ever make in their future lives will be any less or more important, on up to the day when they preselect their coffins. Wood or steel? Tiny plastic dinosaur or miniature packet of sour candy? But no one appears to be attending this station. "Hello?" says the mother, thinking someone might be blocked by the central display of large gifts no one ever wins.

Up from behind the counter, a young woman rises into view, startling the mother a bit. Perhaps she was down there restocking one of the prize bins. The attendant's name tag reads *Janet*.

"May I help you?" she asks.

"Oh, sorry . . . didn't see you. The kids are still looking."

"No rush. It's still half an hour to closing time."

"Thanks." The mother hesitates, glances at her husband, then takes a step closer to the counter and says in a hushed voice, "Um, I hate to say it, but that girl at the laser tag game is really something, huh?" She remembers her name, from her name tag, and says it. "Nanette?"

The customer services attendant is not particularly pretty but she's young. She doesn't wear glasses, and she has a black dot of a mole in the exact center of her collarbone, and a curtain of coppery red hair that falls almost to her bottom. With eyes oddly unblinking, she smiles and wags her head and replies, "I'm sorry, I'm not sure who you're talking about. There *is* no Nanette."

The Toll

The car ahead of Nate's was taking so long at the toll booth, as its driver probably searched in the seat console or dug in his or her pants for change, that he ejected one CD and fed in another. He traded the best of Todd Rundgren for the best of Bread. It was the kind of music he wouldn't dare play on his computer at work for fear of teasing from his younger coworkers, but it was the sweet melancholy stuff of his teenage years, which he had spent in one unbroken yearning mope for love and sex in their delirious and incomprehensible tangle . . . not yet knowing where emotions and lust intersected or parted ways. He knew now, only too well. Both had parted ways a long time ago and departed altogether shortly after that, with his divorce.

As the first music track started, he glanced up again through his windshield at the car ahead, positioned in front of the toll booth's window. The red glow of its brake lights reflected on clouds of exhaust, which billowed and swirled in the frigid night air. It was almost two in the morning, and Nate was returning to Massachusetts from the Foxwoods Casino in Connecticut, feeling dazed from too little sleep, too much Maker's Mark, and losing five hundred dollars. Setting out Friday evening after work, he'd told himself he'd go easy on the drink and cards. Well, he always told himself that, didn't he?

Things had started to look interesting tonight when an attractive Vietnamese woman in her thirties who was also playing poker began flirting with him, but she was sliding down a precarious losing streak, and when she whispered that she'd sleep with him in the casino's hotel if he gave her a thousand dollars to continue playing, he'd withdrawn from her—crestfallen, though he should have known better.

This was getting ridiculous. Unless he'd missed it while changing CDs, he hadn't even seen the car ahead of him roll down its window for the driver to give the toll booth attendant his or her ticket. Through the churning crimson-glowing fog—which seemed to fill the air, almost obscuring the black lines of trees that hemmed in the narrow toll plaza—Nate couldn't make out the driver aside from a black blurred head, and he couldn't discern the toll booth attendant at all. Was there even anyone in there? Could that be why the driver was hesitating, uncertain? Where did toll booth attendants go, he wondered idly, when they needed to pee? Into the dark trees at the side of the road?

Nate glanced into his rearview mirror, imagining that the people behind him must be getting impatient, too. He saw that there was only one other car queued up behind him, but again he couldn't make out the person inside because of the way his own brake lights saturated his car's exhaust with more scarlet light.

The song "Make It with You" was cut off abruptly, in mid-wistful croon, and loud static took its place. Startled, Nate said, "Now what?" He ejected the CD, reinserted it, but it wouldn't play. Had the radio, by some quirk, come on instead? No—he checked . . . he had his system set to CD function. He ejected the Bread CD, fed in the Todd Rundgren again. The static hissed and crackled on. Great—something with the sound system. After losing five hundred tonight, that was all he needed. He stabbed his finger into the power button and the static was gone. He let out a heavy sigh, raising his gaze to the windshield once more.

The longer the three cars idled, and the more exhaust rose up around them, the more intense grew the red glow until it seemed that soon it was all Nate would see . . . like being at the bottom of an ocean of luminous blood.

Yet then Nate spotted something moving through the red fog, coming in from the right side of the exit ramp, crossing from the vacant E-ZPass lane into this lane. The thick red mist made it ill-defined, but Nate took it to be a large deer: dark and thin, with stick-like legs. Its movements, though—somehow strangely jerky and gracefully fluid at the same time—for some reason put him in mind of an immense daddy longlegs. And then Nate realized that this creature was bipedal, striding on just two strangely bent legs. It was hunched forward over two similarly long, thin, oddly bent forelimbs. Its elongated head, which he had first taken for a deer's snout, actually appeared to be tapered to a bony point.

"Oh Jesus," Nate said out loud, but keeping his voice low lest he draw the spidery figure's notice. "Oh man, oh no, what *is* that?"

The figure passed between the front of Nate's car and the rear of the car ahead of him. There it stopped, and Nate's heart slammed on its brakes in his chest when he saw the figure straighten up to its full towering height and face directly toward him—a silhouette in the bloody fog, skinny as a lengthy tree branch in the rough shape of a man.

Static burst from the speakers of his sound system again. Nate jolted, saw that somehow the power light was back on. This time words came through the static, sounding like a computer's synthetic voice: flat, lifeless, inhuman.

"Mr. Forrester," the voice half-buried in static said, addressing Nate by name. "We have a matter to discuss with you."

Nate didn't speak. Maybe if he pretended not to hear the thing, it would go away. How well could it see him in here, through the restless shrouds of fog? His fists gripped the steering wheel more tightly. Could he spin the wheel, stomp the gas, veer over into the E-ZPass lane and escape the toll plaza? Was there enough room between the cars to do that, without hitting the silhouetted figure? Maybe he *should* hit the figure. He flicked his eyes to the rearview again. Was there sufficient space to back up a little, before he tried such a maneuver? Could the driver in back of him see this figure too, or did his car block it?

Or might he be the only one capable of seeing it, because he was simply hallucinating the creature? Had he fallen asleep in his car while waiting for the driver ahead of him to pay his toll? Yes, a dream—a dream. Wake up, his mind screamed at itself, wake up, *wake up* . . .

"Mr. Forrester," the voice repeated, sounding exceedingly patient with its lack of intonation. "Are you listening?"

"Please leave me alone," Nate spoke up at last. His voice sounded to his own ears like that of a frightened child, close to tears. Pleading. He couldn't even summon the strength to feign strength.

"We're afraid we can't do that . . . you have been selected."

"Selected for what?" he blurted to the unwavering, seemingly faceless stick-figure.

"A test."

"Who are you?" Nate demanded, in almost a hysterical screech. It was an alien, wasn't it? An alien that meant to abduct him, subject him to some terrible examination or experimentation. A *test*, it had said.

The figure ignored his question. "There is a choice you must make."

Nate could only groan.

"Are you listening?" the voice droned again.

"What kind of choice?" Nate whimpered.

"There are occupants in the vehicles to the front and back of you. One occupant in each."

"Yes?" His voice quavered, unstable, as though it might unravel into incoherence . . . even as the figure's voice had taken form from hissing chaos.

"We have immobilized your three vehicles and the occupants within them—except for you. The other two are locked in the moment and are not privy to our conversation."

His car was immobilized? Nate shifted his foot from the brake to the gas and depressed it. His car remained idling as if he had done nothing. He pressed the gas pedal to the floor, to no effect. He returned his foot to the brake.

"The choice you must make is this: you must tell us which of the occupants of these vehicles should be removed from the fabric of existence."

"*What?*"

"Tonight, one of these human beings will be removed from existence. They will cease to be."

"But why?"

"Why is of no concern to you. Suffice it to say, it is an experiment."

"But—but why are you asking *me* to choose?"

"That is the experiment," replied the voice. "Isn't it? If we were to choose . . . well, it would be pointless. We wouldn't even be here."

"Is this some kind of trick?"

"Not a trick. A *test*."

"You want me to . . . you're asking me to pick which of these other people you should kill?"

"Not kill, Mr. Forrester. We repeat: to eradicate from existence. So that they will never have existed as a living entity at all."

"But how—how . . ."

"You needn't concern yourself with how, either."

"But what you're asking . . . it's evil!" The last thing Nate wanted was to provoke this creature—and now, rather than being an alien, he took it to be a demon—yet he couldn't restrain himself.

"Evil. Interesting. How so?"

"*How so?* These people have families . . . loved ones . . . they might have children waiting for them at home."

"Indeed. All factors that you must take into consideration when making your choice."

"But how do I know about those factors? I don't know these people! I can't even see them!"

"Try again. What might you tell about them from their appearance? The appearance of their vehicles?"

Nate peered into his rearview mirror once more, to find that a clear spot like a window had opened in the thick icy fog. Through it, he could now see the face of the driver in the car behind him, illuminated by the unnaturally vivid red light. It was the thin face of a young man, maybe a college student, but with his little ginger goatee and eyeglasses he gave the appearance of being intelligent, maybe even scholarly, not the guffawing beefy frat-boy type. Nate could now see, too, that his car was a silver Hyundai. The front license plate was folded under where he'd once nosed too close to a parking lot barrier. A homely little human detail.

Tonight Nate had lost more money than he took home working all week, endless hour after hour at a job he despised . . . and now on top of that he was being asked to murder a stranger? Because that was what the creature proposed, no matter how it chose to express it. Nate might as well press a gun to that's boy's forehead and blow the back of his head off himself. That young man was a son. He might have brothers and sisters. One day soon he might marry, to father children, whom Nate would be murdering, too. No—no—he couldn't do it. He was a gambler, and a drunk, and a loser, yes, he could admit to that—a loser at life, not just at cards—but he wasn't a *bad* person. He was not a *killer*. He would refuse to play this game, this alien experiment into human behavior, or devil's sadistic bargain. He wouldn't damn his own soul.

When he looked forward, however, and saw that the creature had shifted aside a bit to afford him a clearer view of the vehicle idling in front of his own, suddenly the decision that was being thrust upon Nate seemed much easier.

It was a gray Toyota RAV4, and though Nate couldn't see the driver's face, he could now make out that it was a woman with longish dark hair. Furthermore, on the rear window was one of those decals that portrayed a family of stick figures, corresponding to the owner's own family. In this case, an adult man, woman, and two small stick children with smiling faces, like figures a child himself might draw.

There really was no choice which of the two strangers should be evaporated, was there? This woman already *had* children. If Nate should indicate that she was the one to be eliminated, it wasn't as though he would be leaving her children motherless . . . they too would cease to exist, for she would never have lived to give birth to them.

"Have you decided, Mr. Forrester?" asked the voice through his car's speakers. "Do you require a bit more time?"

Another glance into the rearview mirror. No—that boy had been someone's child once, too. He still was. But if Nate pulled the trigger on him, his parents would never have known him, never have held him as an infant, never have kissed his newborn head. Hung his drawings on the refrigerator. Allowed him into their bed when a nightmare woke him in the middle of the night.

"What if I say no?" Nate said. Finally his voice sounded less shaky. Sounded like something approaching firmness. "What if I refuse to choose?"

"Quite simple. Then we will remove both persons from existence—and you can go on your way."

"You son of a bitch," Nate hissed.

"Perhaps you need to give it more thought, Mr. Forrester. Take all the time you want. We are, after all, suspended in this moment."

"You want to see how terrible people are, don't you?" Nate snarled. "You want to see how low we can sink. It amuses you, huh? You smug fuck. You expect it of us."

"As we say, the whys and wherefores of the test are not for you to ponder."

Nate squeezed the steering wheel so tightly that he thought he might wrench it free in his hands. "How about if I choose *you* to be eliminated?"

"We're afraid that is not an option."

"Of course not."

"Only the occupants of the vehicles."

"The occupants of the vehicles," Nate echoed, nodding slowly.

"Yes."

"*Any* occupant of these vehicles I want."

"That is the choice, precisely."

Nate kept nodding, until a hard little smile came to his lips, and he felt his eyes filming over with tears. "Okay," he said. "Then I've decided."

When he told the looming emaciated figure his decision, its voice over the car's speakers said, "Interesting."

*

Troy sighed irritably. It had seemed like an eternity for the woman ahead of him, in the RAV4, to find the two measly quarters that the man in the booth required for the toll. It had seemed so long, in fact, that he had actually dozed off for a moment. In that tiny span he had dreamed there was another car between his silver Hyundai and the woman's gray Toyota, but when he'd snapped awake again he saw that this wasn't the case. Just a second's worth of dream.

Finally, the RAV4 pulled ahead to continue off the exit ramp, and Troy rolled the Hyundai up alongside the booth to pay his toll as well.

Saigon Dep Lam

The first time Lan saw the angry black man, she was waiting on her motorbike at a stop light. The sun hadn't yet risen and she was making her daily trip to a nearby street market to buy supplies for her cousin's little restaurant, where Lan worked as a cook.

Her cousin Nhu had been taking pity on her when she'd given her the job, Lan was certain, because Lan's elderly mother had just passed away and her brother wouldn't do anything for her, but Nhu had also recently lost her best cook and so it seemed a reasonable arrangement all around. Quickly enough, though, Nhu had told Lan how grateful she was that she had taken her on. Lan had lived the first fifty years of her life in Trảng Bàng, and from that district Lan had brought the local pork soup recipe called "bánh canh Trảng Bàng," which had been going over very well with Nhu's customers. Nevertheless, Nhu had asked Lan to keep herself back in the kitchen out of sight. She didn't need to tell Lan why. It was obvious that her appearance might be deemed unlucky and affect the diners' appetite.

Like the myriad interchangeable women who on motorbike or on bicycle or on foot peddled fruit or sold lottery tickets on the streets of Ho Chi Minh City, Lan typically wore a floppy cloth hat and covered her face from the eyes down with a handkerchief. Those other anonymous women wore handkerchiefs or surgical-type masks to protect themselves from bike exhaust and the harshness of tropical sun, but in Lan's case it served also as disguise. Only back in the kitchen, or in Nhu's home, would she take these accoutrements off. As she was thus outfitted, and with the gloom of pre-dawn masking her further, the black man didn't so much as glance Lan's way as he went walking past.

Foreigners abounded in Ho Chi Minh City. Since the American soldiers had withdrawn, Westerners had been a much rarer sight in Trảng Bàng, and so Lan had found herself staring at them surreptitiously over the edge of her mask ever since coming to this city. They inspired in her a mixture of feelings, all of them vague. This man was surely no tourist, however. His clothes were too well worn, looking unwashed as well. He wore a bushy beard and a soiled little cap, and he carried a walking stick—though he strutted along the sidewalk with a kind of vigorous defiance, so he surely didn't need the stick as a cane. Lan suspected it was a visual weapon, to intimidate others into not harassing him. And she suspected he had suffered much harassment in his life. Probably only a few years younger than herself, he was doubtlessly the offspring of an African-American soldier and a Vietnamese woman, and any woman who had slept with an American soldier would be deemed a prostitute, any child of such a union a bastard and outcast. This man's curse was that he had inherited all his father's characteristics; from this distance, at least, he didn't look Vietnamese at all.

The traffic light changed, and Lan drew up her legs and started forward again. She glanced back at the black man as he stalked in the other direction. He frightened her, because he looked surly, even deranged, but she also felt sorry for him. What kind of life must he have lived these past forty-plus years?

As she approached the market, already bustling with activity, she had a fantasy that the man she'd seen wasn't a "con đen lai"—a black half-breed—but an American soldier who had never returned home, choosing to remain in Vietnam. She had heard of such men. But living openly on the streets of Ho Chi Minh City, rather than in some rural area, as the stories went? Not likely, and besides, he had looked too young to have been a soldier. It was just that, having lived so much of her life in near isolation, Lan liked to fantasize and embellish stories to entertain herself. She always kept such flights of fancy to herself.

At the market, despite her hat and handkerchief, she felt eyes crawling across her face like curious ants. Did these people around her think she had no business here, acting like a normal person? Shouldn't she be begging in the street as the maimed so often did?

"You have a beautiful eye," Nhu had told her. It was meant as a compliment, but Nhu's words seemed to Lan to narrow her worth down to a very small spot. Her other eye was a tough white orb set in the patchwork web of scar tissue that covered most of her face, twisting her lip up tightly so that speaking and smiling were equally awkward. Nhu seemed to think it was Lan's good fortune that the napalm had left her that one viable eye. But an eye for what purpose? Seeing herself in the mirror? Seeing others steal looks at her on these market excursions? It was the same as when Nhu bragged to her husband, "Lan was the cutest little girl; I wish you could have seen her." Such a very small spot of her life, those first eight years. Was she even the same person, Lan sometimes wondered, as that beautiful child Nhu referred to?

Heading back to the restaurant above which she lived with Nhu's family, her Honda laden with bulging plastic sacks, Lan envied that black man who had been marching down the sidewalk with his stick like a rifle, so fiercely unapologetic. Although, she considered, that was probably due more to madness than to pride.

*

Neither Lan nor Nhu were Catholic, but many in Vietnam were, and even Buddhists welcomed Christmas—though it was nowhere near the celebration that Tet, the Lunar New Year, would be next month. Ho Chi Minh City was bedecked and bejeweled for the Western holiday, only days away. Lan had never seen the city before at this time of year and was dazzled. It made her think of the popular song "Sài Gòn đẹp lắm"—"Beautiful Saigon"—with its cha-cha rhythm.

Ho Chi Minh City would always be Saigon to its proud citizens, wearing its imposed name like the handkerchief she wore to hide her scars. As she rode toward the restaurant with her daily haul, Lan reflected on the city's duality. Assimilated into a unified Vietnam, but inhabited by people who largely still despised the North. Wealthy tourists shopping at the glistening Diamond Plaza and bustling Bến Thành Market, while homeless child prostitutes hawked their bodies for food and drugs. Unlicensed images of Mickey Mouse and Winnie-the-Pooh on clothing and school murals more prevalent than images of Ho Chi Minh himself, and what must his statue in front of the People's Committee Building think of the city lit up this way? Only blocks away from his statue loomed the great Notre-Dame Cathedral, its twin bell towers still outlined in Christmas lights with dawn not having yet broken.

The song lyrics were doing their cha-cha-cha through Lan's mind . . . "Sài Gòn đẹp lắm, Sài Gòn ơi, Sài Gòn ơi!" . . . when she spotted the black man for the second time.

In the past few days she hadn't seen him again, even though she had scanned around for him as she rode her Honda, but she had seen several other monsters in the area instead.

Because Lan worked long hours, from opening in the morning until closing at night, Nhu had been giving her cousin two days off a week. Up to now, on her days off Lan had kept to the house, cleaning around to help out and treating herself to a little TV: a Chinese costume drama or Korean soap opera dubbed into Vietnamese. She went out only when the city was in darkness, feeling like a ghost—a ghost of an earlier, bloodier Vietnam. But the black man's unabashed fearsomeness had strangely inspired her to be more bold herself, and this week on her two successive days off she had spent a good deal of time just riding around in the naked blaze of sunlight. It had been a guilty thrill, like going out to meet a secret lover.

This was when she had seen the other blighted souls. Like the black man, they too appeared on the sidewalks, as if they had come out specifically for her to see them. They were like signposts, Lan thought.

Sitting on the curb at a street corner, a teenage boy with deformed legs. Lan wondered if the deformity could be the result of Agent Orange. He appeared addled, grinning brightly at passersby like a much younger child. But when she saw him the next day, toward dusk, sitting at the same spot as if he'd never budged from it, he was rubbing at his eyes. Was he tired, sleepy? Were his eyes burning from the long day exposed to glaring sun and vehicle exhaust? Was he even crying? Lan didn't want to think that, didn't want to imagine that the people who apparently dropped him off here to beg were in no great hurry to pick him up again.

On another street corner, a monk sat in his saffron robe, also as a beggar, his head shaven and his face horribly scarred by fire so that it looked like melted wax, his lower lip hanging grotesquely, his eye sockets flat patches of flesh. No doubt a victim of napalm, like herself, but Lan then wondered if he might have failed at self-immolation.

But this morning, in the deep blue murk before dawn, she saw the black man again. Maybe he too had taken a couple of days off from working, if he worked, or begging or scavenging or stealing. This time he was reclining on the sidewalk, propped up on his elbows watching the motorbikes and occasional truck rumble past. Had he slept in that spot last night, or was he only resting a while before he resumed his ceaseless wandering?

Lan experienced the odd impulse to pull her bike up to him and stop. But what would she say? And could he even carry on a coherent conversation? She remained frightened of him. And yet, she felt compassion for this unruly spirit.

She rode past him, continuing on her way to her job, but at that moment she had an inspiration. Because the man was obviously the child of an American, she had decided she wanted to give him a Christmas present.

*

With Christmas only a couple of days away, she couldn't wait until her next two days off to buy the man's gift, and she didn't want to ask for another day off when her cousin depended on her so. She decided to keep on the lookout for some shop along her way to the market that might open early for business. Otherwise, she'd have to hope to find a shop that stayed open later than Nhu's restaurant did. Maybe one of Saigon's large night markets, which blazed and bustled past midnight, with their rows of food stands and diverse wares spilling out from under awnings?

Working in the cramped kitchen, soaked from steam and sweat, she wondered what she might buy the man, never having bought a Christmas present before. Although he might welcome some money in a little envelope, such as people gave out at Tet, that didn't seem personal enough to her. Money would simply be like just another throwaway to a beggar.

She also wondered what she might say to him as she presented this gift. With her scar-tightened lips, she felt more than awkward speaking with people, and though she believed she might feel less self-conscious speaking with this particular person, that might not prove to be the case when she was actually standing before him.

And then she asked herself what exactly she hoped to achieve by giving the man a gift. Did she expect the gesture to soothe his savage heart, calm his bedeviled soul, if only briefly or fractionally? Did she even think her offering might touch him so deeply that his response would be to love her? Love this frightful woman, whom no man had ever loved?

This last fancy caused Lan to go hot in the face with embarrassment, shocked at herself and cursing her childish imagination for slipping its reins. She was only contemplating an act of kindness toward another human being, who looked as though he might benefit from kindness. Should there be any more reason than that simple human connection?

*

On the morning of the 23rd, Lan caught a glimpse of him again as she buzzed past on her Honda. His back was to her, but she recognized his defiant stride, his wooden staff. He was turning into a narrow side street, not far from the stretch of sidewalk where she had seen him those two other times.

She felt the impulse to turn her bike around and follow him, to see if he lived or worked down that way—if he really lived or worked anywhere—but she had already gathered her supplies for the day and Nhu would be waiting for her back at the restaurant, where things had to be prepped before they opened for business. So instead, Lan simply made a mental note of which side street it was.

*

That night, when Nhu had closed up the restaurant, Lan made an excuse about wanting to look for a new pair of sandals and then hurried on her motorbike to a night market, as she had earlier considered. Other night markets in the city might stay open to 2 A.M., but this one was the nearest to the restaurant and closed down at midnight.

Because the market was out in the open, she wasn't the only woman who wore a hat and a mask over her lower face, so her general anonymity and sense of purpose fortified her as she slipped through the throng that choked the aisles, shopping or buying food and drink.

Lan considered buying something useful, like a new pair of sandals for *him*, but that just didn't seem festive. Perhaps a little doll of Ông già Noel—Old Mr. Christmas—but she decided he might find it more childish than cute. Finally, she found what she thought was the perfect gift, and her lips almost stretched into a smile beneath the handker-chief.

It was a miniature plastic Christmas tree, with little colored balls and foil-wrapped presents.

Lan managed to sneak the tree into Nhu's home, and into her tiny room with its mildew-stained walls, without Nhu or her husband and children noticing. Because how could she explain what she had bought it for? If the children saw it, they'd want it for themselves, and of course she'd give it to them and say that had been her intention.

Before she hid it away, Lan studied the tree again. She fingered the tiny gifts, trying to imagine the wonders they might contain. Gifts that a husband might give to his wife. The makeup she had never worn. The jewelry no one had decorated her with. Sexy underwear or sheer stockings, maybe.

But she knew that beneath the foil there were only cubes of Styrofoam.

*

Their tiny restaurant was packed from wall to wall on Christmas Eve. Lan worked almost feverishly in the kitchen to keep up. Coming back from delivering another order to a table, Nhu smiled with satis-faction and related to her cousin, "A girlhood friend of mine, Phuong, married an American and moved to the USA. Two years ago she came back to visit her family with her husband. She told me it's so cold where they live, on Christmas the streets are dead—everyone stays in-side and keeps to themselves. How lonely that sounds, huh? Look at all the excitement tonight. I'm sure it's better to have Christmas in Vi-etnam."

Yes, it was noisy out there on the street; Lan could hear the chaos of sound coming in through the open front of the restaurant, along with the night's heat and the traffic exhaust. Ceaseless streams of mo-torbikes, horns beeping as cars and trucks struggled to press through, pedestrians shouting and laughing, throbbing disco music from nearby cafes. Right now she wished she was out there herself, looking around for the feral "con den lai." She was starting to get anxious.

"Do you think we'll be closing at the regular time tonight?" Lan asked. They usually locked the folding front gate at eleven.

"We'll see if the crowd has thinned out by then," Nhu said. She put a hand on her cousin's shoulder, and no doubt could feel uneven scar tissue through the thin fabric of her top. "I know you're tired, Lan."

Lan assured her, "I'm fine, Nhu." If she couldn't locate him tonight, she'd try again tomorrow after work. But by then, Christmas day would be all but over, her gift all but meaningless.

Nhu returned to the serving area, balancing four plates of food on her arms.

But as eleven approached, Nhu judged that the crush of customers had subsided enough that they should close at the regular time. "You worked so hard today, Lan. You need to go home and rest. Tomorrow will be even busier, after all."

Lan experienced a wave of relief. There might still be time to spot the black man out there somewhere. With the streets so active, why shouldn't he be about as well?

After they had cleaned up for the night and were about to lock the front gate, Lan said, "I think I might ride around a little bit, just to look at the lights."

"Don't forget this," Nhu said, reaching behind her and passing a plastic shopping bag to Lan. It was the bag she had hidden the Christmas tree in. "Who is it for, Lan?"

For a moment Lan couldn't answer, but at last she said in a tiny croak, "A friend."

"Really? I'm happy you've made a friend. You'll have to tell me about her. Or him."

"I will." Lan bowed her head and ducked past Nhu, straddling her Honda before her cousin could ask her more.

*

Each major thoroughfare in Ho Chi Minh City was a single mass of motorbikes, like one immense dragon crawling along, metallic scales gleaming. On the sidewalks swarmed the equivalent in pedestrians, children wearing glowing reindeer antlers or even, inexplicably, plastic Halloween devil horns. The streets with their shops and restaurants and cafes were already bright, but the imported holiday made them extra dazzling ... gaudy and delirious. Christmas lights twinkled everywhere, each Catholic church so festooned with flashing colored lights that a Westerner might think it was a Las Vegas casino, or a mother ship from an alien world.

As Lan got away from the main avenues, though, things gradually grew more subdued. She drove down the street where she had seen the half-breed those several times, but she didn't find him, and doubled back again for another try. Coming the other way was a motorbike with a Vietnamese man dressed as Santa Claus seated behind the driver, on his back a sack of gifts. Seeing Lan notice him, he smiled at her through his fake beard as their bikes passed each other and he called out in English, "Merry Christmas!"

At last, Lan directed her Honda toward the side street she had seen the black man entering that other morning. She found it was little more than an alley, twisting this way and that. Small cement houses crammed cheek-to-cheek, with open fronts giving a peek of their interiors, where Buddhist altars glowed with Christmas-type lights themselves. The alley boxed in the smell of food, of incense, of tropical night; the lurid and sensual air of Vietnam.

She rode along slowly, met by only half-curious looks from those walking the narrow street or seated inside the open front rooms of their homes. She didn't spot the man she sought, within or without. She turned down more micro-streets that branched into new directions, becoming lost in an unfamiliar maze.

Turning yet another corner, she came upon a street that had strings of white Christmas lights suspended over it, row upon row, forming a kind of tunnel of light. Lan was drawn this way and passed under the arched ceiling of light, intrigued to find out where it would lead her.

The streets had phased into a somewhat wealthier type of neighborhood, some of the houses now possessing high walls and iron gates. Here, Catholic families had set up large nativity scenes, having formed caves of metal foil perhaps to simulate ice and snow. Within these foil hollows sheltered oversized replicas of the baby Chúa Giêsu Kitô, a cloned army of foreign saviors, all with their pudgy arms outstretched.

The narrow side streets became even more subdued, the noise of the city increasingly distant, fewer and fewer people out walking, more walls to hide the fronts of houses. Lan heard TVs and music playing quietly on the other side of those walls, sounds that seemed more lonely than comforting. The walls were topped with spikes or glued shards of broken glass. The alley Lan was currently in came to a dead end, where an especially large and ambitious nativity scene had been set up. But the smiling child no longer charmed Lan into forgetting her mission. As she turned away to retrace her path, she began to despair of finding the black man tonight and delivering the gift she had for him.

The lighted dioramas in this dark labyrinth, with their painted plaster figures, now seemed to Lan more like the eerie scenes of a ghost train ride, such as those she had heard existed at big amusement parks like Suối Tiên and Đại Nam Văn Hiến. Now, sure she had failed in her venture, she just wanted to find her way out again. Back to her tiny room above the restaurant. She would give the pathetic plastic tree to Nhu's children.

She was angry with herself when she realized a tear was forming in the corner of the one eye Nhu called beautiful.

Lan backed her bike away from the dead end, turned the handlebars, and rode the Honda down the passageway and around a corner. But soon she grasped that she had taken the wrong path. She was now in an even darker, quieter alley formed from the back walls of houses, without any Christmas lights or even smiling plaster faces to offer her company.

She longed to find that tunnel of white light again, a landmark that she knew would funnel her toward more familiar surroundings.

So around another corner . . . and Lan soon found herself at another dead end, but this one composed simply of a dark wall streaked even darker with mildew. This neglected space was almost a tiny courtyard, though one formed more by chance than design.

Once again confronted with such a tight space, Lan had to stop her bike and walk it around to face the other way. This time when she had turned it around, however, she saw that a dark figure was moving in her direction slowly, gradually shuffling its way out of the shadows and into the meager light that penetrated the alley.

When the faint illumination fell upon the figure's face, she saw it had no real face to speak of. That was how she recognized this man. He was the saffron-robed monk she had seen begging on the street corner by day, his face a thick mask of scar tissue, his eyes melted away leaving only blank flesh.

He scuffed his sandaled feet along, reaching out his arms ahead of him like the oversized Christ dolls.

Though she bore a resemblance to him, the monk's appearance frightened her, and her instinct was to remain still and silent so he wouldn't be able to hear her and approach her directly. Though surely he couldn't want to hurt her. Surely, if anything, he would only want some money, which at another time of day and in another location she would have been happy to offer.

As Lan stood there astride her bike, poised like a deer paralyzed by terror, another figure detached itself from the shadows pooled along the opposite side of the alley, yet this figure was low to the ground . . . crawling on its elbows, and dragging its twisted, useless legs.

Lan drew in her breath sharply when she discerned it was the teenaged boy she had seen on two successive days, begging on another street corner, smiling with a younger child's innocence at passing traffic. Unlike the monk, the boy could see her, and he beamed that same smile at her now. Again, though, in this place and at this time of night his huge grin only caused a shiver to go through Lan.

A third silhouette, moving weirdly into the light. This young man was missing one arm and one leg, perhaps having stepped on a forgotten landmine. He was using a single crutch to hobble along. He grinned at Lan, too.

A girl perhaps ten years old crept forward, smiling shyly, maybe self-conscious because lingering poison from the dioxin Agent Orange had caused her eyes to be spaced twice as far apart as they should have been.

Lan had felt an increasing need to flee, a growing panic, as these figures and several more who were compromised in other ways emerged from the darkness, apparently intent on closing in a half-circle around her, with only the dead end wall behind her. She thought she should gun her motor and plunge between them before that happened. But they all halted a short distance away, facing her expectantly.

As they stopped there, forming their half-circle, Lan finally realized that the "con đen lai" was amongst them, holding his staff in one fist like a proud explorer who stood at the crest of a mountain in an uncharted land. He was not smiling, as most of the others were, but neither did he look filled with fury as when she had seen him in the past. Like his companions, he merely watched her as if in anticipation.

In that moment, Lan was convinced that the man had previously taken note of her, too, after all. And that he had led her here.

She swung her leg over the back of the Honda's seat and unhooked the plastic bag she had hung on the bike. Her silent audience seemed to lean in with greater interest as she reached into the bag. Looking up at them to observe their faces, no longer afraid of those faces, Lan drew out the plastic Christmas tree, decorated with its tiny foil-wrapped packages.

The teenage boy with the useless legs barked a single delighted laugh. The girl with the terribly far-spaced eyes smiled more broadly.

Lan saw that the black man was staring intensely at her eyes, one dead and one alive. He nodded at her. One more thing to unwrap.

As Lan set the tree down on its stand, on the street in front of the half-circle, with her other hand she reached up to pull her hat away. Then she removed her handkerchief as well.

Distantly, the six bells in both of the twin towers of the Notre-Dame Cathedral rang out deeply over the beautiful city of Saigon.

It was midnight.

It was Christmas.

The Green Hands

4. The Imperatives

Two imperatives overshadowed every other thought, during every waking moment: *Run* and *Never stop*. For Zetter they were really a unified concept, a single rule.

At one time the belief was that all sharks needed to keep moving constantly or they would drown. Zetter had read this was no longer deemed to be true, except for perhaps certain types of sharks . . . but it was true for him. He had to keep running, or he would die.

In the beginning he'd believed that he was only at risk at night, and so he had relaxed his guard during the day. Until he had found out, almost too late, he wasn't safe in the daylight either.

In the beginning he'd also believed that it was only adult Caucasian males who sought to catch him, to seize him with their venomous green hands, because at first those were the only types of Green Hands he'd encountered. But he'd learned this, too, was not true.

Here's how he had discovered both things.

2. The Mall

Zetter liked malls, because they were thronged with people. Though the Green Hands were people, too, most people weren't Green Hands, and he was certain his pursuers didn't want witnesses who might possibly interfere or impede. They would be wary of coming at him in plain view of others.

That didn't mean they wouldn't try to put their hands on him surreptitiously when others were around. On one early occasion, he had been walking toward a subway train to board it along with a crush of other people, when peripherally he saw a hand reaching for his elbow. Someone a little behind him, to his right. The hand caught his eye because it was softly luminous, as if a dim bulb inside it illuminated translucent skin . . . but this pale luminosity, as always, was like that of a glow-in-the-dark toy: phosphorescent green in color. He had cried out in alarm and pushed roughly against the people in front of him. He'd knocked down a middle-aged woman. A young black man had sworn at him and tried to punch him in the mouth, but had missed and struck his shoulder instead. All that mattered was that Zetter had just managed to elude the extended hand. He never looked back to see the person who had tried to touch him; he just broke free of the line of people and went bolting off down the subway platform for the nearest steps up to the street.

Since then he knew that while it was comforting to have a lot of other people around, it was not a good idea to get too boxed in. It was like those situations where a woman gets groped in the press of bodies on a tightly packed train or bus. Best to keep his distance, so he could see the Green Hands coming for him.

On this day he was at a large, sprawling mall with multiple levels. He didn't know the name of the mall and wasn't even sure which city he was in. He was already rationing his funds at this point, having emptied out his bank account shortly after he'd begun running, so for dinner he only allowed himself a small cup of coffee and one plain doughnut in the food court. Then, because he was so weary it was as though a filter of TV snow hung before his vision, he crossed his arms on the sticky table and rested his head on them. Yes, it was a risk—it was always a risk to sleep, anywhere—but he was not a machine. *Never stop* had to allow for at least teases of rest. He could only run for so long before he needed to recharge, so he could run again.

Because his senses were so attuned now to the presence of others, he jolted awake a split-second before the person looming over his table could reach out to put a hand on his shoulder. Maybe he felt their presence displace the air, or caught a nearly subliminal whiff of perfume. In any case, he sat up, startled and wide-eyed, and scraped backwards in his chair.

"Whoa, easy," the female security guard said, holding up the hand she was going to touch him with. "Just wanted to ask if you're okay— you've been asleep at this table for a couple hours now. Are you waiting for somebody?"

"Two hours?" he replied, his head packed full of cotton.

"Yeah, that I've noticed. The mall's closing for the night, so I'm afraid you'll have to move on. Do you need to call someone?"

"Closing down?" Zetter looked to either side of him. All the tables that had been occupied when he'd first sat down with his frugal meal (by families with small children, teenage boys acting obnoxious to impress the girls in their pack, people who were not *alone,* were not *running*) were empty now. A Latino man and a Latina woman in rumpled blue uniforms, on opposite ends of the food court, were spraying down and wiping the table tops.

"Yes, it's just past nine-thirty. The mall's closed. You'll have to leave now."

He stood up and slipped his arms through the straps of his backpack. He kept the backpack with him whenever he left his car, in case he was ever in a situation where he had to abandon the vehicle. This had happened a few times, but he'd been able to steal back to the car later.

"Okay . . . sorry," he muttered to the security guard, shuffling past her blearily, trying to remember in which direction an exit might lie. The floor plans of several malls he was better acquainted with overlapped in his mind, coming unbidden, confusing him even more instead of helping.

But despite the disorientation brought on by having awoken abruptly after too little rest, Zetter found his way downstairs to one of the mall's exits without any difficulty. Along the way, barred shutters were being drawn down over all the shop openings. Manikins, many of them faceless or even headless, stood frozen behind store windows like museum displays re-creating the life of an extinct alien race. Their poised, motionless, unnatural hands made him feel anxious.

The spring night air was cool, with the faint smell of new life struggling to gain its foothold. The moon was full, the craters that caused people to liken it to cheese—in the way that humans often trivialized things greater than themselves—seeming especially vivid. His car looked remote and small, served up on a dinner plate of lamplight surrounded by empty darkness. He started across the lot toward his vehicle, glancing all around warily as he moved, like a soldier crossing a clearing. When he'd come here this afternoon he'd had to park far away because these empty slots had all been filled.

Pine trees bordered the far side of the lot. It was the trees he watched most suspiciously. Any second now he expected to see a figure come running out from those dark trees: a clean-shaven white man in a neat business suit, eyes gleaming too feverishly, his grin too wide, and his arms held out in front of him, fingers hooked like talons, hands glowing a brighter green because the surrounding air was so dark.

He was now equidistant between the mall's entrance and his car cringing in its yellow pool. A crisp breeze came up, ran over him like water, and gooseflesh rose in its wake. He kept watching the trees as they grew closer, like a line of approaching figures garbed in black robes with peaked hoods. But he also kept shooting looks to either side. The wind caused an empty soda bottle to clatter across the pavement behind him, and he whirled around . . . relieved to find no smiling man in a black suit stretching his arms out to him, only paces away.

At last he reached his car, tossed his backpack onto the passenger's seat, locked himself inside, and exhaled a heavy shuddery breath.

He still felt vulnerable, poised out here on an exposed plateau of darkness. Even with the lights off inside his inactive car, and him slumped down in gloom, the Green Hands would still be able to recognize the vehicle itself. If enough of them came . . . if they grew bold enough . . . if they were to smash his windshield with stones and grope in through the holes . . .

Sleeping some more in his car was not an option, anyway: he could see the revolving red lights of a security vehicle as it started making its closing-time sweep of the lot that encircled the mall like a moat around an abandoned castle. He would be rousted a second time if he didn't remove himself first. Better to get the shark swimming again. He had no destination, but he had half a tank of gas at present, so he could afford to drift aimlessly for a bit until he might spot another place where he could rest a little—preferably, once the new day broke, when he believed it would be safer.

So he got the car rolling and pointed it toward one of the lot's exits, before the roving red lights could swing in his direction.

The side road he nosed along soon flowed into a highway. He went with its current, a dark ribbon of night, nearly empty but for distant red taillights floating like airborne embers. The full moon rode the sky alongside him, as if pursuing him.

He put on his radio for a semblance of company, but the FM was just as noisy with grating static as the AM. When he thought he heard a man's voice say *Zetter* behind the layer of static, he quickly shut the radio off.

How did they know his name? How did they know him at all? Why did they want *him?* What had he done to them? What *was* he to them?

Yet he knew he wasn't the only one they'd targeted. Maybe all his life he'd brushed shoulders with people hunted, haunted, by the Green Hands. People whose harried, tense faces he'd dismissed as merely the manifestation of an anxious, anxiety-ridden society.

He knew he wasn't their only target because he had seen them touch someone else with their green hands.

Until then he'd never known of the Green Hands—never suspected their existence, never heard so much as a rumor of them.

It had happened like this.

1. Deirdre

It had been a Sunday evening. Who, he'd wondered when his wife Deirdre went to answer the front door, would be ringing the bell at this time? His sister, living in Rhode Island with her husband, would never come unannounced—though perhaps an old friend or two would, despite his dislike of unexpected guests. He heard Deirdre's voice in their tiny front hallway, but didn't catch the words. Curiosity roused him from lounging in their bed watching TV, and he went to go look for himself.

Deirdre had left the living room door halfway open, so through it he saw her in the hallway, standing at the threshold to the front door, though at this angle he couldn't see who was speaking to her. He hung back to listen.

Deirdre's coppery red hair was mussed, and she had pulled on a bathrobe because they hadn't changed out of their sleep attire for the entire day, too comfortably lazy to even shower. Deirdre was forty, but to Zetter's eyes just as attractive as when he had met her at twenty-five. Too attractive, he often fretted. They had argued over the years because of his jealousy, his insecurity. He was the first to admit that he was jealous and insecure. Who wouldn't be, with a wife as good-looking as Deirdre? He always imagined how her coworkers must covet her. He sometimes checked her cell phone and laptop, and when she caught him at it their fighting would be long and awful. Conversely, she didn't seem jealous at all, and even that would eat at him; didn't she value him as he did her? Despite not sharing his affliction, did she comprehend that if she were ever to cheat on him, he would be utterly abandoned, lost in the world? That if the only person he really loved could betray him like that, then no other person could ever be trusted again? Maybe she would have sympathized more if her parents had been unfaithful to each other, as his had. They were both gone now, his parents, their own fighting only stilled in death, their twin stone plaques in the earth disingenuously serene.

When he and Deirdre fought about his anxieties—especially when he gave voice to these fears and, in doing so, more than implied accusation—he would feel physically corrupted afterwards, as if guilt were an actual poison he'd masochistically injected into his own body.

Yet even now he wondered: was this person at the door a persistent lover she was trying to shoo away? Some coworker so obsessed and bold he would even try to see her at the house, or who might not realize (through Deirdre's intentional omission) that she had a husband at all?

Watching his wife as she looked out into the evening's deepening murk, Zetter could make out her words at least. She said, "I'm sorry, I don't understand. What are you saying?"

Then Zetter saw an arm reach through the threshold toward his wife's chest, as if to take hold of a breast. His heart rocketed in his own chest . . . but Deirdre seemed just as startled. She flinched back from the reaching hand. The stranger's arm was covered in a black sleeve, such as that of a business suit, with a white shirt cuff peeking out its end. The suit made Zetter flash, irrationally, on the idea of Jehovah's Witnesses come to sell them salvation. But there was another detail: the hand moving toward his wife appeared to glow faintly, a pallid bioluminescent green, in the gloom of their front hallway.

It all happened in a moment. Deirdre didn't recoil far enough, and the hand with its firefly glow pressed flat against her sternum, the V of bare skin between her breasts, and Deirdre disappeared.

There was the barest sliver of a second in which Deirdre, poised at the doorway, seemed suspended between existence and nonexistence. In that eye-blink she appeared as a negative image of herself, the same phosphorescent green as the hand that had touched her, the hand that had then been promptly withdrawn. She was like an afterimage burned by the sun on Zetter's eyes. Then Deirdre ceased to be, and the place where she'd been standing in her bathrobe and tousled red hair was empty.

The person who had touched her then stepped through the open doorway, out of the night and into the hallway, as if to occupy the space where Deirdre had been.

"Hey!" Zetter said in dazed protest, gaping.

The man who had stepped into Zetter's home turned his head to grin hugely at him, his gleaming eyes unblinking and fervid. He appeared to be younger than Zetter, perhaps in his thirties, with neatly cut sandy hair and a nicely fitted black business suit. His tie was green. His hands were green. He raised both of them and extended them toward Zetter, starting for the half-open door to the living room in which Zetter stood.

Zetter couldn't reach the door in time to close and lock it. Instead, he whirled in the opposite direction, streaking through the dining room and into the kitchen, and the back door of the little house he had shared with Deirdre for over a decade. He heard the grinning man behind him in pursuit, but somehow Zetter had the presence of mind to scoop his car keys off the kitchen table before he threw open the door and burst out into the darkness of his back yard. His driveway was just around the corner of the house, though his feet almost went out from under him on the slippery grass.

He got the car door shut just as the grinning man slammed his body against it, hands splayed open against the glass. They glowed more distinctly out here than they had inside the house.

The man was still thumping his hands across the windows and the car's body as Zetter got it started and screeched out of his driveway, onto the quiet side road where his humble little house squatted.

In the rearview mirror, Zetter saw the black-suited man still chasing after him, sprinting down the center of that drowsy little residential street, hands groping at the air, white grin reflecting the streetlights.

Zetter had never looked back since.

And he carried that final flash of Deirdre with him, like a strip of negative from which one no longer has a print.

3. The Rest Stop

He drove on the highway for an hour and forty minutes. He was vaguely conscious that he had crossed a state line. He had rolled his window down to let in the brisk spring night air, to keep himself from nodding off, regretting that he hadn't hidden in a toilet stall in one of the mall's department stores, to nap there sitting down until the mall opened again in the morning. Finally he gave in to exhaustion and pulled the car into a rest stop. He considered going inside the service building to buy another coffee to keep himself awake until daylight, but he didn't think any amount of coffee could accomplish that at this point. He parked his car at the far edge of the lot, sank down low in his seat, and pulled a soft orange blanket over himself. It was the blanket Deirdre would cover herself with in the car. Deirdre had always complained of being cold, even in the warm months. He would tease her about it.

He pressed a corner of the blanket to his nose, to see if he could detect a ghost of her perfume, the scent of her hair, some lingering essence, but there was nothing. It just smelled vaguely of himself.

Sunk in his seat, tightrope walking the fine line between the waking and dream worlds, he found himself staring at the car's closed glove box. He seemed to recall there was a pair of Deirdre's winter gloves inside, made from soft leather. He wondered if those would retain any of her scent, but he couldn't bring himself to reach out and open that little hatch, to take the gloves out and confront them.

He dreamed that he had forgotten to roll his window up again. He dreamed that a man stood just outside the car, a man with sandy hair, reaching in to touch him on the head like a faith healer. He snapped awake with a gasp in his heart, but saw that the window was closed and no man dressed like a Jehovah's Witness stood beside the car. He also saw that the sun had come up, though it was still low enough in the sky to indicate the day was young.

He was cramped, but he felt a little better for the rest. His stomach complained, however, and so did his bladder. A headache had developed while he slept, too. Caffeine deprivation was the primary cause, he figured; he was addicted to coffee. Now was the time to get some, and he'd need to gas up again before he got back to moving.

So Zetter slipped out of his car and, hands on his hips, stretched far backwards and then from side to side to work out some of the kinks. While rotating his head on his neck, to the accompaniment of grinding creaks, he saw three children playing in the parking lot, not very far from him. His car was still solitary here at the edge of the rest stop lot, so he presumed these kids belonged to one of those vehicles parked nearer to the service building, occupying themselves while their parents fetched them some breakfast sandwiches or such inside.

Seeing that he had emerged from his locked car, the children stopped whatever it was they were doing to raise their heads and look directly at him.

Zetter returned their gaze and saw they were two girls and a boy, ranging from maybe six to nine, with dark complexions and jet-black hair—perhaps Indian? Huge dark eyes in solemnly beautiful faces. The morning was very cool, so they wore padded winter coats, with their hands in mittens. They had been kicking at something on the ground between them.

Zetter saw that their object of interest was a dead animal that had been flattened by a car in the lot, so long ago that its fur was faded, its species unidentifiable.

"Hi," Zetter said, as they stared at him without blinking their out-sized black eyes. He was already taking one step backwards toward his car.

As one, the three small children broke into big white smiles and pulled the mittens off their hands, off their small green-glowing hands, to let them drop to the pavement. Then, as if at the sound of a starter gun, they charged at him, their mouths silent but their eyes seeming to giggle exuberantly.

He made an instantaneous decision, though it was more animal instinct than strategy. He knew he didn't have time to slip his hand into his jeans pocket for his car keys, extract them, unlock his door (even though his key chain had a remote), open the door, duck inside, close and lock the door before the trio of children were upon him. So instead, he turned in the opposite direction from his vehicle and ran, sprinting, hoping his long legs would carry him well beyond their reach so that he could swing back around toward his car again, this time with more of a space between himself and his pursuers.

Daylight? Children instead of adults? *Nonwhite* children? Two of them *female* children? Either there had been all sorts of Green Hands all along, or else the original beings had spread their condition, their corruption, like a disease.

He ran in the direction of the highway, and in his frantic state of mind even considered forsaking his car and flagging down someone else's vehicle. But what would he tell the driver if he proved successful? (Though he knew it was more likely he'd only inspire anyone who saw him into increasing their speed.) Would he tell them he was being chased by three homicidal tykes, the touch of whose stubby little fingers would unmake him?

Still bolting toward the highway, before he could start arcing to the right to circle back toward his vehicle, Zetter saw a tractor-trailer truck coming up fast on his left, having peeled off the highway onto the ramp to the rest stop. He managed to dig down in himself for a further surge of speed, to get past the truck before it could cut him off. If he had to stop abruptly to let it rumble past him, that might be all the time the children needed to catch up to him.

Yet he made it across the width of the exit ramp to the guard rail, where he did have to skitter to a stop lest he topple himself right over it onto the highway. He heard the truck driver lay on his horn and thought the man must be angry at him for having dashed right in front of him. But as the truck's air brakes hissed, Zetter heard a series of thuds and thumps, and even through the driver's closed window he could hear the man yelling incoherently.

Zetter turned toward the vehicle, which had come to a stop and loomed idling, to see the driver half jumping, half falling from his cab. He could also see several small dark heaps underneath the length of the trailer. Hoping that he wasn't misinterpreting what he saw, Zetter started jogging back toward the truck.

The driver had dropped to hands and knees to look under his vehicle and cried out, "Oh my God, no . . . oh God, no! *No, no, no!*"

But Zetter wanted to cackle. He wanted to whoop, *"Yes, yes, yes!"*

The truck had struck all three of the children who had been pursuing him. He couldn't have planned it better if he had tried. One of them was still pinned under a rear wheel of the tractor, little more showing that an outflung arm. The other two, further back, were flat-

tened like the dead animal they'd been playing with only a minute before, the whole of the intestines pressed out of one, the head of the
other so squashed and emptied out it was just a sleeve of skin, and all
this spread along smears of blood with the fanged pattern of tire
tracks. Zetter could only tell the two bodies under the trailer had been
the girls by their long hair.

Maybe he giggled, because the driver suddenly jerked his head
around to look up at him. The stocky, middle-aged man—with his
white-stubbled jowls and a baseball cap like a souvenir from a mundane
life that was now irretrievably behind him—had tears in his eyes. Zetter
wondered if the man was crying for the children or for himself. Zetter
hoped he wasn't smiling; he couldn't tell. The man wailed at him,
"They just ran right out in front of me! You saw it, man, didn't you?"

"Yes," Zetter comforted him, coming a few steps closer. "It wasn't
your fault."

"Will you tell the police that?"

"Of course," Zetter lied. He had no intention of staying here long
enough to be questioned by police.

"Were they . . . they weren't with you, were they? I thought they
were running after you."

"No."

"They weren't playing with you?"

"I didn't even see them. I saw a moose on the other side of the
highway." Zetter pointed. He was in Maine, right? If not, he hoped the
story didn't sound too absurd. "At least, I thought I did, so I was running to have a better look. I bet those kids saw it, too. They were
probably doing the same thing."

"Oh God," the driver bawled, looking around again at the three
children he'd killed. "I can't believe this . . ."

Zetter dared step closer to the driver, and therefore to the nearest
of the bodies: the boy crushed under the rear tractor wheel. He helped
the driver stand up, taking his elbow to support him. It was a strange
sensation, touching another human being after having been so careful,
in recent times, not to allow anyone to touch him under any circumstances. The man fished out his cell phone. "I'd better call the police,"
he blubbered, like a big child himself, though other bystanders were
now gathering all around the truck and numerous cell phones had al-

ready come out. Zetter saw a teenage boy squatting down to shoot video of the smeared bodies with his phone.

With the driver distracted by his call, Zetter approached the child pinned under the wheel, until he all but stood over that outflung hand. It was of extreme interest to him. The miniature hand with its slightly curled fingers was intact except for a deep gash in the center of the palm, almost like stigmata. But the detail that so intrigued Zetter was the fact that, in death, the boy's hand no longer glowed green. It was the same brownish skin tone that his face had been.

"It's *awful*," a woman was sobbing hysterically. "Where are their parents? Does anyone know their parents?"

"Why would they run in front of him like that?" some man behind Zetter asked.

The driver looked up from his cell phone. "They saw a moose," he sobbed.

Zetter was about to turn away, figuring now was a good time to make his escape before the police arrived—and with the crowd growing thicker, the driver wouldn't as readily notice the departure of his witness—but something else about the dead boy's hand reclaimed his attention. Was the skin of his palm actually moving slightly, the lips of the laceration pulsing irregularly?

Then a tiny head pushed out of the wound: the head of an insect, with feelers probing the air. The head was luminous green, even the two great eyes. Horrified but mesmerized, Zetter continued watching as the rest of the insect struggled out of the wound in the boy's palm, like a moth emerging from its cocoon. It wasn't a moth, however, but a large wasp, entirely colored that pale phosphorescent green, though slicked red with blood. It flicked its wet wings as it poised there on the boy's cupped hand.

Zetter wondered if the boy had only been a host, and if he was now gazing at the entity that had possessed the child. Was that why the boy's dead hand was no longer luminescent: this fleshly vehicle could no longer serve its purpose?

The wasp scuttled in a half-circle, as if to face Zetter directly. He backed off several paces. Thank God its wings were too wet for the thing to take flight just yet.

In the meantime, Zetter took flight instead, running off toward his car. He thought he heard the truck driver call after him, but in the mounting clamor of voices he couldn't be sure, and he didn't look back to check.

He stopped for gas and coffee in a small town, after taking an exit further down the highway.

5. The Endless Crime

He was in a motel again. He hadn't bothered to take in its name. They were all interchangeable by now. Once again, he wasn't sure what state he was in. He figured lower New Jersey; perhaps Delaware.

It was good to be showered again. He called for a pizza delivery but wished he owned a handgun as he answered the door to accept it. How could he apply for a gun permit, though, the way he jumped between states? And he had no idea how one went about obtaining a gun illegally, except to steal one. But the exchange of pizza and money went without incident, and he sat down on the bed to eat while he watched TV.

No news stories about mysterious assailants with green hands, whose touch caused people to vanish from this world. Did the authorities know about the Green Hands but conspire to keep the general public unaware?

In all this time he hadn't caught any news stories about a missing wife and husband from Massachusetts, their home abandoned without anything having been packed. Either he had missed any such story or the authorities had squashed that information, too.

He sat in just a T-shirt and boxers he had bought in a mall after the escape from his home. On the bedside table lay his wallet and the stainless steel Swiss Army watch that Deirdre had bought him for his birthday eleven years ago. It was a little scuffed but still handsome. Its hands were frozen at 11:59 P.M. He could have had the battery replaced at one of the malls he'd been to, but since he avoided unnecessary human interaction he had been putting it off. Anyway, it seemed appropriate to him that he should appear to be moving outside the flow of natural time.

After he finished the pizza and a bottle of soda, he lay back in bed and continued watching TV, having settled on a true-crime series, the theme of which involved the critical first forty-eight hours of a homicide investigation. A suspect was brought into an interrogation room, a camera near the ceiling recording the session. Zetter became engrossed in the proceedings but dozed off during a commercial. When he opened his bleary eyes again, another person was being interrogated. At first he thought this was an accomplice, until he realized that the earlier episode had ended and this was a new one. There was no doubt a marathon session of episodes of this program underway. Though he regretted not seeing the outcome of the last episode, Zetter got caught up in this one. A man shifted restlessly in his chair as a detective pressed him about the shooting death of his wife. The suspect swore that in the darkened living room of their home he had thought his wife—returning home late from visiting a friend—was a burglar.

The detective insisted the husband had shot his wife intentionally, aware that it wasn't a friend she had been visiting, but her lover.

At some point Zetter fell asleep again. Later he woke up again and resumed watching. Once more it took him a few minutes to realize it was yet another episode, yet another crime.

This recurred several more times through the deep of night, into the small hours of the morning. One crime blended, unresolved, into the next until they all seemed to be a single crime—complex, convoluted, ultimately insoluble—involving countless perpetrators, countless victims, a crime that was ongoing and never ending.

6. Blackout

Zetter had parked his car in the lot of a large bookstore that was perched on a hill like a fortress in a very hilly area of this city, which to his mind demonstrated humankind's insect-like determination to flourish in any terrain or environment. He didn't know this ashy gray city's name and was still not certain what state he was in—both literally and figuratively—but the bookstore at least offered him a welcome sense of familiarity. He and Deirdre had often visited several Massachusetts branches of this same bookstore chain, and though each store varied slightly in its individual character, overall they were pretty much uniform. A common Sunday routine for them had been to go to the bookstore to browse around and have a cappuccino in its little café before going across the street to the supermarket for some grocery shopping.

He sipped a cappuccino now, standing by his car, looking out over the unknown city as its lights multiplied, the mellow purple evening shading toward full night. The summer air was thick, enveloped him as if to drown him slowly in its humidity, but it further reminded him of weekend excursions and vacations with his wife. Car headlights advancing in strung beads of gold and receding in beads of ruby streamed along the distant, steep streets. Golden light glowed through the bookstore windows that faced onto the parking lot, and inside Zetter could see people flipping through magazines in that section of the store. Inside the building, a little Asian boy maybe five years old pressed his palms and nose against the glass, staring out at the pretty evening like Zetter.

But as if to masochistically spoil this tranquil moment for himself, Zetter was reminded of one of their Sunday bookstore visits, when a masculine voice had said with pleased surprise, "Deirdre," and they had both looked up from the magazines they'd been perusing to see a man who was younger, taller, more trim, more nicely dressed than unshaven Zetter in his casual Sunday T-shirt and shorts. This man was grinning at Deirdre and entering into enthusiastic chitchat with her. Deirdre was suddenly bubbly and animated, too; and though she introduced the man as a former coworker from her previous job, after that the two of them had gone on as if Zetter wasn't there, as if he had altogether ceased to exist, until finally he had simply returned to paging through his magazine, without really seeing what those pages held, his face gone hot inside, his jaw clamped too tightly.

Later, they'd argued in the supermarket across the street while buying the food they meant to eat together, in one of countless rituals in the life they shared—arguing itself a recurrent ritual—their voices growing so loud that people turned their heads to look at them, and by the time they arrived home that evening they'd gone from raised voices to not speaking.

Zetter glanced over at the little boy still squashed against the glass as if suction-cupped there, gecko-like, suspiciously expecting to catch the boy staring at him, but the child was still dreamily gazing off toward the urban vista, those scintillating rivers of gold and red. Zetter turned back to look upon the sprawling, sparkling city, too.

And then it stopped sparkling. All the city lights that had proliferated as the sky darkened were extinguished simultaneously, extending to the limits of the horizon. The only lights that remained were the headlights and taillights of the traffic streams that crawled like immense, bejeweled millipedes.

Had the city's electrical grid become overtaxed this sultry summer night? Too many air conditioners running?

He heard voices behind him, looked around warily at a couple with paper coffee cups in their hands, who had just emerged from the bookstore and unlocked their own car so as to depart. They too were gazing off toward the lightless city. "Huh," Zetter heard the man say to the woman. "Maybe a solar flare, huh?"

"Maybe a drunk hit a pole and brought down a power line."

"Nah. . . . Look, it's too widespread for that."

"Mark," the woman said, her tone edging toward nervousness as she shot a look toward the now darkened bookstore, "I don't like this."

"Something's wrong," Zetter said, as if joining in their conversation, but he only said it under his breath.

"Something's not right," Zetter heard the man named Mark say to the woman.

The couple got into their car quickly and started it up.

Zetter looked from their car to the bookstore windows. They were now like thin sheets of ice covering a starless black void that reached back unto infinity. There, still pressed to the glass, were two tiny hands. Hands that glowed green against the blackness of oblivion.

Zetter fumbled with his keys, unlocked his car, and got himself inside. Through his windshield, he saw the couple in their car already heading for the parking lot's exit. He started his own vehicle and began turning it in a wide arc to point it toward the exit. This action brought him nearer to a wooden fence that bordered the far side of the lot, where the hill fell away sharply. With this fence close on his left, he peeked out again at the darkened city. Something about the scene that stretched below him caused him to brake for a moment and to study it more carefully. He then realized what he was seeing.

Those lines of headlights and taillights were no longer flowing. The lights still glowed just as brightly, but they had all come to a standstill, as if in a still photograph of a city.

Could a solar flare, he wondered, shut down car engines, too? But even as he asked himself this, he knew this occurrence was not due to any conventional celestial event.

He got his car moving toward the exit again, once more glancing at the black windows lining the bookstore's flank. Those little green hands suction-cupped to the glass were gone.

As he came up on the lot's exit, he saw that the couple had pulled their car over to the side a little and put it into park, with the motor idling. Its interior was dark. Just as Zetter's vehicle came parallel, both the driver's and passenger's doors opened and the couple stepped outside again. They no longer held coffee cups in their glowing green hands. With their faces contorted into grins that threatened to split their cheeks, the man and woman extended their arms and threw themselves upon Zetter's car, pounding its hood and windows with their palms.

He thrust his foot against the gas pedal, and the man slid away off to one side. The woman, more toward the front of his car, was pushed over and went down below the line of the hood. The car jounced roughly as it went over her . . . first the front tires, then the rear. Zetter didn't stop or look back, not even to see if the man with the crazed clown grin was chasing after him. He sped down the hill toward the main street.

There, ahead of him, he saw the street was clogged with unmoving traffic. Idling cars with their headlights and taillights gleaming. As he approached the bottom of the hill, he suddenly slowed in speed, for he saw that the doors on all those unmoving cars were swinging open.

Just before this steep access road to the bookstore joined the main street, there was a little residential road that branched off to the right. Zetter veered his car onto this tributary, grateful for it, his heartbeat a desperate, incoherent splutter.

In his rearview mirror, as he turned onto the offshoot road, he saw overlapping figures in unknown numbers silhouetted against the headlights, leaving their cars . . . and breaking into a run en masse, like a group taking part in a marathon.

The side road was narrow and bumpy, the pavement split and potholed as if great tree roots underneath had stressed the pavement, though it was only a matter of frost heaves and neglect. His car bounced as if he were running over more scattered bodies. He passed several dark houses that crouched among clumps of black trees. And then he came to the road's end. It was a cul-de-sac.

Zetter swore and pounded the steering wheel with the heel of his fist. He cranked himself around in his seat to look out the back window, but trees now blocked the lights of the street except for gold and red twinkles showing through here and there, like stars in alien constellations. Too dark. If any figures were already racing along the twisty little side road, he couldn't see them. Probably none were close, just yet; otherwise their hands, glowing disembodied, would give them away. But this was only the scantiest respite; he knew they'd catch up with him at any moment.

Even if he could back up or turn the car around, what was the point? The traffic that had come to a standstill in the major street would block his way. And all those many drivers . . . they'd block him, too.

Run. Never stop.

They had boxed him in at last. Where could he run to now—into the trees? With all the freshly made Green Hands abandoning their cars, hundreds of them, maybe *thousands* of them closing in on his position from all over the city—perhaps, by now, every inhabitant of this city—they'd simply fan out and surround him. It was only a matter of time.

It was finally time to stop. Maybe it would be better to cease to exist, at any rate . . . put an end to this nightmare existence.

That was what his mind said, but his body followed the biological imperative to survive, and he was already lunging out of his car and rushing toward the nearest of the darkly squatting houses whose properties formed the cul-de-sac. The first point of egress that presented itself to him was the garage adjacent to this house. The overhead door was shut, but the beams of his car's headlights showed him a door to the side of that. He turned its brass knob, found it unlocked, ducked into the garage, and shut the door after him. He flipped the latch in the knob to lock the door, then faced the gloomy cavern he had entered. Just enough illumination from his headlights made its way through the overhead door's little windows to reveal an array of gardening implements hanging from a rack bolted to the wall. Rakes, hoes, long-handled spades, and a pitchfork with five curved tines. He took this down and balanced its weight in his hands.

He could only hope that at least temporarily he had thwarted his pursuers, who wouldn't know which of these houses, if any, he had stolen into.

His victory was briefer than he'd thought. Where the garage's back wall met the house proper, a door was flung open and a man appeared in its threshold. Gray-haired, big-bellied, wearing a comfy Homer Simpson T-shirt and sweatpants and a grin like a gleaming scythe blade. And green hands, as if they had been dipped in some phosphorescent chemical. Without a word or exclamation, without any accusation for Zetter's trespassing—indeed, his smile seemed to *welcome* Zetter joyously—the gray-haired man jumped down the two steps from the house to the oil-stained cement floor of the garage and came at the intruder with luminous fingers spread wide.

The man all but flung himself onto the tines of Zetter's pitchfork as he swung it around in front of him. The five prongs entered the man's jowly throat, and that stopped him in his tracks. He even blurted, then started gurgling, and pawed at the air like an insect with a pin through it, though his grin didn't so much as twitch. Zetter jerked the tines free, but before the man could stagger forward he jabbed the pitchfork into his lower face, tearing through flabby cheeks and stretching his lips back from his grinning teeth. Again Zetter tugged the prongs free, only to stab them into the man's face again, higher this time, into his eyes. The squelch of his pierced orbs and the scrape of bone made Zetter's stomach roll onto its back, but he held tight to the pitchfork's shaft and followed the homeowner to the garage's floor. His brain impaled through the orbits of his eyes but still wearing that Cheshire Cat smile, the gray-haired man convulsed violently as though he clenched a live power cable in those bright white dentures of his. Zetter kept him pinned to the floor, putting weight on the pitchfork's handle. Finally the man was still, and Zetter let go of his weapon, stepped back panting. The tines were still stuck in the dead man's skull, the handle bobbing close to the floor.

Zetter considered using one of those gardener's spades to hack off one of the man's glowing hands and use that to light his way into the blackened house itself, but already both of the dead man's hands were losing their pale luminosity. Zetter recalled the hand of that boy crushed by the truck at the rest stop, some months back.

Vague shadows passed in front of the murky little slit windows in the garage's overhead door. He heard the brass doorknob rattling. Without wasting any more time, Zetter rushed past the body of the first person he had ever intentionally killed (*the first?* part of his mind questioned) and plunged through the doorway the homeowner had appeared in. He shut this door and locked it behind him, too.

The interior of the house would have been entirely dark, had it not been for the shining green hands drumming at all its windows.

They hadn't been tricked as to which house he had entered. They surrounded this one, probably more and more of them coming by the second, streaming onto the obscure back road from all those vacated cars bejeweling the streets of the city. They slapped the flats of their hands against every ground-floor window, the combined green light showing through curtains, shades, venetian blinds. But why didn't they find themselves rocks, bricks, other objects to swing against the glass? Even a fist might break a window. Windows seemed to foil them, or confound them . . . maybe even made them timid about applying force. All this time Zetter had thought it was simply their inability to break the safety glass of his car's windows, but now he realized it was something more than that, something unaccountable. A window was a portal that showed you another place, beyond the place you were in. Perhaps they were even reverential toward windows.

He didn't want to put any great trust in this theory, though. Even if they were impeded by windows in some strange way, they might still shatter one unintentionally through all their slapping against the panes. He needed to make himself more secure. The house had no second story, but . . . a basement? The door to a basement, if it had one, would be in the kitchen. So, by the misty greenish glow that penetrated the house, he found his way into the kitchen and there located a door that, when opened, revealed a darkness with the mildewed smell of an underground place. He descended the first few steps and shut the door behind him, but found that it didn't lock. He cursed internally. Yet what choice did he have now? Better to keep descending. Maybe there was a small room he could lock or barricade himself in; at the very least, a closet to conceal himself in. Maybe there were more weapons, even guns.

Or maybe he had painted himself into a corner that no biological impulse for survival could prevail over.

The cellar was in deep yet not total gloom, for once again that fungal green illumination entered through several small windows spaced along the walls, at the level of the ground outside. Even here, maybe squatting low or even lying on their bellies in the grass, the Green Hands drummed their hands against the glass.

A billiard table stood in the center of the main room, which was a playroom with an old sofa along one wall, a hanging dartboard, and a refrigerator perhaps stocked with beer. Zetter picked up a pool cue and held it like a spear while darting looks around him. An adjacent, smaller room showed a water heater hulking in the corner, and a washer and drier against one wall.

The tattooing against the cellar windows, and those upstairs—he could hear it through the low ceiling—increased in tempo, grew wilder, until surely the glass couldn't take much more and every window would explode inward simultaneously. Yet then, suddenly, it stopped altogether. Everything was still.

Had they given up, then? Had the glass truly defeated them?

The green glow had subsided along with the drumming, swallowing Zetter in a darkness he actually welcomed, but now the glow returned. Instead of thumping against the windows, this time the hands pressed flat against them and remained there unmoving. Were they going to try to push the panes out of their frames, instead of smashing them? Zetter couldn't tell if any pressure was being exerted.

He turned and stepped into the laundry room, which he found had its own door, standing fully open. He closed it, but again it had no lock, proving itself useless. He looked about for things to use to barricade it shut . . . for all the good that would do against a crush of bodies, once the Green Hands got inside. For sooner or later, one way or another, they must. The windows down here were too small for anyone but perhaps a child to crawl through, but the windows upstairs, not to mention the doors, were another matter. And they might have no compunction at all about smashing down the doors.

It was while checking to see if he could disconnect the washer and dryer, to push them against the door, that he glanced up at the single tiny window in this room and saw not only hands pressed against its dirty pane, but the squashed nose of a little boy's face. A little Asian boy of about five years. Grinning like a larval Buddha.

Zetter had grown breathless from his exertions, and from terror, so when he shouted at the child's face his voice was ragged. Close to cracking, close to weeping.

"Why me? Huh? I'm nothing special! *Why me?*"

The child stared as if into his core, but of course made no reply. Despite or because of this, Zetter kept on.

"If I did something . . . if I did something wrong, I didn't mean it! Okay? I'm sorry!" At last he broke into sobs. *"I'm sorry!"*

A crease in the center of the boy's left palm seemed to widen and deepen, showing black inside, like a little toothless echo of his grin.

Zetter thought the tears that had welled up in his eyes were distorting what he saw, until he realized that the lips of this little vagina-like slit were pulsing irregularly. Then a tiny head pushed out of the bloodless opening . . . pushed straight on through the window pane as if it posed no barrier at all. It was the head of an insect, with feelers probing the basement's damp air. The head was luminous green, even the two great eyes.

Horrified into silence, though tears still trailed down his cheeks, Zetter watched as the rest of the insect struggled out of the portal in the boy's palm, like a moth emerging from its cocoon. It wasn't a moth, however, but a large wasp, entirely colored that pale phosphorescent green, slick with slime or mucus. It flicked its wet wings as it poised there, on the inner surface of the cellar window.

Before the wasp could take to the air, Zetter threw open the laundry area's door and leaped back into the playroom, meaning to slam the door shut and trap the wasp in the smaller room.

He found, though, that the air in the playroom was filled with swarming, soundless wasps, swooping and circling, glowing as beautifully as the fireflies he would catch in a paper Dixie cup in his backyard as a child.

Zetter began shrieking in the voice of panic, an animal-like sound he had never made nor heard before, waving his arms madly in an attempt to bat the wasps away from him. But they converged on him, covered him as he blindly stumbled for the stairs that led back up to the kitchen. The wasps crawled on his clothing, snagged in his hair.

All the while, the green hands remained pressed to the little basement windows, the black orifices in their palms still gaping open, like watching eyes.

Zetter tripped over something, fell forward, caught himself before he could crash to the floor, all the while wildly slapping at his head and body. In spite of his efforts, one of the wasps scampered down the back of his collar. Another crawled halfway into his left ear. Before any of the others could sting him, however, one of the insects in his hair scrambled down his forehead and injected its stinger directly between his eyebrows, as if to punch open a pinhole-small third eye there.

Zetter jolted up straight as if electrified rigid, his eyes bulging wide. This reaction transpired in but a fraction of a second. His left hand had been raised in front of his face to swat at his head again. In that microsecond he saw his hand frozen there before his eyes, and it appeared as a negative image of itself, but colored the same phosphorescent green as the wasp that had stung him.

And then Zetter's hand was gone—along with the rest of him—as he blinked out of existence.

PART TWO: OTHER WORLDS

The Green Hands

0. Out of the Blackness

Though he couldn't say why, when he came to consciousness he was surprised to find himself alive. Then again . . . was he alive? After all, might ghosts feel a kind of consciousness?

Yet surely ghosts couldn't detect scent. The air he drew into apparently corporeal lungs (and ghosts didn't need to breathe, either) was damp, with the taint of mold and old mud. Maybe the lingering effects of some past flooding. He thought of flooding because he seemed to recall he was in a subterranean place. Yes, a cellar. His back was pressed to this cellar's cold stone floor—unless it was a slab in a morgue, or in a burial vault, that he lay on instead.

He sat up slowly, bracing his hands on the cold surface, sliding them around in the utter darkness. No, not a slab; indeed, he sat on a floor. But he knew nothing of the dimensions of the room he occupied. The walls and ceiling might be very close, or miles away for all he could tell as yet. He considered testing the space around him by calling out, and hearing how his voice sounded—whether it was tightly contained or echoed away into the distance—but he was reluctant to call attention to himself. He might not be alone here, and he had a vague impression that not long ago he had been pursued by others—others who meant him great harm, or at the very least meant to alter him in some way he did not want to be altered.

Standing upright now, he felt at his body and acknowledged that he was wearing clothing, though he couldn't picture what it looked like. Now that he directed his consciousness to his feet, he understood they were shod. Timid about bumping into some unseen object and tripping—maybe even falling into a well or down a flight of stairs to a yet lower level—he at first just shuffled around in a close circle, peering into the void that encircled him in the hope that he'd catch at least

a glimmer of distant light, one spot where the blackness shaded hopefully toward gray.

Nothing of the sort, though. He was therefore left with no choice
but to select a direction in the directionless black and start moving in a
straight line so as not to simply circle back on himself. When he came
to a wall, as surely he must, then he would have some grounding, and
he could feel his way along it—eventually, it had to be, to a door.

He only hoped that this door, when he came to it, wouldn't be
locked. For might he be trapped now, in this place where he had apparently taken refuge from those unremembered Others?

He got himself started, with tentative little steps like those of a
very old person, holding both his arms straight out ahead of him, waving and groping like the probing antennae of a giant, blind cave insect.

Shuffling steps, shuffling steps. This was definitely no close space.
Eventually, ahead of him he heard the patter of dripping water, and as
he continued along the dripping came alongside him, so that he could
detect a faint echo as the drips plopped into an unseen puddle on the
floor. Then the dripping fell behind him and was gone. Silence again
except for his cautious scuffing steps.

He had no idea how much time had elapsed since he'd begun
moving. A half hour? An hour? Longer? Nor did he know how long
he had been down in this underground place, where he had hidden
from the Others.

At one point, something alive scuttled across the top of his left
foot. It was big enough to be a rat, but he had the impression of more
legs than that. He let out a yelp, which echoed off into the gulf, and he
broke into a run for several yards, afraid that there might be more such
creatures, maybe even a whole swarm of them. But he got himself under control, reminding himself of hidden wells and sudden flights of
descending stairs.

Then, there it was: the faintest, ghostly suggestion of light straight
ahead. He wasn't imagining it; when he blinked his eyes or experimented
by shutting them, the pale gray glow disappeared. Had he been lucky in
his choice of direction, or if he'd headed a different way would he have
still encountered light, perhaps even sooner? It didn't matter now: all
that mattered was reaching this source of illumination.

As the light grew slowly more distinct—and accordingly, he was

able to walk toward it at a quicker pace, without his previous trepida-
tion—it brought with it other things that also increased in intensity.
For one, the scent of mold he now took for granted was being replaced by an outdoors kind of smell, of open air and perhaps country-
side. And what bore along this scent was a cool breeze ... just a
whispery hint at first, but growing steadily into brisk gusts that penetrated into the cavernous chamber he had awoken in. Whenever these
irregular gusts rose up, they whistled through whatever aperture—be it
door or window—gave them ingress.

The light was now strong enough for him to make out litter on the
floor around him: brown leaves mummified into crumbling fragments,
which crunched under his soles along with a grit of dirt that had blown
in over an untold period of time. Still, the light didn't define this immense space any more than total darkness had. He still couldn't make
out a ceiling if he looked upwards, nor walls around him. The ceiling
was too high up, the walls to the rear and sides of him too far away.
And yet, he had seen no columns to support the ceiling of this unthinkably vast room. No furnishings. No features that might define its
purpose. This structure struck him as a place that had been gutted and
abandoned a long time ago, or else built a long time ago but never finished or occupied.

A clean outline of bright light took form from the previous dif-
fused glow. It was a doorway, open to the outside with no door hinged
to it any longer, if there ever had been. The dead leaves formed a carpet here, which he waded through ankle deep.

He came to the threshold—twice as tall as himself—and stood
framed in its outline, to gaze out upon the scene presented before him.

A little beyond where he stood, a flight of stone steps—as bone
pale as the inner and outer walls of this structure proved to be—
wound down the steep face of a hill like the spine of a buried dinosaur.
These steps passed between bald outcroppings of rock and were overgrown with long, leached yellow grass that eventually swallowed the
base of the staircase altogether, where the foot of the cliff met the
shore of a sea or enormous lake. Small misshapen trees with gnarled
black bark grew here and there atop the hill, close to the structure, and
tenaciously clung to the severe slope, their dead brown leaves mostly
blown away by the chilly gusts off that body of water.

These details he only absorbed later, however. What first commanded his attention, and filled him with quaking awe, was the sky. Though he could grasp no memory of his life before attaining consciousness in this empty building, not even his name, he knew that he had never before beheld a vision like the one now revealed to him.

The sky was overcast, as though a milky cataract lay over it. Because it picked up the glow of the red sun, the sky's color was a uniform pale orange. And that sun—it was at least five times the size it should be. That is, if it was even the sun he had once known. He recalled the term "red giant," but if he had somehow leaped billions of years into the future and his own sun was approaching that phase, shouldn't his world be much hotter than he remembered it—not cool, as it was presently? Could the swollen, inflamed aspect of this star—whether familiar or alien—only be a trick of the atmosphere, magnifying its appearance?

The giant red circle gave the impression more of a flat disk than a sphere, like a trepanned wound in the sky, welling with blood. Its fire was so dull, it didn't sting his eyes to gaze directly at it. Below, the sea-or-lake presented an inverted reflection of this scarlet sun and the surrounding orange sky, its water stirring languidly, drowsily, as subdued as the molten disk.

Feeling estranged from the concept of time, he didn't know as yet whether the sun was rising, like a great hot air balloon, or setting under its own weight, to drown in the body of water.

And yet this titan sun was not what filled him with wonder mixed with terror.

A multitude of objects was suspended in the sky, like a bucketful of pebbles tossed up and caught in a still photograph before they could fall back to the ground. These many objects were people. People, floating high above him, directly overhead, and extending far out above the water until they were mere gnat-like dots against the orange sky. Hundreds of them . . . no, *thousands* of them.

They were not drifting, borne along on a current; they did not turn or twirl as if dangling from strings. The people sprinkled throughout the air were as fixed as insects in amber. Every body was suspended face downward, arms and legs somewhat bent, as if they had been flash-frozen solid while crawling on hands and knees. And each person wore an identical white robe, with a cowl pulled up over their head, throwing the face into shadow. They were all barefoot. The deep hoods and loose robes made it hard to distinguish which might be men, which might be women. Smaller, children-sized figures of varying age were included in the throng.

Because he couldn't see the faces, even of those hanging directly above him, he couldn't tell if these individuals were alive and in some sort of suspended animation or dead. Their flesh might be putrefying for all he knew, or even long mummified, though he doubted that from the looks of their feet—the hands being hidden in the baggy, too-long sleeves of their robes. Their naked feet ranged in shades of pigmentation, indicating a mix of races, but none of them looked to be in a state of decay. And the white robes were pristine, not stained with purge fluids.

Even if they weren't decaying or desiccated, he still had the sense that these people had been in this state for countless years, even eons, accounting for the abandoned appearance of the edifice he had found himself in, since surely these were the people who had built and utilized it. What calamity had befallen them? Or had they *aspired* to their present condition, given themselves over to it? Perhaps they had been halted, mid-rapture, on their ascension to some brand of heaven . . . or because they were corporeal, this was the limit of their ascension. It could be that inside their quiet shells these beings knew bliss.

Then again, they might be trapped against their will, silently raging to be free.

They might even be conscious of him. Their eyes—were they open? He stared hard at the figures directly above him, stepped further away from the building to get a better look. He saw the dull red blaze of the sun reflected wetly inside the cowl of one of them, like twin embers. Yes, the eyes of this one, at least, were frozen open.

Now that he had stepped away from the building, he moved closer to the edge of the cliff where the stone stairs zigzagged down its face, then turned to look back to get a clearer sense of the structure's layout. It loomed tall and wide, running far off in either direction, but it was mostly just an unembellished block of pale stone. In fact, one might even believe it was carved from a single gargantuan rock—or had been shaped from the summit of this steep hill—for no individual blocks composed its walls. A castle or fortress, utilitarian in the extreme? Yet there were no crenellated battlements atop it, and no windows. He could say nothing of its other sides, but on this face he saw only one aperture: the doorway he had stepped through.

Maybe it was a great mausoleum for a dead king. Or a dead god.

Or maybe it was a kind of gateway.

The word *mall* came to him: a sprawling construction where many wares could be purchased. The building reminded him of that, but completely hollowed out, an empty skull, the last of its material goods sold long ago. Objects that had proved their ultimate insignificance by having since crumbled to dust. Were the people in the air the past consumers, now risen literally and figuratively above the need for material comforts?

The only important thing was that right now the building promised shelter if need be. He felt he could return inside and spend the night there, but he dreaded its complete darkness. Better to sleep on the floor close to the doorway and hope for a little light from the stars, or the moon . . . if those heavenly bodies could cut through the solid overcast. Currently, though, he was curious as to what else might lie in the vicinity, and he decided to venture forth a bit—though not so far that he couldn't easily return to the structure when the sun fell. He hoped it was dawn, and not dusk, so he'd have more time in which to explore.

Since the building dominated the top of the hill, and he spied no further entrances along this face—which seemed to extend unto infinity in either direction—he chose to descend the stone staircase to the edge of the lake-or-sea. This he began doing, picking his way very carefully lest his foot catch in the long tangles of grass, or in case one of the gusts that buffeted him from time to time, coming off that body of water, caused him to lose his footing, tumble the rest of the way down, and break his neck in the process. These surges of wind would stir the robes of all the suspended people, causing them to rustle and snap like myriad hanging flags.

The last steps were fully smothered under the long matted grass, so he switched over to the face of the hill itself and made it down to the shore intact. He was grateful to be at this level, because it put the dangling people that much higher above him than they had been when he'd stood atop the cliff. But now, which direction to take? He looked up and down the shoreline and in either direction saw nothing of note as of yet. Just the thin, pebbled strip of shore, where a line of dead plant matter had washed up over many years, humped and slimy like an immense, decaying worm strung along the surf. The surf itself, as he had noted earlier, was lazy, dreamlike, as if its low rolling waves were composed of a liquid heavier than water. Would an ocean be this tranquil? A lake, then?

Arbitrarily, he decided to take the left-hand direction.

He walked for a fair distance, until he noticed that the sun had without a doubt lowered in the sky. The end of the day, then, not the beginning. He felt a bit anxious about being caught out here without shelter when night fell, these people all hanging over his head.

And the people were just as evenly distributed across the sky here as they had been back at the cliff. They receded in every direction, silhouetted like black stars against the sky, which was deepening from a pale to a pumpkin orange. Did they fill the lowest stratum of the atmosphere around the entire globe? Maybe not just thousands but millions, *billions* of them?

Having confirmed it was sunset, he had just decided to make his way back toward the titan structure surmounting the hill when he noticed something a little further ahead, where the terrain had started to become more even. Set back from the water, almost lost in a congregation of those stubby black trees, was that a small white building of some type?

He quickened his pace to reach it, hoping to find it abandoned, hoping to find it an alternative source of shelter in which to spend the night. And sure enough, it was a small structure: a house or cottage, its walls built from mortared stones, worn by water, smooth and white as skulls. The roof shingles were black, maybe coated with tar to keep out water, unless that was simply the color of the wood, judging from the trees the cottage hunkered within. There were no windows, and the structure was so small it might actually be more shed than cottage. There was only a door, again made from thick planks of black wood. Having reached the door, he put his hand on its rusted metal handle, and it squealed open on ancient hinges. Unlocked. He had tensed up inside, fearing someone might be within, but he hadn't really expected it. It would seem all the occupants of this world were lodged in the air.

It was too much to expect there would be food and water within;

he'd have to deal with those issues tomorrow. He assumed this place was as long abandoned as the fortress building. He was relieved just to have a more confined shelter in which to pass the night.

He was just about to step inside when from behind him came a thunderous sound. It was like the mournful lowing of a cow that had fallen into a deep pit, magnified to a near deafening level. He whirled around, heart paralyzed, as the sound kept rumbling on like an avalanche. Far out in the water he saw a tremendous shape break its orange surface—a vast black mass that seemed to roll over ponderously until it started sinking away again. If it was a whale, then like the inflamed red sun it appeared much larger than any whale he had ever known about. Just as the huge creature was beginning to submerge, the lowing sound somehow trailed away into a mechanical buzz-saw noise like the drone of a cicada. This buzzing vibrated inside his head just as the deeper tone had done. But when the leviathan had fully slipped back underwater, the cicada sound turned muffled, receded, vanished. The air and water were still once more.

He ducked into the cottage and slammed its door. How could he know whether or not that beast was amphibious and might make its way to shore?

He would have been in total darkness, except that he had noticed there was a narrow window in the wooden door, covered on the inside by a movable panel. He slid this open to let in the red-orange glow of sundown. Enough light entered through the slit that he could see a heavy plank leaning against the inner stone wall. He retrieved this and set it into its waiting brackets, barring shut the little building's heavy wooden door against the night.

0. Moonrise

Before the sun descended below the line of the horizon altogether, submerging itself as the leviathan had done, its lurid light allowed him to assess the interior of the cottage. There was no bed, no other furniture than a crude but sturdy table in the center of the single room, with two chairs made of the same charred-looking black wood. A few wooden shelves were mounted on the walls, but they were barren. A hunter's or fisherman's cabin, used only occasionally? There was a small fireplace, but its hearth too was empty. He could rectify that tomorrow, collect branches to burn to keep warm and over which to cook food, if he could find anything edible. He might sample the water to see if it was salty, though he was reluctant to drink even fresh water with monsters dwelling beneath its surface.

Almost in a corner of the floor, to the right of the fireplace opening, he discovered a trapdoor of black wood, held shut with an iron bolt. Hoping to uncover some supplies stashed away, he pulled the rusted bolt aside with a fair degree of effort. Taking hold of the iron ring in the center of the trapdoor, he hauled it open. Immediately he leaned back on his heels, away from the smell that puffed up at him on long bottled-up air. Musty, moldy, it reminded him of the atmosphere inside the fortress building, but more concentrated.

It was a well of inky darkness. Without a lantern or candle to see by, all he could discern were the top few corroded iron rungs of a ladder set into the side of a shaft of unknown depth.

He shut the trapdoor again and, though it was an effort, shoved the bolt back in place. Who could say what might come up through that shaft from the darkness otherwise?

He returned his attention to the room he found himself in.

The floor was gritty with dirt that had blown under the door, the table top a little less coated, so he swept this with the sleeve of his shirt, deciding to use the table as his bed. But after his apparent sleep inside the fortress building—and he had no idea how long that sleep had been—he found he wasn't tired enough to shut his eyes just yet. Instead, he paced the cabin, around and around the table, careful not to trip over the slightly raised edge of the trapdoor, trying to focus his thoughts . . . thinking about ways he might gather food, ways he might fashion a club or spear from stones lashed to tree branches . . . frequently pausing to peek outside through the door slot, as the upper curve of the sun was swallowed by water turned black as outer space.

The sky itself retained the faintest milky glow, however, as if the unbroken cloud cover emitted its own luminosity, and against this he could just barely make out the forms of the nearest of the white-robed people. He heard the distant fluttering of their garments, like wind in a ship's sails.

Now that he was no longer moving, exploring, the scope of the desolation he had encountered settled on him with the unfelt but crushing weight of the cosmos, and he experienced a deep loneliness. How much more bearable his disorienting and frightening situation would be with just one person beside him! A woman, with whom he could talk and share decisions, who could offer him comfort just as he would offer her protection. He required no other person than that. Then he might feel more than merely contented; he might even feel happy. Just the woman he loved and himself, with no other person who might intrude on their relationship, no one to lure her away into betrayal, no one to compel her to break their bond, break his heart, break his mind into shards.

Ah, but it was only a fantasy, he knew. He was damned to be alone. Utterly and eternally alone.

Upon his latest peek through the slot in the door, he saw two things had changed out there. For one, the sky's pale glow had begun to take on a subtle greenish hue, as if the painter's blank canvas of cloud cover were reflecting and diffusing a light source that was thus far out of his view. And the other new development was that all the people who had been hanging in the air were slowly floating feet first down toward the earth.

His first impulse was to slam the door panel shut, to block out the uncanny sight, but at the same time he was mesmerized and felt he needed to see what this development would lead to.

Then he shuddered hard in response to another thunderous blast of noise, such as he had heard earlier. Again, outlined against the faintly green sky, he saw that the same vast creature—or one of its kind—had broken the surface of the water, just as the feet of the lowering people were about to touch the drowsy, slow-motion waves.

Most of the robed figures who descended toward the water penetrated it and, without resisting, calmly slipped below the surface out of view. But those who came down upon the exposed portion of the enormous animal as it rolled over immediately went on all fours, as if to catch hold. They bent their heads so low, he had the impression they were touching their foreheads to the creature's body out of reverence. Might they even worship the thing?

It hardly seemed possible, but as the leviathan continued rolling over and submerging anew, its lamenting cry grew even deeper, more profound, rattling each nerve in his body like a sapling violently shaken in angry fists. Again, this heavy bass moan morphed somehow into a cicada sound, which was like a chainsaw cutting through the side of his skull, but thankfully this was drowned out as the great beast slid completely beneath the surface. With it vanished those several dozen robed figures who had managed to cling to its body, like remoras riding on a shark.

Yet many other of the hooded figures had alighted on dry land—the shore and further inland—and he saw them start wandering around aimlessly, stiffly, cowls concealing their features, long sleeves concealing their hands as their arms hung limp at their sides. They didn't bump into one another, but neither did any of them converse with or in any way acknowledge anyone else.

Some had landed close to the cottage and turned slowly to face in its direction, as dreamy in their movements as sleepwalkers. Seeing this, he ducked down below the level of the slot in the door and reached up to slide its panel shut as quietly as he could manage.

Enveloped in total darkness, he could hear the movement of bodies close outside, shuffling across the pebbly sand, rustling through tall beach grass, seemingly even brushing against the stones that composed this little building. He hoped these beings were so accustomed to this shed-or-cottage being abandoned that they wouldn't try to gain entry to it. (For, in their numbers, how could they not force their way inside eventually if they desired to do so?) He prayed that they had not been conscious of him before the sun had sunk and they had become active, despite their apparently open eyes.

Time went on . . . maybe several hours, as he sat on the floor with his back propped against the door. Now, finally, he was growing tired, exhausted by the enormity of all he had experienced since awakening. Deciding that in his current situation he was no more at risk asleep than awake, he rose, approached the table, and stretched out upon it with his head resting on his bent arm.

For a while he couldn't sleep, too unsettled by the sounds of moving bodies outside, in effect surrounding the little cottage. At last, though, exhaustion won out. He dreamed.

In his dream, he was in a comfortable little house, lounging in bed watching TV. TV . . . ah, yes . . . the dream reminded him of the existence (long past?) of television, but he couldn't quite make out what he was seeing on its screen, which fizzed with a veil of static, behind which dark figures jerked erratically, perhaps in some kind of experimental dance performance.

Somewhere beyond his bedroom, an electronic bell rang. With a sigh of lazy irritation, he swung his legs to the floor and left the bedroom, walking through the weirdly familiar house toward its front door. Impatiently, the bell rang again. He sighed again.

He opened a door to a tiny hallway. Out here was the front door to his dream abode, and he pulled the door open to see who was calling on a Sunday evening . . . for he knew it was a Sunday evening.

Just outside, standing in a pool of yellow light with the deepening murk of evening behind her, was a woman wrapped in a bathrobe. Her thick, coppery red hair was mussed as though she herself had just risen from bed. She was very attractive, despite the unnaturally huge grin that seemed to deform her lower face.

The woman thrust her arms out at him. Startled, terrified, somehow he knew he must not let her touch him, and he was already jerking back and slamming the door shut. Her hands were apparently prosthetic, but useless—made of glassy green jade, with smooth unmoving fingers. When the door banged hard against her wrists, both jade hands were dislodged and one of them dropped to the floor of the hallway at his feet. It shattered . . . stray fingers skittering across the worn floorboards. He managed to get the door closed, and he bolted it.

He stooped to gather the broken hand and disconnected fingers, and he carried the pieces into the kitchen, where he put them all into a white plastic shopping bag. As he did so, he noticed there was a ring stuck on one of the fingers: a gold Claddagh ring, with two hands holding a stylized human heart. The heart had a diamond in its center.

He tucked the bag containing the smashed jade hand and the diamond ring in the back of a kitchen cabinet. Though he didn't bang the cabinet door shut, the sound of it closing was as loud as a gunshot.

He awoke with a start and sat up on the table with his heart thudding, thudding, as if the woman from his dream was thumping ineffectively, without hands, at the locked door of the cottage. He almost expected to see her shattered jade hands lying on the floor, but of course he could make out nothing in this utter darkness.

Not quite utter. A line of dim greenish light demarcated the bottom edge of the cottage's door.

He could still hear the shushed, scuffing movements of bodies outside, passing through the bleached grass, nudging against the cottage's stones. But that green light tugged at his curiosity. Getting down from the table as quietly as he could, he stole to the door, drew in a deep breath, clamped it off in his lungs, and slid the door's peephole panel aside just a bare crack. He neared his eye to it, ready to flinch back in an instant if need be. He feared a finger or a stick being thrust through the slot unexpectedly.

The source of the green illumination was immediately apparent.

While he'd slept, the moon had risen, full and blasted with craters. Not corresponding to his memory of a much smaller moon, it appeared to occupy the same amount of sky as the swollen sun. How could that be? While a star could enlarge over time, a moon would not . . . unless its orbit was decaying and it was drawing gradually closer to the world it circled. This was, of course, assuming he was on the same world upon which he vaguely recalled having lived.

The bloated moon's bottom edge lightly touched the water's horizon, like a stupendous child's balloon buoyed there. And the moon was a phosphorescent green.

He thought of the words *green cheese*. He didn't know why. Maybe because he was growing increasingly hungry.

The moonlight enabled him to make out the figures milling about the beach in the near and far distance, their white robes picking up the green glow. Dozens of them just within his narrow range of view.

One figure stepped directly in front of the peephole, its face only a foot away, though its features were lost within the shadowed frame of its hood. Was it peering back at him through the thin gap? He had instantly hunched down below the peephole, poised at the cliff edge of panic, thinking: *This is it. This is it. Now they come.*

But they didn't come in numbers to pound or press against the door. He heard dragging, somnambulant footsteps as the person just outside the door continued along.

Still bent below the spy hole, he edged its panel ever-so-gently closed again.

After a time—after his heart had subdued itself—he returned to the table and stretched out upon it once more. If he dreamed again that night, he didn't recall it the next morning.

0. Carcasses

When he again awoke, he sat up sore and achy on the surface of the wooden table and saw that the red-orange light of dawn had replaced the night's fungal glow at the bottom edge of the cabin's bolted door. He slid down from the table, went to the door, and cracked the panel over the peephole slot.

All the robed figures had already risen back into the sky, once more hanging there motionless but for the rippling of their garments in the gusts off the water. Glinting drops still fell from the sodden robes of those miraculously undrowned people who had formerly been submerged in the water. He rather regretted not having witnessed the moment at which they all rose—might there be something to learn from the spectacle?—but mostly he was relieved that they were once again off the ground and inert. He felt it was safe to venture outside again and turn his attention to finding food and water. His stomach was like a piteously begging dog, and his throat was parched, his dehydration having brought on a deeply stabbing headache.

He unbolted the door and stepped out from the cottage into the bloody glow of the monstrous sun that still hung low in the sky—as if its sheer bulk wouldn't permit it to float any higher—and noticed something anomalous further down the shore in the opposite direction from the fortress on the high hill. It was impossible not to notice: a titanic black shape lying just at the attenuated edge of the water.

He was certain, without hesitating to consider any other possibility, what that great mass was. It was either the very same leviathan he had seen the descending figures alighting upon last night or else one of its brethren.

Shutting the door behind him, he set off down the strip of stony beach, following like a trail the dark humped band of slime that marked the border of the lake-or-sea, toward that much larger humped dark form.

The languorous surf lapped around the massive shape. The closer he got to it—and the more colossal it became, like a battleship run aground—the more nervous he felt. What if the beast still had a spark of life in it? What if it should suddenly rear up, swing toward him? Once again he considered that it might be amphibious . . . might merely be basking in the morning air, not dead. But he detected no movement or sound of any kind. And as he drew nearer, he saw other things that convinced him he had nothing to fear from the behemoth.

The beast lay on its side, its back toward him, and its smooth upper surface was covered with small, ragged craters, showing a yellowish layer of muscle or blubber under the rubbery black flesh. Red blood had run out from these circular wounds and down the animal's curved body, turning the water around it pinkish.

He had no doubt that the figures who had come down from the sky upon the beast had inflicted these injuries, though he didn't know how. Had they dug their very hands into its meat? And though the wounds were so numerous that in places they overlapped and combined to form larger wounds, were they really so severe as to have proved lethal?

When he had finally walked far enough alongside the creature, in its shadow, to arrive at its head, at least one of his questions was answered—that being the exact cause of its wounds.

The beast had a long, narrow lower jaw like a sperm whale, lined with pointed ivory teeth the span of his hand. Its bulbous head was more like a pilot whale's, however, and the beast had four eyes on this side: one large black orb, with three smaller black eyes arranged around it. Was it the same on the opposite side? He couldn't tell, with its heavy head lying on its side in the thin surf. For now, he switched his scrutiny to the two human bodies that had been crushed between the spider-eyed animal's great jaws.

They were two of the people who had floated down from the sky last night like parachutists, maybe among those who had clung to the thing's back, but they had slipped off. One was a young male, the other a middle-aged female, their robes torn and bloody. The creature's jaws had crushed them so badly through the midsection, its teeth stabbed into them, that loops of bluish intestines had been squeezed out from between the monster's clamped jaws, one drooping end stirring in the water. The eyes of the pair were already turning grayish.

Yet both blindly staring corpses were grinning. Their bared teeth were stained red, with shreds of black flesh and yellow meat or blubber caught between them.

If there had only been one body, he might have thought that the person's lack of hands was the result of deformity or an old injury. But the torn robes of both dead people were disturbed in such a way that he could see the man was missing both hands, revealing only smooth stumps, and the woman had no left hand.

Behind him in the grass he found a length of dead branch, and he took off his shoes so as to wade into the water a little and poke with the stick at the sleeve covering the woman's right arm. In so doing, he revealed another rounded stump.

He looked up at the figures hovering above him. So none of them had hands inside those long baggy sleeves, then?

Last night, the descending people hadn't clung to this beast with their hands but with their teeth, when he had thought they were lowering their foreheads to its body in reverence.

He could only imagine what might have happened to him last night, had he been vulnerable outside when they became active and settled to earth.

Were they *all* grinning inside those deeply shadowed hoods?

He looked down at the behemoth again, blood still trickling in thin rivulets from the myriad bite marks in its towering body. He noted that no flies had come along to buzz about the carcass, or even the intestines festooned across its jaw. It seemed that in this world the only living things besides plant life were the robed people, the leviathans, and himself.

His moaning stomach hoped this was not true. But if it were, that there would be plant life that was edible. And so he continued moving along the shore, away from the beached carcass and the fortress further back, in search of whatever might sustain him.

0. The Betrayal of Time

Further inland from the water, now that the terrain was only mildly hilly, forest predominated. Tall grass and brittle underbrush—which itself looked as though it had perished of thirst—gave way to more and more trees, until finally the woods closed around him, shutting out even the gold-glinting suggestion of water. These trees of the forest proper were less stunted and contorted than those that grew near the water. They were taller and straighter, and the trunks of many of them as thick around as ancient oaks, but their bark was still a charcoal black. The leaves clinging to their branches, increasingly blotting out the pale orange sky and the figures suspended in it, were just as brown and shriveled as those that formed the thick bed covering the ground under his feet: layer upon layer of brown, decaying leaves. The uppermost layer he scuffed through was dry and crunchy, but beneath that the leaves moldered, damp and smelling of slow disintegration.

Experimentally, he squatted down and pawed through the leaves, digging deeper, scooping them aside, slippery dark masses that he disliked touching, in search of insect life. Normally, wouldn't one find scurrying pill bugs, silverfish, millipedes, other creatures that thrived in rotting leaf litter? Maybe even a salamander? Nothing—and when he came to the black soil he dug into that as well, but again without discovering earthworms or any other forms of life. The idea of eating worms, especially while still alive, was revolting, but he was growing desperate. He was not starving to death yet, but it was a real concern.

Had all these animal forms gone extinct naturally, he wondered, or had the robed people—perhaps immortal—eaten them all over countless ages, night after night upon descending to the earth?

He suddenly recalled the creature he had felt scamper like a tickling hand across his shoe in the fortress building. Did animals shelter in there, safe from the robed people? Or had he only imagined that sensation in the darkness? It was worth investigating later, at any rate.

And when he returned to the water's edge, he considered that he himself should sample the flesh of the beached whale-thing.

For now he stood erect again, continued venturing deeper into this deciduous forest.

He found no acorns as he kicked along through the leaves. He was also hoping to encounter mushrooms growing on the forest floor, but as yet he had spotted none. What he did start to see, however, were thick, woody plates of bracket fungus growing on the trunks of some of the trees. He couldn't recall if he'd ever heard these were edible. Maybe? Perhaps certain types? He vaguely recalled some were used for medicinal purposes, but he didn't trust his memory when he didn't even know his name.

He broke off a small chunk from the outer edge of one of these growths and nibbled on it gingerly. It was tough, and tasted much the way the leaf litter at his feet smelled: musty, moldy—the concentrated

essence of forest. But he gnawed some more and broke off more pieces to eat later on if he didn't develop a stomach ache or vomiting,
pushing the fragments into his trouser pockets.

He came upon a clearing, where again tall bleached grass grew.
Boulders rose up from the grass here and there as if randomly deposit-
ed by some long retreated glacier, their flanks blotched with pale cir-
cles of lichen. Here he could once more see the multitude of robed
humans caught unmoving in the air high above him. But it wasn't the
sight of their bodies that suddenly unnerved him; it was the deepening
pumpkin orange color of the sky.

Could it be possible? Was the sun, unseen behind the trees encir-
cling the clearing, already descending? He had thought he had awakened to dawn, not the waning of afternoon! Had he really slept that
long, then?

No . . . no . . . he didn't believe he had. Somehow, the sun did not
cross the sky in this place, this time. Instead, in defiance of any laws of
physics and behaviors of the universe that he recalled from his past existence, the sun seemed only to struggle up a short way into the sky before its great mass dragged it back down again into the same spot on
the horizon. The days were short-lived, half-dead things. It was the
night that went on and on . . . the night that thrived and reigned.

He would ponder this maddening enigma later, when he was secure behind a bolted door. For now, he must get back to the cottage
before the sun descended all the way.

Before the grinning people without hands descended.

He turned away from the clearing and plunged back into the
woods. He had continued all this way in a straight line—he *hoped* in a
straight line—and he must retrace that trajectory, lest he become lost
and helplessly exposed out here.

He forgot his hunger, forgot even his throat-cracking thirst. He
would have no time to stop and sample the flesh of the slain leviathan.
Two imperatives overshadowed every other thought: *Run* and *Never stop.*

0. The Descent

Low-slung tree branches seemed to grab at him to impede him,
clawing at his cheeks and forehead and neck. He slipped once on the
slick leaf litter under the deceptively dry upper crust, and went down

hard with the air knocked out of him. He scampered back to his feet, though, and continued racing onward, dodging between the close columns of live wood.

He began to despair that he had got himself turned around somehow and was only running deeper *into* the forest . . . until he started to see those goldish glints through the trees that told him the lake-or-sea lay straight ahead. At that point, however, the woods had grown so dark that several times he almost collided with the black trunks, veering around them at the last moment and one time bashing his shoulder badly against rough bark. The fragments of sky seen through the dead foliage overhead had gone from deep orange to purplish. Was there still time to make it all the way back to the cottage? He entertained the thought of climbing up into one of the larger trees and hiding amongst its boughs to pass the night, hoping that the grinning people would not spot him up there once they'd returned to the earth, but no . . . no . . . he couldn't risk it. He had to reach the cabin—it was the only way he might survive.

The tantalizing liquid sparkles seen through the trees were growing dimmer, like cooling embers. The sun had almost sunk below the horizon.

Then, just like that, he burst out into the open air, thrashing through tall dried-out grass, with the inky body of water spread before him. The purplish sky had that subtle milky luminescence, against which dangled the innumerable robed men, women, children.

He sprinted along the shore . . . huffing frantically, doing his best to ignore how his throat grew ever more parched as he gulped air into his lungs . . . defying the wild drumming of his overtaxed heart. The muscles in his legs burned, and his skull was a solid ball of pain. His whole body seemed bent on betraying him, giving him up as a sacrifice.

The leviathan was still there, of course, there being no high tide to draw it back into the water. It would no doubt rot where it lay. He was grateful for the sight of it, however grotesque, and more grateful for what he could now see not too much further beyond it: his little cottage made of white stones.

Still, he didn't know if his legs could carry him that far. He wheezed curses at himself. Groaned encouragement to himself. Come on . . . he was almost there . . . he could make it . . .

The sun had entirely vanished beneath the line of water, fully submerged like one of those colossal creatures after they had briefly surfaced. In its place the sky was taking on that greenish tint he had noticed the night before. This time he understood it foretold of the later rising of the great green moon. He realized now that the moon would rise from the same spot into which the sun had sunk and take its exact place in the sky, as if they were two very different faces of the same gigantic orb.

The people suspended in the air had begun their dream-slow descent.

Run. Never stop. He panted entreaties to a God he doubted he had ever believed in before, and who probably didn't exist anymore even if He once had. *Dear God . . . please God . . .*

They were floating steadily lower, all of them at the same rate, as if tethered to invisible marionette strings. Maybe it was God who was their puppet master.

He thought he was going to vomit. He thought his bowels might let go. His legs were boneless—how could they continue to support him? He was weaving from side to side as he ran, like a drunken man.

Lower . . . lower. He didn't dare look up at those directly above him, lest he trip over something in his path, but he saw those ahead of him, their bare feet poking out from under their robes. The empty black hollows of their long gaping sleeves.

The sky shaded darker by the second, even as its subtle green stain became more distinct.

The stone cottage was not much further now . . . and yet, the descending people were just above its roof. They were going to come down directly in his path, blocking him . . . cutting him off . . .

Grinning. Biting.

Somehow, somehow, he managed to find a surge of energy, a spurt of adrenaline that jetted through him, and he flung himself forward crazily, sobbing a loud cry of desperation.

One bare foot brushed against his shoulder. They were coming down all around him. He dove between them, dodged around them as he had the trees back in the woods. They seemed disoriented for a moment as their feet were planted solidly, getting their bearings as they awakened, but he could *feel* their eyes snapping alert as their gaze fell upon him.

He had closed the cabin's door when he'd left earlier to explore—but what if the little structure's rightful owner had returned in his absence? What if the door was bolted on the inside?

He fell against the door of black wood, and it gave inward without resistance.

He spun around to find one of the robed people, a woman, stepping through the threshold, her eyes wide and gleaming inside her cowl. Her grinning teeth were clicking together rapidly. He snatched up the length of wood leaning beside the doorway and rammed its squared end into her nose, crushing it. Blood poured down over her bared teeth, but her grin didn't even waver as she stumbled backwards. He slammed the door shut and dropped the thick board into its brackets to bar the door from being opened inward.

But immediately, he heard the wood creak as weight was pressed against it.

He didn't even have the strength left to climb onto the table and stretch out. Instead, he crumpled to the floor and curled in on himself, wheezing like a man in his final moments. He retched, but nothing came up. It only seemed to tear the dry tube that was his throat.

The ceiling creaked, too. Trickles of dust pattered down. They were on the roof.

He heard them scrabbling at the outer stone walls, all around him. The creaking of the door became more pronounced. The board rattled a little in its brackets.

They were going to get in, hands or no hands. It was only a matter of time. Surely, before the sun rose again and they rose with it into the sky.

He wished he had a weapon. At this point, not so as to fight back against the horde, for that would be beyond futile, but something with which he might kill himself. A knife to open the femoral arteries in his legs, for instance. Suicide would be vastly preferable to having their many mouths on his body . . . their teeth clamping into his flesh.

Then, suddenly, he propped himself up on one elbow, as if a voice had clearly called his name—a summoning voice that offered him an avenue of escape.

He turned to face toward the back wall of the murky room, near the cold fireplace, where that trapdoor of black wood was set into the floor.

He scrambled to hands and knees, crawled over to the spot, and found the trapdoor with his desperate, clawing fingers. Taking hold of the rusted bolt that secured the hatch, he drew it back with one strong jerk, then he lifted the trapdoor open by the ring in its center. He was again met by that expulsion of fetid air; but this time, instead of being repulsed, he welcomed it. He couldn't see the rungs set into the side of the shaft below him—indeed, he couldn't even discern the outline of the shaft's opening—but he swung himself around, stuck a leg out and then down, and probed with it until his foot settled on one of the rungs. He leaned his weight onto it, fearing the rung might tear loose from the wall and he would be pitched into uncertain depths, but the thing held. Gripping the edge of the opening, he lowered himself down, easing his other foot onto the next rung.

Before he descended too deeply to do so, he reached up blindly, found the trapdoor again, and eased it down into place over his head. He found no bolt on its inner surface to slot home. Without a means of locking the hatch on the inside, he may have only postponed his demise for a short time more, painted himself into an even tighter corner, but he held on to the hope that this inset ladder was here for a good reason—that something *more* lay below.

Distantly above him, he thought he could hear the robed people thumping at the cottage's door with their knobby stumps, but the sound was muffled through the thick wood of the lowered hatch.

He hadn't counted them, but when it occurred to him to wonder how many rungs he'd already descended, he guessed it was twenty. Even as he thought this, his right foot encountered a flat solid surface instead of a rung. He had reached the shaft's bottom. He turned away from the ladder, holding onto one rung with his left hand just in case it was only a shelf he stood upon, a narrow ledge, before the shaft continued downward. Tentatively he stuck his right foot out further and further, sweeping it to one side and then the other. No—it was a floor, he was sure of it. Finally he let go of the rung and edged forward a few steps, reminded of his time seeking to escape from the lightless interior of the gigantic fortress or mausoleum.

He shuffled along this way for a time, still wary of blundering into a sudden pit or further descending shaft or stairwell. Yes, he might have been in the fortress again . . . except for the fact that his sounds came back to him very closely, intimately, as if he were in a confined space. Testing this theory, he stretched his arms out to either side of him, and in fact both hands touched solid walls, cool to the touch like stone or concrete. He was apparently traveling along a narrow corridor or tunnel.

Then he came to a place where the tunnel formed a T. He might have walked nose-first into the wall in front of him here, had there not been a faint light glowing from somewhere down the left-hand branch of the T. The right-hand branch was pitch black. Though the dim glow down the left branch was of a green tint, and he feared that might mean moonlight—which might mean he would be stepping outside into the night, vulnerable to attack—he felt he had no choice but to go where the light could show him his path. If it proved to be an open doorway through which the robed people might enter, he'd quickly retreat and retrace his steps, to grope his way down the right-hand branch instead.

The glow increased in brightness, revealing to him the outlines of the tunnel, which had a low curved ceiling. Gradually, he could tell that the light emanated from certain spots spaced along the length of the tunnel. He believed these must be windows, letting in the moonlight.

When he approached the first of these sources of light, however, he found that it was not a window offering a view of the night outside, but a thick glass panel as tall as himself and just as wide: one surface of a tank like a large aquarium, set back into the wall of white stone. He couldn't tell where the tank's lighting originated from, and decided it was the green liquid filling it that generated the luminance.

Suspended in this glowing green fluid in no orderly fashion, but more or less evenly spaced apart, were a multitude of human hands of varying size and skin tone: the hands of elderly persons, with fat veins under thin wrinkled flesh; tiny pallid infant hands tipped with delicate fingernails; hairy male hands, slender female hands. All of them were floating motionlessly in the aquarium, their slack fingers slightly curled like those of sleeping people. Or dead people. Where the hands had once been—or should have been—joined to wrists, there were no raw cross-sections of meat and bone. Where a severing wound should have been, there was only smooth, rounded flesh. As if the hands had been seeded and grown in this vat, had never been attached to a body at all.

Were their cells still alive, but in a kind of suspended animation? Had they been preserved for some future use? To be grafted onto the arms of the possibly mutated, handless people outside? Or had they been *removed* from those people? If so, as punishment? Or perhaps in a willing sacrifice, an act of religious contrition? Was it their way of gradually divesting themselves of their human shells, toward a purely spiritual existence? But why save the discarded appendages, then?

He pondered that if it was some type of preserving or nourishing fluid the hands resided in, shouldn't they all be heaped in a great mass like lobsters at the bottom of the tank, not hanging there in one place this way? So was the solution viscous, thick?

He stepped a bit closer to the glass, almost touching his nose to it, the green radiance painting his own hands as they hung by his sides. And that was when it struck him. It was not the medium the hands were stored in that produced the green glow. It was the hands themselves, filling the entire aquarium with their luminescence.

Turning away from the tank, he continued down the corridor and was unsurprised to find that the other lighted panels spaced evenly along it from that point on—the panels set into the left side of the tunnel corresponding to the spaces between the panels lining the right side of the tunnel, for a staggered effect—also proved to be tanks filled with luminous hands pickled in viscous solution.

He continued on and on, the corridor seemingly endless, past aquariums housing enough hands to equip all those robed people he had seen outside. The only change he encountered in his surroundings was a bit of damage to the tunnel, giving him the impression that it was of extreme age. He'd come across cracks in the ceiling, some that curved down along the walls between the tanks, and ultimately he saw tree roots that had pushed through the wider of these fissures, black and bristling with hairs, looking like giant centipedes. The musty, moldy odor of these underground passages was more intense now, apparently invading with the roots, if not emanating from them. The smell of the wildness of life, or the decay of life, or both.

From the ceiling further along, one quite large tree root as thick as a bough had snaked its way in over time, hanging so low that he had to duck under it and sweep its dangling, off-branching lesser roots aside with his arm, like a curtain of limp tendrils.

Broken bits of stone littered the floor, fallen from the fissures, and under the giant root he found one sizable chunk with a pointed tip like a prehistoric hand axe, which fit nicely in his palm. It wouldn't be of much use if a horde of robed people came charging down the corridor suddenly, but it was at least a shard of comfort.

A short distance beyond the spot where the root had breached the ceiling, he discovered another, more profound sign of damage to the tunnel.

An even greater root had come down through the ceiling inside one of the tanks, like a monstrous black anaconda covered in long hairs, and exerted enough pressure over time to push the glass panel out of its frame. This had toppled into the corridor, where it lay on its face intact. The preserving medium had burst free, massed thickly both at the bottom of the tank and where it had spilled out onto the fallen glass panel in chunky, gelatinous mounds. It gave off a strong smell like semen. Without the glow of the hands that had once occupied the tank, the gelatin was a dead fishy gray, not green.

Without the hands that had once occupied the tank?

He looked up and down the corridor, unconsciously squeezing the rough-edged hand axe more tightly. They couldn't have rotted without leaving bones, could they, however long ago this damage had occurred? Had the robed people taken them so as to reattach them? Or, ravenous as they were, would they even *consume* them?

He resumed walking. The tanks beyond the ruined one were intact, filled with their gelatin and their placid dreaming hands, and the invading roots became less frequent, until even the cracks eventually tapered away. He might have believed he'd come back around in a full circle, except for the corridor's unerring straightness.

Then, abruptly, he stopped moving, standing dead still. He listened as a sound came to him, where before there had only been his own footfalls.

It was a distant purring or soft rapid pattering. Was that a rainstorm, drumming the earth somewhere above his head?

But it wasn't above his head. It seemed to be coming from far back down the tunnel he had been traveling through. He stared back that way, yet saw nothing aside from the green light shining into the corridor, occasional tree roots hanging down, and that one fallen glass panel heaped with thick gray jelly.

Though it was still muted and remote, the sound was growing steadily louder. It wasn't rushing sea water, was it? Flooding through this tunnel? But it didn't sound like advancing water. He couldn't form a mental image of what it might be. He was torn between lingering to see what might be revealed and quickly resuming his path forward.

Then, as the pattering noise grew more pronounced, more immediate, he finally saw what caused it—and his course of action was decided.

Far back down the tunnel, a low wave was advancing, but it wasn't water or any other liquid. This quickly approaching tide glowed green, its radiance rushing along the corridor like the light of a train barreling through a subway tunnel. Though they were still too distant for him to make out their individual shapes too well, he knew what these things were that made up the glowing tide: a swarm of human hands, scurrying on their fingers like tarantulas.

He spun away and bolted.

He was afraid of slowing his momentum, or even tripping over an unseen obstacle such as more fallen rubble and thus flinging himself onto his face; but he still couldn't resist glancing back over his shoulder from time to time as he ran, to gauge whether the green hands were gaining on him. So far, he was maintaining the same amount of distance between the horde and himself, but he was running pretty quickly and so must they be, scurrying like a solid mass of rats from a fire below deck on an old wooden ship. The hands had flowed over and around the fallen glass panel and the mounds of jelly without impedance. In their fever to reach him, the hands were not only scrambling across the floor but over one another's five-fingered bodies, some of them even occasionally hopping into the air, briefly, above the general stampede.

How many were there? It seemed more than that one emptied tank could have contained. Had other tanks in this subterranean system been compromised as well?

He prayed for another T intersection . . . another choice of directions, so that he might confuse his pursuers . . . at least have some kind of option. Better yet, he prayed for a door, or another ladder taking him upwards out of these tunnels. Yet so far he had seen none of these things.

Until, finally, ahead of him he spied a staircase—a flight of steps shaped from the same unbroken white stone as the walls and floor. The last of the tanks set into this tunnel cast its illumination through an open doorway and onto the first of these ascending stairs.

With his hoarse panting sounding like sobs, he dredged up a seemingly final reserve of energy, as when he had been racing to reach the cottage before the robed people came down from the air. He hurled himself at the stairs. When he reached them, he started charging up them without even breaking stride.

The staircase was lengthy, angling up and up, but he could see a closed door of black wood at the top. It was not really that much farther from reach now. Yet . . . what if the door proved to be locked?

The hands would have him, then. But what would they do to him? Claw him to pieces—or carry him outside, as a swarm of ants cooperate to hoist large objects, to deliver him to their grinning, voracious masters?

Maybe it would be better if it was simply over. No more running, no more hiding. No more hunger, no more confusion. Or loneliness.

He didn't dare risk another look behind now, but he heard them flooding up the stairs after him. Were they closing the distance between him and themselves at last? Even if the door wasn't locked, if it was stuck in its frame the effort to dislodge it might give the hands the extra few seconds they needed to overtake him. At least he saw no rusty bolt on this side that needed to be wrestled back—just a handle like that on the door to the cottage.

Yes, they were very close behind him now, he could tell. The green stain of light on the walls around him was washing forward, growing brighter, as myriad fingertips thumped against white stone, and fingernails scratched for purchase, and skin rubbed across skin in a lustful frenzy. He thrust out his own right hand ahead of him, his fingers spread to catch hold of that iron handle. At some point he had dropped his useless hand axe, after having held it so tightly that its jagged edges had sliced his palm, now greased with blood.

His bloody hand slipped through the handle, clenched it, and he pulled. The door wouldn't budge.

Incandescent green on the walls, brighter and brighter. It made his own body fluoresce green.

He yanked hard, tugged again, howled in misery—until he realized the door was meant to swing out, not in. He shoved against the ebony wood instead and almost tumbled onto the grassy ground beyond. He caught his balance, spun around, saw the hands pouring over the top stair, and slammed the door shut. They thudded against it, clawed with their nails. He knew that when enough of them came and piled up, compounding pressure, they would push the door open . . .

No—there was a thick iron bolt on this side. With an internalized whoop of joy, he slammed the bolt into its slot.

Grinning, he turned away from the door, rested his back against it, and gulped at fresh air. Now he could take in his surroundings—the scene that lay before him.

It was still night. The robed people were not suspended in the sky, though thankfully none of them stood here atop this shaggy high cliff with him. The cliff overlooked that body of water that was either a great lake or the sea.

To his right, the grass-fringed cliff ran on extensively while also rising higher, away from the ridge of exposed rock into which the black wooden door was set. At last, at this steep hill's summit, an immense monument or sculpture rose against the night sky. He thought it must be as tall as a building of a dozen stories.

The monument was in the form of two vast human hands, gracefully slender and exquisite even as they loomed awesomely. The hands had been shaped in a cupping gesture, arcing away from each other fluidly. Though he was distant from them, and the tint of green moonlight might be tricking his eyes, he had the impression the hands were carved out of solid jade, polished and sleek.

The monstrous, pitted green moon was aligned with the upturned palms of the hands in such a way that it seemed as though they had been designed to uphold it in the sky, cupping the ghastly sphere as if it were a diseased human heart, to be offered as a sacrifice to the cosmos.

A mysterious sense of familiarity came over him as he stared at this towering idol. He was moved to tears and stood up more erect, away from the wooden door, trembling all over violently.

Despite this, a movement in the tall, pale grass around his ankles drew his attention. Maybe it was the shifting green glow down there that had caught his eye. He looked down and saw a many-legged creature like a large crab or giant spider, impeded by the grass but struggling closer to his shoes.

It was one of the disembodied hands. It had slipped through the threshold before he had been able to get the door of black wood closed and bolted.

He wanted to cry out, but his lungs seized shut to trap the air, and before he could back away the hand pulled free of the encumbering grass and scampered onto his left foot.

At this touch, even through the material of his shoe, he was jolted as if electrified rigid, his eyes bulging wide. This reaction transpired in but a fraction of a second. In that microsecond, looking down at his body and legs and feet, he appeared as a negative image of himself, but colored the same phosphorescent green as the hand that had touched him.

And then he blinked out of existence.

0. A Ring

He snapped awake with a gasp in his heart and sat up in the seat of the parked car he had been slumped down in, covered with a soft orange blanket.

Through the car's windows he saw that the sun had come up, though it was still low enough in the sky to indicate the day was young. The sun was not monstrously engorged, so it seemed that it would have no trouble rising fully into the sky, as a sun should do.

The car sat at the edge of a parking lot, distant from other vehicles that were grouped closer to a gas station and the adjacent service building of a highway rest stop. He didn't recognize this place, however. Didn't know the number of this highway. Didn't know which state he was in.

He didn't know the make of the car he sat in. He realized he didn't know his name.

His disoriented gaze settled on the car's glove box to his right. Would there be something inside that would tell him who he was and why he was here, sheltering in a parked car? He had an intuition that this would be so, and thus reached to it and popped the small compartment open.

Resting atop a small stack of papers and the car's owner's manual was a package wrapped in a plastic shopping bag. He drew this out, into his lap, and opened the mouth of the crinkly white bag to see what it contained.

Inside was an object sealed inside a quart-sized plastic freezer bag. He gazed down at the thing clearly visible within.

A mysterious sense of familiarity came over him as he stared at the treasure, the memento, secreted inside the package. He was moved to tears, trembling all over violently.

Inside the freezer bag—discolored with decay, even though the bag being supposedly airtight—was a severed human hand. It was slender, the hand of a woman, and it wore a ring—a gold Claddagh ring, with a diamond mounted in the central heart, which two graceful hands cupped as if to uphold it as an offering to the cosmos.

Good Will toward Men

1. The Five Stages of Drowning

He didn't know for how long he'd been drowning.

The liquid he was suspended in wasn't water, being of a more viscous nature and of a smoky gray tint throughout. Still, it was fluid enough that it had filled his lungs when he'd been thrown from the edge of the crater in which the liquid formed a wide, deep pool.

Though his body was in truth only an illusion, a spiritual representation of the physical vessel his soul had occupied in life, when the Demons that he and the other Damned called the Torus had cast him into the gray pool he had experienced much of what was called the five stages of drowning.

First Stage: Panic, as he thrashed his arms in a futile attempt to keep his head above the surface. However, in life he had never learned to swim. Even as he splashed frantically he recalled his older brother, an experienced swimmer, teasing him and calling him a baby for not even allowing their parents to support his body in the shallow end of his Aunt Marge's swimming pool. He'd cried, all but hysterical, when his father had tried to carry him in. This panic stage lasted about forty-five seconds, if eternity could be said to be portioned out in the terrestrial sense.

Second Stage: As his head sank below the surface, he held his breath in an attempt to prevent himself from ingesting fluid. Here was where a difference occurred between drowning in Hades and drowning in the earthly world. In life, he would have likely lost consciousness now due to lack of oxygen. However, in the afterlife his sham body only pantomimed the functions of a material body: he experienced hunger and thirst but didn't require food or drink; his heart beat, but his body didn't actually utilize the mock blood it drove through him;

he seemed to breathe but didn't need air to survive because he was immortal. And so, he was only too horribly conscious of the stages that followed.

Third Stage: Despite his mind being aware, after about a minute and a half of trying to hold his breath his body persisted in its emulation of mechanical processes and went into respiratory arrest. His mouth gasped open and his lungs filled like sacks of sand. He sank lower in the gelatinous fluid until it grew darker around him. He finally hung in a shadowy oblivion between what lay above and what lay below. Below was ominous blackness. Above, if he tilted back his head, he saw the silhouetted curve of the crater's rim and the ambient golden glow of the air, though the ceiling of the sky itself—an inverted sea of molten lava—was covered by a blanket of dense black clouds. Also silhouetted against the fiery air were several of the gigantic Torus beings, looming there like statues and seemingly gazing down into the pool, though they had no eyes, their heads darkly outlined as great zeroes.

Fourth Stage: His spiritual body went through the motions of hypoxic convulsion, going rigid and jolting with spasms as if he were being electrocuted. A thick white foam rose up from between his lips, and he didn't even have the breath to dislodge it by blowing it away. Unlike a drowning mortal, he did not suffer sodium deficit or potassium excess or fallen calcium levels, because he was no longer comprised of chemicals, but he could feel his imitation heart stutter to a halt and go still like a rock in his chest.

Fifth Stage: Death. But he was already dead, so he dreamed.

2. The Sea of Memory

Though he never truly slept, sometimes in a sense there were nightmares. Unbidden, bad memories would push their way to the forefront of his mind, like scarred black whales breaking a calm surface to spout geysers of blood. However, if he relaxed his mind sufficiently that he achieved something like meditation, something like a self-imposed coma—internalizing his consciousness completely, forbidding it a peek at any window—he could distance himself from his surroundings and situation, so that for all intents and purposes he was *away*. (Dare he even say . . . *free?*)

Because damnation was eternal and the passage of time so difficult to gauge—there was no day or night—he would never know for how long he had been in one of his *away* periods before being disturbed from it. For there were disturbances. The Damned did not share this pool of perpetual drowning with each other only. Every now and then he would be roused from his dreaming state by a vicious tug on his foot or hand, nose or ear. His eyes would snap open to see that a large eel-like creature had clamped onto him. Only one of an endless variety of infernal life-forms, this creature had a long, segmented body like a human spine of black bone, its black head with its four white-glowing eyes composed of two matching halves resembling the heads of human infants, twins conjoined at the mouth, so that the lower jaw of each was the upper part of the other. Their shared mouth was full of needle teeth, and the eel would tear away a hunk of flesh or maybe even a few toes or fingers before it swished away again into the depths below, or to feast on another of the Damned.

He could only be grateful that apparently just one of these animals haunted the pool, and not a whole school of them in an unending feeding frenzy. He could only be grateful that, given time, his mock flesh would regenerate, the perception of physical agony would recede. He had taught himself to be thankful for such things, as a coping mechanism.

He was always grateful when he could return to his dreams.

He dreamed of, or rather remembered, his childhood. The Sunday drives his father would take him and his mother and brother on, after church, with no destination in mind, stopping for ice cream or to play in some little park they'd never been aware of before. He remembered Christmas mornings, bleary from too little sleep but high on adrenalin, sitting cross-legged on the floor near a live (or rather, undead) tree almost lost under the cheap mortal magic of tinfoil icicles reflecting multicolored fairy lights, he and his brother admiring (sometimes jealously) each other's presents as they tore the shimmering skins from them.

He remembered his adulthood. He could clearly see his future wife's breasts the first time she'd let him expose them, in his car in a parking lot outside a steak house where they'd just eaten; could almost feel their softness again, smell their warmth, taste their dark nipples, hear her little sigh.

He vividly recalled being drunk at his wedding dinner, blissfully disoriented as he stared into the pink-lighted miniature fountain tinkling under their elevated wedding cake, thinking, "I'm a *husband* now."

. . . And vividly recalled thinking, "I'm a *father* now" as he watched his blood-slick son emerge from inside his mother, bluish as if born dead (and from his first breath, already on the lifelong path of death like all mortals) . . . the doctor rushing him to a table to suck out the meconium he had aspirated. Seeing his airborne son's penis, he had told his wife, "It's a boy!" The doctor had paused, swung around with his son aloft, and said, "Oh yeah, it's a boy," and then had continued to the table.

. . . And dueling with his seven-year-old son with toy light sabers in a department store, falling to the floor mortally wounded and looking up to see a pair of parents watching his performance from the end of the aisle.

. . . And walking into his son's room (*no, not this again!*) and seeing the fifteen-year-old hanging from his neck (*oh no no no!*) with his toes just lightly touching the floor, as if he had been frozen in a graceful leap upward, a leap *away,* an arrow caught in flight, never finding its mark. A document left open on his computer, a confession of his shame. An account of his seduction at the edge of twelve and three subsequent years of abuse by their family's priest, Father Gordon MacArthur, who was already on administrative leave as his diocese investigated him in regard to several other allegations. The rope choked off his son's voice, his bulging tongue gagged him, but his document poured forth a gush of words. In the document that cast its blue light upon his hovering body, making of him a ghost bearing witness to its own testimony, the boy apologized to his parents. He couldn't face them when they found out, couldn't face his classmates should his name be released or leaked, couldn't face this mortal realm of betrayal and grief any longer.

. . . And walking up behind the man on the sidewalk, barking his name (*Father MacArthur!*) because he wanted the priest to see him, to *know* him, and, when the man turned, shooting him with a .357 Python in the belly. Standing over him while the priest curled himself around the bullet like a fist. Listening to him whine and whimper and grooooan before finally . . . *finally* . . . pointing the revolver again, this time at his head.

. . . And then (*this again . . . always this again*) lifting the gun's muzzle to his own temple, while he heard people screaming across the street, while he sobbed out loud an apology to his wife, who was back at their home unaware, his son's mother, whom he had failed because he hadn't protected their child from a predator, because he (*Damn him! God damn him!*) had insisted his family attend church every Sunday just as he had as a child, insisted they believe in its words, and in the messengers of its words, and the promises of eternal love and justice and reward, and he had pulled the trigger, and like a bullet through a skull, a bullet through some mysterious veil, he had fired his soul *here*.

3. The Dubious Rescue

A stern finger poked his shoulder to arouse him from his dreams.

His mother? Was it already time to go to school again, the weekend gone so soon? He groaned inside.

The finger poked him again, hard, in the side of his neck. *"Mom!"* he wanted to protest. How could she hurt him this way? It wasn't like her. He opened his eyes, and at the same time the finger curled and hooked him with a pointed nail under the edge of his jaw, puncturing his skin. It ripped upward, tore free, leaving a deep gouge along his cheek.

With his eyes open, he saw in front of him the void of grayness and remembered where he was with something so much more than a groan inside him. It was more like the howl of a man plummeting down a bottomless pit, forever and ever and ever.

He also saw the shadowy form of another Damned man not too distant from him, like himself suspended in the thick solution. This man was thrashing his limbs as if drowning; had he only just been tossed into the pool by the Torus? But no . . . he was being towed upward on a taut black cable, as if being rescued. So why was he resisting? Then he realized that wasn't a cable. It was a long, rigid pole of iron. He realized this even as a similar pole caught him in the left eye socket with its hooked end—which in his dream he had taken for a finger that had previously failed to snag his jaw—popping the jelly orb therein and taking hold of bone.

Then he himself was being hoisted up toward the surface. He himself flapping his limbs like ineffectual wings. He would have sucked fluid into his lungs, in his attempt to scream at the pain, had they not already been filled to capacity.

The shock had jolted his heart into beating again.

As he was reeled in like a fish the outer air brightened above him . . . and as the fluid around him correspondingly appeared lighter, with his remaining eye he saw a half dozen other Damned—men, women, a girl of maybe twelve—being pulled up by hooks caught in their flesh or bone, too. He imagined other Damned behind him were also being drawn upward. A ring of the giant Torus were arranged around the circumference of the pool, effortlessly working their long metal pikes.

Then he was breaking the surface, sputtering, trying to sob. Hand over huge, gnarled hand the Demon that had snared him pulled him toward shore. Identical to all the others, the Torus was twice the height of a human, its body hidden under layers of black leather robes imprinted with glowing white insignias that emitted wisps of vapor, its eyeless head a great circle of amber-colored flesh with the vague shadow of its O-shaped skull visible within.

He was dragged away from the rim of the crater, and with a deft flick of its wrists the Torus unhooked its pike from him. He was left floundering, blood running from his eye socket and the gouge in his cheek. He rolled onto his side and began vomiting up the gray fluid that had filled his lungs for however long it had been. Beside him and all around the perimeter of the pool, other Damned were doing the same.

The pain and the violent effort of his body to empty itself caused him to lose consciousness in a way he had never done while floating, as if in outer space, in the drowning pool—but just before he did so he saw there were other, smaller beings standing in a cluster off behind the ring of towering Demons. These beings were not dressed in black, but in robes of white.

4. The Visitation

He awoke as if from a night's sleep in his mortal life—on his back, atop a narrow bed (*was this his childhood bed?*), dressed in dry clothing. He saw, though, that this was not his childhood bedroom. It was a tiny barren cell, three blank walls with the fourth wall, facing a corridor beyond, comprised of iron bars covered in three-inch spikes. A series of grooved tracks running along both the ceiling and floor accommodated each of the bars, so that the wall of bars could be cranked closer and closer to the cell's occupant—this advance done either swiftly, or with excruciating anticipation over slow daily increments—inevitably pinning and crushing the prisoner against the pocked and bloodstained back wall. He knew this because he had been a prisoner of one such cell in the past, before being dragged to the pool of perpetual drowning.

So had the Torus realized at last that he had learned to overcome his panic and physical discomfort in their deep well, and even achieve periods of tranquility? He had heard that the Demons liked to vary the torments in Hades, lest the Damned become too accustomed to any one of them. He experienced a more acute sense of despair than he had known for some time. Was his new punishment to take place in this crushing chamber, or was it only a temporary holding cell until he could be moved to another of Hades' infinite regions, presided over by another of Hades' infinite races of Demons?

It wasn't that his clothing had dried out, but that he had been dressed while unconscious in a brand new uniform of long-sleeved black top, loose black trousers, thin-soled black shoes like Kung Fu slippers. Gone was his old waterlogged uniform, threadbare and torn by bullets and blades, his old shoes with holes in the imitation matter that composed their soles (which didn't heal up on their own, as did the holes in the imitation matter of his soul). He was at least thankful for these . . . gifts.

He sat up on his cot, felt at his cheek where the groping pike had lacerated it. Smooth once more. He realized he was seeing with two eyes again. The only scar remaining, that always remained, was the conflated symbol branded on his forehead that announced his doubly damning sins: the sin of Murder, and the sin of Sacrilege for having killed a servant of the Creator.

As he was feeling around his regenerated eye with his fingertips, he became aware that he was hearing a distant murmur of voices from somewhere out in the corridor. Curious but apprehensive, he got to his feet and crept closer to the thorny bars.

The voices were somewhat louder, echoey with the corridor's acoustics, but from this angle he couldn't see anyone . . . just a few other cells like this one, facing his. They were untenanted, however, with their doors standing open. Leaning closer to his cell's door in the hope of making out the unknown speakers' words, he curled his hands around two of its bars between their spikes . . . and the door shifted forward, swinging out a little. He had been left in an unlocked cell.

What kind of trick was this? Some diabolical game? Were those apparently human voices meant to lure him into a trap?

He eased the door outward some more, grateful that its hinges didn't squeal, and dared to poke his head into the corridor. His reactivated heart was pounding at maximum power.

To the right the corridor went on a good ways, showing only more abandoned cells, but the sounds had come from the left and in this direction he was met with an unexpected sight. In an open intersection of corridors, about twenty Damned—all in fresh black outfits—stood facing a group of six human beings in snowy robes with the hoods drooping behind them like crumpled wings. These were undoubtedly blessed souls—people who had died under the good graces of the Creator. *Angels*. The only time he'd ever seen Angels before, they were tourists venturing into Hades on safaris to hunt the Damned. Evidently Paradise grew boring.

Standing to either side of the Angels, no doubt to protect them from the Damned, were two taller figures wearing cone-like red hoods, through the eyeholes of which a white light glowed, their bodies also cloaked in red. They carried assault rifles. These were obviously Celestials, the equivalent of the Demons: entities that saw to the needs of the Angels just as Demons saw to the punishment of the Damned. They were said to be more terrible than Demons, but like Demons they could be destroyed—*killed*—because they had no immortal souls. And what Damned didn't dream of killing Demons and Celestials?

One of the Angels, a corpulent elderly man, bald but for a semicircle of white hair tucked behind his ears, looked over and spotted him and motioned to the others. Even the hooded Celestials turned his way. He felt the irrational urge to dive back into his cell . . . as if that would protect him if those crimson-robed warriors came striding down the corridor.

Another of the Angels, a tall woman perhaps in her early sixties, with silver-white hair flowing to her shoulders, smiled and raised a hand to gesture to him. "Come here, sir . . . don't be afraid. We bring you season's greetings!"

5. The Most Wonderful Time of the Year

He hesitated. The tall woman, who must have been model-beautiful in her younger days and was still striking—poised and sapphire-eyed—gestured again but maintained a patient and gentle tone. "Come on, don't be shy now. What is your name, sir?"

He was reassured that at least the Angels didn't have guns. Obediently, he started down the corridor toward the unlikely party. When he was close enough for his nervous voice to be heard he said, "Andrew Nabors."

"Andrew! Did your parents name you after Andrew the fisherman, brother of Peter, son of Jonas?"

"I don't know."

"Any relation to Jim Nabors?" the corpulent man asked in a wheezy voice, grinning.

"Not that I know of," Andrew said.

"Andrew, my name is Eva," said the woman, apparently the leader of this group. Andrew resisted the urge to ask if her parents had named her after the first woman. "This is my son, Patrick." She indicated the corpulent man, who had obviously died many years after his younger-looking mother. Eva went on to introduce the other members of her party . . . aside from the nameless Celestial escorts.

Andrew nodded to each Angel in turn and at the end muttered, "Nice to meet you." He noted that the other Damned were watching him expectantly, as if he might tell them what was going on, their faces no less uneasy than his own. Several of them were children. One of the Damned women held a boy of maybe five in her arms, straddling her hip. Surely not her own child, because—as was clearly not the case in Heaven—one of the punishments of Hades was never to allow family members or spouses to be reunited in death. Hades was vast enough that they could be distributed impossible distances from one another, that even an eternity of traveling might not be traversed. The boy made Andrew think of his son at that age, and the thought of the boy's fear compressed his heart in a vise.

"Well, Andrew," said Eva, "you were the last we were waiting for. Now that we've all been properly introduced, why don't we go on to the main hall to talk about the reason why our little expedition came here today."

The Damned followed the Angels through a series of corridors until they entered a large chamber with a high arched ceiling that Andrew hadn't seen when he'd been briefly held in this facility before. The room was undecorated, windowless, but a long table made of black wood from infernal trees, with benches pulled up to both sides of it, dominated the floor. A miniature cloud, glowing white, billowed and knotted in upon itself in the air above the table, giving the room its illumination. Were banquets held here for visiting Angels? Meetings for Demonic officials? In each of the room's four corners, unmoving as titan suits of armor, stood a Torus Demon with a spear. The vapors curling from the sigils on their robes were like an audience of ghosts lurking furtively at the fringes.

Eva turned to face them all, passing her smile from one to the next, and announced, "Today, my friends, is Christmas Eve."

Another of the perks of Heaven? Andrew wondered. The passage of time was charted, known?

No one reacted, except for the dark-skinned boy on the woman's hip, who twisted around alertly in her arms. In life he might not have celebrated that holiday, but he obviously knew of its festivities. Seeing the child's instinctively eager reaction out of the corner of his eye squeezed from Andrew another dollop of pain.

When no one said anything, Eva went on, "A group of us in Paradise have undertaken to forego our own Christmas celebrations this year to bring them, instead, to unfortunate souls like yourselves. We call ourselves the Carolers, because in life some of us—myself included—went door-to-door singing carols outside people's homes on Christmas Eve." Her smile grew more beatific at the memory. "There are presently almost two hundred of us. Because Hades is so immense, we can't possibly reach out to all of you, but we hope for more volunteers to join the cause in years to come. Nevertheless, we Carolers have spread ourselves out as best we can, and our particular group has chosen this place—chosen *you*—for our visit."

Some of the Damned exchanged wary looks. When was the trick

going to be revealed, the trap sprung? Andrew, however, felt Eva and her group were sincere. He had grown up with religion. He recognized the missionary, the evangelist, the midwife to those who would be born again. But it was too late for any of them to be born again, wasn't it, when in Hades they had been consigned to eternally die again . . . and again.

Eva looked a bit embarrassed or disappointed that no spontaneous exclamations of gratitude, nor even a single smile, had greeted her announcement, but she soldiered on. "Tomorrow morning is Christmas, and we'll have some festivities for you . . . some special surprises. But for now, we want you to enjoy the anticipation that makes the night before Christmas so magical. We invite you to interact openly with each other, to talk freely and move about this facility as you care to. There will be no punishments, no torments, nothing to fear tonight. This respite is our gift to you. Tonight you can reflect on your lives . . . on Christmases past. We encourage you to sing songs together, play games! And we most certainly invite you to talk with us as well. I'm sure most of you have regrets about decisions you made in your lives. We will listen to those regrets with open hearts, and you may find a degree of comfort in the telling. Confession is good for the soul, and it's unlikely that in life or thereafter you've ever taken the opportunity to truly confess—to confront your sins in a manner that is contemplative, that doesn't simply involve the punishing consequences of sin." She spread her arms, palms upturned, saint-like. "We welcome you to talk of this, or any other thing you may care to express."

"Ooh," her son Patrick wheezed, looking toward a doorway at the far end of the great room. "Here come some treats!"

Into the chamber came a procession of a dozen Demons of a smaller size than the Torus, better adapted to this structure's maze of narrow, low-ceilinged corridors. They were very much like old but still powerful chimpanzees, shaved completely hairless, their pale and stubbly bodies and even their faces luridly and colorfully tattooed with scenes of the Holocaust, and child molestation, and the tortures of Inquisition. Overlarge penises swung between their legs as they loped along. They often ravished female and male Damned alike, even the children, and the Damned had nicknamed their species Rapes. But now, incongruously, they bore platters of illusory food for illusory bellies. Breads and crackers and cheeses, ruby-red grapes and other infernal fruits that didn't quite correspond to earthly varieties. Earthen jugs of wine, water, and milk derived from infernal animals. Pastries and candies and nuts. The platters were laid out along both sides of the banquet table. Then, with a few flashed snarls at the Damned and a couple of barking cries, the Rapes turned and waddled out of the room again, their great arms swinging at their sides.

"Please," Eva said, waving her arm like a woman revealing a car behind a curtain on a game show, "enjoy yourselves!"

6. The Breaking of Bread

Though some of them no doubt suspected poison, or razor blades or broken glass secreted in the food, not one of the Damned refused partaking of it, so strong was the hunger they constantly suffered. The young woman who had taken it upon herself to care for the little boy sat him beside her on the bench and plucked grapes for him.

Partly what reassured the Damned was that Patrick and a couple of the other Angels were digging into the feast themselves. "Mm," he mumbled, chewing, "this is a helluva good cheese!"

"Patrick," his mother warned, casting him a chastising glance. She continued speaking with one of the Damned who had approached her, a timid-looking man who had died in his seventies. He had revealed that he was a newcomer to Hades, the drowning pool having been the first of the punishments meted out to him. In a quavering voice he had confessed his sin: in life he'd been an atheist.

"Is it true," he asked her, "there's no Satan . . . never was? Only the Creator?"

"Yes, Richard," Eva replied. "A truly loving and strong father knows when to spank just as he knows when to caress." She laid her hand on his shoulder. "One cannot blame Him for their fate; one can only blame himself. Those who sin bring about their own punishment. They wield the sword against themselves."

"I'm sorry I didn't believe, Eva, I'm sorry!" Richard sobbed, breaking down. "Now I know better! Why do I have to suffer for all eternity just because I made a mistake—a stupid, blind mistake?"

Listening in on their conversation, chewing a cheese sandwich he'd put together, Andrew cut in before Eva could reply. "In life, supposed-ly, we can be forgiven for our sins if we confess to them and repent. Why can't we be absolved after our deaths, if we feel contrite?"

"Oh, Andrew," Eva said, facing him, "by then it's too late: judg-ment has been cast. The opportunity to die in a state of grace has passed, but the opportunity was there. May I ask you—and of course you needn't answer if you'd rather not—what sin brought you here?"

Andrew put down his plate, and his voice gained strength, defi-ance. "I shot a man—a priest who'd been abusing my son, and who knows how many other boys, for years."

"I'm sorry to hear about your son. Did you kill this priest while he was attacking your child, to defend him?"

"No. I hunted him down after the fact. I shot him in the street. And for that, for killing that monster, I'm here. I was a devoutly reli-gious person in life, but here I am. And I strongly suspect that Father Gordon MacArthur is at this very moment enjoying Christmas Eve in Heaven, attended by a flock of golden-haired Celestial slave boys. Is that true, Eva? Did he make it into Paradise?"

"Andrew," Eva sighed, "I don't know of this man. But if he felt honest regret in his heart for his actions, if he made confession and paid his penance in life—*in life*, before you killed him—then yes, An-drew, he would have."

"I see. Sure. Make some bullshit insincere confession, go through the motions, and why not? So tell me this: how about my son? Where is he now? Because I forgot to tell you this part, Eva: my son was so distraught over what that scumbag did to him that he hanged himself. He killed himself, only fifteen years old." His voice choked on the last few words.

"Oh, dear," Eva said, wagging her head sadly, her tone that of a compassionate doctor relating that a loved one's prognosis was dire. "If he committed suicide, then I'm sorry to say he'd be denied en-trance to Paradise."

"Of course!" Andrew blurted, though this news was not unsus-pected. "Of course he would!"

One of the two Celestials, who had been lingering nearby, shifted forward and raised its assault rifle a little, but Eva waved it back.

Andrew lowered his voice to a hiss, pointing toward the child eating grapes, who was oblivious to their conversation. "What about him? What could he have done at his age to deserve being here?"

"He told me his name is Ravinder," Eva whispered, leaning toward Andrew. "I'd say he was born of Hindu parents. I'm sorry, Andrew, I know how this sounds, but I don't make the rules. The rules are not kept secret, though. In any part of the world where people live, people of any color or creed, who is not aware of the Son's words, whether they choose to follow them or not? 'No one comes to the Father except through me.'"

"And that poor kid has to be tortured for eternity because he didn't defy his Hindu parents and say, hey, fuck that, this Jesus guy is for me?"

Eva recoiled slightly, her expression gone chilly at his profanity. "You talked about contrition, Andrew, and forgiveness. May I ask you another question? Even if you could be forgiven for murdering that priest, and ascend from Hades to Heaven, can you tell me you are truly sorry for having killed him?"

Andrew didn't even have to think about it. "No," he said flatly. "I'm not sorry."

"Well, there you go."

7. The Eternal Night

None of them sang songs or played games that night, after the Angels had all left through that doorway at the far end of the banquet hall, presumably to retire to more comfortable quarters than the Damned had access to. They did, though, break off into pairs or little groups to talk in subdued tones while continuing to pick at the feast. Only a couple of them sat alone, perhaps reflecting too much on Christmases they had known in their mortal existence, one old woman weeping quietly and continuously.

Within Andrew's earshot, a man approached the young woman tending to the small boy and asked haltingly, "Would you want to share a bunk with me tonight?"

"I'm caring for him," she said, nodding at the child.

"Well . . . couldn't someone else watch him? How about just for an hour?"

"Sorry."

"I'm just looking for a little comfort," he said, his voice catching.

"I'm comforting *him*."

The man drifted away, mumbling. Andrew thought he might next ask one of the older Damned women, or the men, or even the twelve-year-old girl, but he didn't.

Eventually people began leaving the hall, seeking cells in which to indulge in the luxury of undisturbed sleep. Andrew heaped a dish with more food, though he was full almost to discomfort, and took it with him. He didn't think he'd find the same cell he'd woken up in but imagined it didn't matter. He settled on a cell that was unoccupied, with an unoccupied cell to either side, but with other people close enough at hand along the corridor that he experienced a faint measure of reassurance at their presence. He closed his cell's door most of the way, but not entirely. It felt good to know it didn't have to be closed all the way.

He set the plate down, removed his shoes, stretched out on his back with his fingers laced behind his head, and gazed at the ceiling with its striped rows of grooves for the bars to pass through when the wall of spiked bars was cranked forward. But not tonight. No such tortures this one night. Tomorrow was the birthday of Christ. But . . . hadn't Christ died for their sins?

So why did they have to die infinite deaths to pay for their own sins? How did that work?

He realized he had never understood religion at all. That it was unfathomable except, perhaps, to the alien mind of the Creator. If He even understood Himself.

Andrew had almost dozed off when a stealthy shuffling from the corridor caused him to angle his face that way. It wasn't Santa Claus with his sack. It was one of the Rapes, the front of its body tattooed with a scene of lingchi, the Chinese torture of Death by a Thousand Cuts. The simian-like Demon, its eyes entirely black, curled back its upper lip in a snarl-like leer and pointed one finger at him. Its member was erect, the head protruding between the bars. It might as well have said to him, though it said nothing, *"Soon . . . soon enough."* Satisfied that Andrew had seen it, the Rape turned away, loping off down the corridor presumably to look in on the next prisoner.

Andrew thought, *So much for Eva's promise of one night of peace.*

He got out of bed and, though it wouldn't lock, he closed the barred door all the way.

Then he returned to his bunk, finally fell into a doze.

He dreamed of Eva, in fact. She was crouched down compassionately beside several African children with cadaverous faces, emaciated limbs, bloated bellies, flies crawling in and out of their nostrils. They stared back at her benevolently smiling face with glazed yellow eyes.

She was handing each one of them a Bible.

8. The Holiday

"Wake up, my friends!" Eva's cheerful voice, her hands clapping, like the nicest drill sergeant in the history of humankind. "Rise and shine!"

She appeared beyond the spiked bars of Andrew's cell. "Time to get up, Andrew! Merry Christmas to you!"

He sat up on his bunk with a groan and was thankful Eva and her companions continued on toward the next occupied cell so he wouldn't have to return her greeting. He put on his shoes, stepped out into the corridor. Others were doing the same.

"Everyone on to the hall!" Eva called back to those behind her.

They trailed after her like a train of obedient, groggy children. They followed her into the great hall, where she swept around to beam at them and watch their reaction.

The hall had been transformed as had Ebenezer Scrooge's home upon the visitation of the Ghost of Christmas Present. A feast had been spread upon the massive table of ebony wood that put to shame the party snacks of the night before. Heaps of steaming vegetables, golden roasted birds, more bread, more fruit, more jugs of beverage. The centerpiece was a whole roasted boar with rows of fantastical tusks curling out of its jaw, rows of horns curling out of its skull.

And in the middle of the table stood a Christmas tree, its trunk fitted into a heavy iron candle base. It was a coniferous tree, like an evergreen, but its needles were obsidian black. The infernal tree had been decorated with pine cones painted gold and silver. Throughout the black branches flashed tiny red lights. These, Andrew recognized, were an infernal insect, a bioluminescent beetle like the earthly lightning bug. Except that these beetles, which inflicted a nasty bite, drank the blood of the Damned. Somehow they had been directed to lie passively upon the branches of this beautiful, this terrible, Christmas tree.

The miniature cloud that provided the hall's light had condensed greatly until it was a mere disk, hovering just above the top of the tree like a crowning star, or a halo. So concentrated, so radiant, it was hard to look at directly.

"Merry Christmas, everyone!" Eva and the rest of the Carolers cried out as one.

The tree—and the Angels—went barely acknowledged as the Damned dug into their repast. Andrew found himself standing beside a portly white-haired man who was piling his plate with several types of mashed vegetables. This man said to Andrew, "I'm a Jew. Do you know what I used to do every Christmas day? I'd volunteer to serve meals to homeless people. Not to insult, but how many Christians do you think ever spent one day feeding homeless people? So do you know why I'm here in Hell?"

"Because you're a Jew," Andrew said.

The man chuckled humorlessly. "Mm-hm." He pointed his fork at the boar carcass. "And I'm not touching that thing. Not kosher."

While the Damned feasted, true to their name, the Carolers serenaded them with Christmas songs. They were able to goad only the twelve-year-old into singing along with them, robotically, her expression shellshocked. Mercifully, she had probably lost her mind many years ago. Andrew had heard her tell Eva in her ghostly, empty voice that she'd died from a scarlet fever outbreak in 1874.

"O Christmas Tree! O Christmas Tree! Thy leaves are so unchanging!"

Andrew heard one Damned mutter to another, "I hate them worse than the Demons."

"What?" said the other person.

"The Demons don't talk to us. They aren't full of shit. They don't lie to us. They don't lie to themselves that they care about us."

"Thou bidst us true and faithful be, and trust in God unchangingly."

After the Damned had eaten much—the boar a torn, partly skeletal ruin—and after a good number of Christmas carols, Eva went to the door at the far end of the hall and motioned for several Rapes to enter. Between them they pushed an odd contraption on wheels. Within an elaborate brass setting that was also the framework for the mobile cart rested an apparently glass orb the size of a basketball, cloudy gray marbled with milky and inky swirls, like the globe of an alien world.

"Friends," Eva explained, "this is another gift we've arranged for you. It's a device normally reserved only for use by Demonic administrators. This is a scrying ball, which can be used to view scenes greatly removed from the viewer . . . in Hades, or Heaven, or even in the mortal world. For our use today, those who lent this fantastic device to us have adjusted it in such a way that any soul who gazes into it will be able to view a loved one, alive or dead, to whose soul they're connected. The scrying ball can detect and trace that connection." She let this sink in, watching her audience's faces. "We've arranged for each one of you, if you choose, to be able to view one loved one . . . whether they be alive on Earth, or whether they've passed on to one of the afterlives."

The Damned still stared mutely. Still absorbing, chewing their food dumbly.

"Who'd like to go first?" Patrick asked, sweeping his arm toward the globe like a stage magician asking for a volunteer for the box of piercing swords.

Finally, one of the Damned raised her hand and stepped forward. She approached the device meekly, Eva taking her by the arm to help position her. Leaning forward hesitantly as if she expected to see some rotting corpse's face swim up in the glass, she asked, "Do I have to tell you who it is I want to see?"

"The scrying ball will know," Eva told her.

They all watched her as the woman watched the sphere. They couldn't see what she was seeing—from where he stood, the globe looked unchanged to Andrew—but within seconds the woman clapped her hand over her mouth and behind it said, "Oh! *Ohh!*" Tears flowed down her cheeks. After a few seconds more, one of the Angels helped her walk to the table and sit down. The woman cast a longing look over her shoulder, back at the globe.

"Who's next?" Patrick asked, looking quite satisfied, like the proud inventor of some remarkable new invention, or a car dealer who had just made a sale.

Another of the Damned stepped forward.

Andrew came up alongside Eva and said, "You can't let Ravinder look into it. That would be cruel, Eva, not a kindness. What's he going to see? The mother he'll never be reunited with?"

"I understand that he couldn't put something like that into perspective, Andrew," she replied. "That's why he was given the toys instead, for his gift." Indeed, earlier Patrick had handed the little boy several gift-wrapped packages to open, containing miniature cars and jointed little figures, toys such as children in Paradise no doubt played with. Contentedly, he sat on the floor playing with them even now.

"How thoughtful of you," Andrew said. "How concerned. And tomorrow, when our special holiday is over, do you know what will happen to Ravinder? A Rape will grab those toys away and smash them on the floor in front of him . . . right before it sodomizes him."

"Stop it!" Eva said.

"Do you think I'm lying? I'm just telling you how it is here. Why wouldn't they do that? And what could you do to stop it? Order the Rapes, order all the Demons in Hades, not to touch the boy's toys? Never to harm him again? You don't have that kind of power, any more than you have the power to take that one boy back with you to Heaven."

"I've done what I can for him, Andrew!" Eva snapped, tears warping the surfaces of her brilliant blue eyes. "I've done what little I can to relieve your suffering for a day or two at least!"

"A day or two of *eternity*? And will we at least have this respite to look forward to again next year? No . . . you already told us you Carolers are spread too thin. Next year it'll be another spot of Hades you'll visit. Right?" She didn't dispute this, only looked at him in helplessness, tears streaming. "You should have just left us in the pool. We were better off in there, without your *mercy*. Why do you think they let you come here? They knew it was only a new kind of torture. Whether you wanted it this way or not, you're just Demons with halos."

"Oh, Andrew," Eva sobbed, wagging her head.

He brushed past her, toward Patrick and the scrying ball. "Okay, let me have my turn. Let's get this punishment over with. The sooner this farce is finished, the better."

Patrick glanced at his mother dubiously, but she nodded at him. The Angel shifted aside so Andrew could stand over the orb and look down at its glossy, clouded surface.

But it didn't remain clouded for long.

9. The Gift

The sphere became clear, became a lens, revealed to him a distant scene. It was obviously a landscape in Hades: an arid lakebed of dried mud split into tiles, as if the party of people he saw moving across this hellscape were walking upon the vast scaly body of the Creator/Satan Himself. There were three men and two women in this little group of Damned in their dusty and torn black uniforms. One of them carried an assault rifle, identical to those of the Celestial guards in this room. Another carried a compact sub-machine-gun. Several of them wore swords in scabbards . . . swords such as many races of Demons carried. Swords that had to have been stolen, like the guns, either from Demons or Celestials. Demons or Celestials who had been *killed*.

One of the members of the party, with a pump-action shotgun in his arms, was his eternally fifteen-year-old son. His tongue no longer bulged from his mouth, his toes no longer touched the earth ever-so-lightly. He tramped solidly, determinedly, across the desert floor, his eyes squinting and hard. He looked to be in search of something.

More Damned to join their little band. More Demons to kill.

His son wouldn't be aware that his father had killed himself after his own suicide. Wouldn't be able to reach his father even if he did know, no matter how long he and his friends marched. But he was fighting back. Defying the keepers of Hades. Defying the order of the Creator. He was young. Defying was what the young did.

Gray clouds spiraled in to cloak the orb once more. Andrew staggered back from the scrying device, turned toward Eva with tears on his own face to mirror hers, but he was also grinning. "Thank you, Eva," he said. "That was a wonderful gift you gave me, after all."

She pivoted to watch him, uncomprehending—only he had seen the vision in the orb—as he crossed the great hall to seek out his cell and wait for the end of their holiday.

10. The Gray

One more gift awaited the group of twenty Damned, come the next morning.

Eva and the other Carolers had departed. They'd tried to round everyone up to say goodbye first, but Andrew had avoided them. He heard from the young woman who had been a temporary surrogate mother to Ravinder that Eva had gently taken his toys back, promising to return them next time she saw him. A lie, but Andrew appreciated that she had done this, rather than have Ravinder lose them in the way he had described.

The Rapes led them all from the building, outside again, and from there the looming Torus took over, conducting them along a trail back to the crater. Back to the drowning pool. Andrew had never been so grateful—that is, aside from his glimpse the day before into the scrying ball.

When one of the Torus picked him up and hurled him into the pool, he didn't resist. As his lungs filled and he sank, his body fought against it but his mind did not.

He welcomed the gray void. Welcomed the dreams.

The Temple of Ugghiutu

Summer storms would often attack the Great Plateau with all the un-expectedness and devastating rage of a bored god once again angered by human indiscretion. On one occasion Nir had been tending his herd under a bright, if hazed, sky . . . only to be racing desperately a minute later to lie in a stream bed as twin cyclones came snaking across the horizon. Several of his goats had been swept up in one of the whirling black titans, their bodies flung or carried so far that he hadn't seen a trace of them after the funnels had marched into the distance . . . again, like the striding legs of some towering deity.

This summer it had been calm—too calm. There had been a drought, and the fields had gone a dry, brittle yellow. Nir had been letting his herd drift further from his village every day, until at last he was camping at night under the sky, contemplating the stars that seemed so tiny, so silent and placid, but which the priests solemnly advised were each and every one a seething inferno, its own raging hell. Each with its own demons, perhaps.

His drifting eventually brought him near to the eastern edge of the Great Plateau, where the general flatness of the land became rocky and broken before dropping off sharply altogether. Here, in the shade of towering outcrops of jagged stone, a little more shielded from the sun, the grass was not as yellow. Nir's lean goats grazed anxiously in what seemed by contrast fields of plenty.

But as if they had trespassed upon some holy land, black clouds like rolling mountains came, billowing and spreading like ink under water. Nir saw the sheets of rain that were sweeping in his direction like a solid wall from the west. Forked tongues of lightning flickered as if from a writhing mass of gigantic snakes in the heavens.

Nir urged his goats into a chasm in the tortured rock, thankful that his herd was of small, nimble goats and not of cattle. He hoped for a cave, or at the least a protruding shelf of rock to cower under when

the deluge passed this way. But the rains came quickly, and though the
walls of rock to either side did protect him to some extent, he and his
little flock were still pounded by the torrents. He didn't fear lightning,
down in the chasm, but this fear was replaced by another when there
came a clattering around him. At first he thought it was the hooves of
the goats, echoing off the walls, until he saw the white pebbles of ice
bouncing off the stone floor around him. Hail. Soon it was pelting
him, and one stone struck his shoulder with such force that it was like
having a cane brought against it. The offending stone, when it fell to
his feet, was as large as a fowl's egg.

The goats continued on ahead, until the floor of the chasm sloped
upwards. Nir followed them, hoping their instincts would guide him to
a better shelter. He tucked his head into his shoulders as larger and
larger stones crashed around him, wincing when one missile impacted
against his backbone. He saw a stone the size of a man's head fall from
the sky and shatter against one wall of the chasm like a skull thrown
from a great height.

The slope ended in a rise, and Nir mounted it. His goats went on
ahead, trotting across an open stretch, but Nir stood rooted on the
spot. It wasn't the fear of venturing into the open that gave him pause,
but rather the imposing sight that had been revealed before him.

Though he had never seen the structure before, he knew it from
the sermons of priests and the boasting of youths who had stolen out
to the east edge for a look. Those youths, that is, who had returned,
and those youths who had been able to find it. For it was said that the
Temple of Ugghiutu was not always to be found on the same spot.
Sometimes it was here, sometimes there, sometimes nowhere to be
seen. The priests said the temple alternated between this world and the
world of Ugghiutu, the ancient god to whom some unknown worshippers had erected the structure. One youth had said he never found the
temple where it had last been reported, but saw a broad path dragged
through the dirt as if the temple had been pushed by an army off the
edge of the Great Plateau . . . yet when he went to look over the edge,
he saw nothing at all below.

But here was the temple now, perched on another rise a short distance from the rim of the plateau, looming through a rippling caul of
rain. It was an edifice like no other Nir had seen, its style of architec-

ture nothing like the work to be found in any village or town he had ever visited, or even like any of the other ruins scattered here and there across the Great Plateau.

It was all made of a dark purple stone, as others had testified, smooth and glossy as if each inch of the great building had been obsessively polished by hand. It had few sharp angles, few straight lines; instead, it flowed and curved, bulged and tapered, fluid and symmetrical in some awesome alien way. There was a great central dome or rotunda, and spires or minarets of spiraled design swirling upward to end in points. There were few windows, round or oval-shaped, and there was but one door. Those who returned said this door was always sealed tightly shut. Those who didn't return, it was said, had found the door open.

The door was open, and Nir's goats had already begun filing inside the building as if they had been called by some other herdsman within.

Nir almost called out to them. But another peal of thunder blasted his ears, the flash of lightning illuminating the temple, better showing off its weird color. The hail was not just painful now—it was deadly. It was a definite danger, one to be dealt with immediately. The dangers of the temple were the stuff of myth. Those who hadn't returned may have ventured from the Great Plateau altogether or been killed by men rather than the spirits of some ancient cult. Or been killed by a hailstorm, for that matter.

Nir depended enough upon animals to trust their instincts, their sensitivity. If his goats found the temple inviting, then he would follow them. His mind made up, Nir tucked his head in even more and dashed out into the open, up the slope toward the Temple of Ugghiutu, which loomed larger and larger until Nir actually plunged into its dark interior.

*

The goats milled in the large foyer, not straying far. One started up a ramp to a second story, but changed its mind and rejoined the others. Nir took a quick count of the beasts as he twisted and wrung out his long hair in his fists. Only two animals were missing in the storm— unless they had entered the temple also and, more adventurous than their fellows, had wandered off to other chambers.

Nir peeled off his soaked jacket and wrung it out also, draping it over the edge of the ramp. His bare arms were chilled and he rubbed them as he looked around him. Though it wasn't the central rotunda, the foyer had a domed ceiling lined with arches of support. Even the arches had smooth, rounded edges. Sharp angles must have been anathema to the people who constructed this wonder. Their aesthetics were not so based on mathematical geometry, obviously, as on the more graceful forms of nature.

Off from the foyer, two dark corridors disappeared into the depths of the temple. One was so narrow a man's shoulders might brush the sides, making Nir wonder what size the worshippers of Ugghiutu had been, but the other was a wide hall with a vaulted ceiling. Down its length, on either side, it was flanked by a row of columns of that same purple stone. Each column was surmounted by a fluted capital, carved to look perhaps like coiled vines. The hall stretched off into utter blackness.

Nir had heard every variation on the legends. Most agreed that the worshippers of Ugghiutu had performed sacrifices of both beasts and humans in this place, supposedly extinguishing entire tribes of primitive men and women. Others said these poor victims were not killed, but spirited away to that other plane where Ugghiutu himself made his home. There, the human men would become slaves, the women playthings. But sacrifice was the preferred version. And yet, the worst version of all held that the cultists of Ugghiutu still existed—that they had not died out centuries before, leaving the temple abandoned, but still dwelt in its deep recesses, keeping from the windows, venturing out only at night. Lying in wait for some foolish youth to come through the door when they were wont to leave it invitingly open.

Nir looked out again at the storm. The rain was so heavy that he could not see the jutting rocks of the chasm through it. He heard hail clicking against the dome far above him. Thunder rumbled, as if from within the very depths of this building itself.

He was no foolish youth, nor was he a brave warrior. But Nir was a man, curious and questioning. A little exploring he would do . . . just a peek into a room or two beyond this foyer. Not so much that he would become lost. Yes, he could remain here like the goats until the storm had passed, but he was not a goat. He was intrigued by this alien place, despite the myths, despite the flutter of his heart and the way his blood seemed to skitter through his veins. This place made his thoughts skitter through his brain. He had never in his life ventured off the Great Plateau, with its great flatness, its great sameness. What he saw here would sustain him for years to come, and his children when he fathered children; and his grandchildren after them would have a tale to listen to in wonder, a tale other than of tending goats day after day on the mind-numbing emptiness of the grasslands.

The darkness at the end of the tunnel gave him pause, however. He turned and glanced up the ramp the one goat had half ascended. At its top, he saw a window letting in the dark light outside. It was enough light to make up his mind to take that direction, and Nir put his first step upon the ramp as timidly as if it were a tightrope across a ravine.

He stole up higher, craning his neck to see into the second floor of the temple. If the cultists were still in existence, if indeed their method was to leave the door open to lure travelers, they might be hiding in that chamber even now, knives in hands, cowls over their heads, shading faces that might be human, or might not. But then, if they wanted him, they could just as easily burst in upon him in the foyer, couldn't they? Overwhelm him before he had a chance to dash out into the rain? He tried to convince himself that it was of no more risk to continue up into that new chamber.

Nir had his own dagger, and he held it before him as he padded to the top of the ramp.

The oval window was to his right. It had no glass, and the rain made the floor a pool, hail clattering in. Nir shielded his face and rushed quickly past it. The chamber was lit weakly by another portal at its end, this one also letting in the storm. Other than that, the walls were empty. No tapestries, no paintings, no weapons on display or sculptures in alcoves. There were no furnishings. The place had been gutted, it would seem—abandoned at some distant time. But why?

No cultists lurking. Encouraged, Nir pressed on stealthily past the second window and through a threshold into another room.

This chamber was larger, and surprisingly well lit. The cause of that was a wonder all its own. The domed ceiling was a cap of crystal, thick and wavy, distorting the view of towering spires outside, the view further distorted by the rain flowing in heavy curtains down its sides.

Lightning flashed outside, illuminating the room more brightly.

Nir turned to touch the stone of the place for the first time. It was so smooth it was slippery, yet not as cool as he expected it to be. The purple was marbled with streaks and veins of white, subtle in most places but sometimes forming patterns like lace or great spiderwebs fossilized inside the rock. This circular room's walls had odd nodules protruding from it at random, some small as nuts, others large as melons, and not carved separately and inserted into the walls, but carved from the walls themselves. In fact, Nir realized at last, he saw no seams in any of the walls where they might have been assembled from various pieces. Even the floor and ceiling merged smoothly into the walls without angles, without seams. As impossible as it was to contemplate, it would appear that the temple had been entirely carved out of one immense boulder of that strange purple stone—so alien a mineral that Nir wondered if it had fallen from the stars.

He passed under the huge lens, gazing up through it and listening to the hail against it. Again, a threshold on the opposite side, and he stepped through it dagger first.

Another ramp, this one spiraling upwards to a yet higher section, perhaps inside one of the shorter towers. Nir began to ascend. His knife inadvertently scraped against the wall as he advanced, and he flinched.

The room when he came to it was long and seemed infinite; another hall extended into blackness, but with a ceiling so low Nir didn't have to bow his head yet felt that he should. There were no cobwebs to worry about tangling in his hair, however. Perhaps even spiders whispered amongst themselves of Ugghiutu's temple.

Nir halfheartedly started down the hall. A little light came up the spiraling ramp behind him from the room with the lens, but the darkness ahead seemed more than his eyes could adjust to. Another few steps and he had decided it was best to turn back. But then something to his right bent his gaze there.

It was a small pit in the floor, against the wall. Nir took one step closer to it and became paralyzed at the contents of that pit.

Bones. Ribs curled like great fingers poised to clutch at him. Skulls grinning to mock his fearful, still fleshy expression. The half-crushed skull of some large animal, perhaps a cow. Bones picked so clean that their very color had been sucked away, from ivory to bleached white.

Sacrifice, Nir's mind hissed at him. Sacrifice . . .

His gaze lifted. A bit beyond the pit was another; another beyond that; and yet another, to the left. These small pits, all filled with skeletons and skulls, stretched off at intervals on either side into seemingly limitless darkness.

Yes, Nir decided, it was time to return to his goats. And perhaps the chasm could afford him enough shelter after all. If the goats wanted to remain here until the storm abated, let them. Stupid animals—what did they know?

Nir turned to retrace his steps, and thunder grumbled behind him. It was a very near sound. It was thunder in this very room.

And there was a clattering, but not of hail. Nir whirled around, brandishing his dagger before him, so puny a weapon that it might as well have been a feather.

Even before he had fully spun about, he felt the floor shift beneath his feet.

It was some ingenious trap, for the floor was sinking away, sinking below the level of the many pits, so that these began to spill their cargo of bones across the floor in the clatter he had heard. The floor began to disappear under the tide of bones. And yet, it did not sink consistently. Where once it had been flat and even, now it sank lower in some places and bulged higher in others even as Nir watched in frozen disbelief. It was as though the hard, solid stone had become some pliable clay. It still seemed solid as ever beneath his feet, but he did not want to remain to see how long that lasted. Again, Nir whirled and this time bolted, even as the tide of bones began to pour toward him.

He nearly tripped plummeting down the spiraling ramp. A skull rolled past him, ahead of him down the ramp. Nir jumped off the side of the ramp, dropped the rest of the way, and tore into the chamber with the vast crystal dome.

The hail had stopped. The rain was slowing, the storm passing as swiftly as it had come. Thank the Elder Gods! Nir dashed on, across the polished floor—this one, so far, still motionless. But the walls . . . if only the walls were motionless. Peripherally, not daring to look directly, Nir saw that those strange nodules distributed across the walls were moving about aimlessly, like kittens playing under a blanket. But he didn't hesitate to examine the phenomenon, plunged on into the next room . . .

. . . and was flying up into the air, his feet skidding out from beneath him. He fell painfully on a bed of hail and water. He had forgotten the two open windows in this chamber. In falling, he struck the back of his head sharply against the hard floor, and his knife went spinning out of his grip.

He lay on his back, dazed, and felt the floor vibrating beneath him. The entire structure trembled subtly as if an earthquake had come. But worse still were the audible rumbles, the groans in the depths above him. Not of thunder. Spirits of cultists, perhaps—if there ever had been cultists dwelling within this place.

Nir forced himself to his feet and staggered on, careful when he reached the second window. The rain had stopped altogether now, he saw, and the sun was even beginning to show as the black wall of clouds drifted on. Nir saw that the grass outside was carpeted in a gravel of hail and was about to stumble on when something else about the scene held him.

It was the shadow of one of the temple's spiraling towers, lying across the hail. As he watched, the spire's shadow was coming apart, the twisted spiral untwisting, coming undone like the coils of a rope. The coils threw shadows, and the shadows writhed and undulated like great tentacles in the air.

The room jolted. Again Nir nearly lost his footing. He gripped the edge of the window for support and saw the landscape shift outside. Slowly, it began to crawl past his eyes.

The temple was moving—moving toward wherever it was it vanished to, when it could not be found.

The realization was enough to shake Nir once more out of his paralysis. He hurried on and gratefully reached the head of the ramp in the foyer.

He saw three things all at once, which whisked the blood from his veins, the breath from his lungs, and the hope from his heart.

In the vaulted hallway branching off from the foyer, the fluted capitals atop the rows of columns had come alive, the coils uncoiling, wavering, a forest of hungry limbs. Worse still, the foyer itself was empty. The goats were all missing. Had they left the building or vanished forever inside it?

That all depended on when the door had shut. Because it was shut. And even from here, Nir could see that it was useless trying to force it. Its edges had smoothly merged with its frame, leaving not a seam.

He was trapped. His tales for children trapped here with his seed. Just his lucky goats, maybe, to sketch at least a bit of legend about him. The legend of another curious fool.

But Nir heard a loud crunching behind him and realized what it was: the bed of hail, crushed beneath the temple as it dragged itself toward the plateau's edge. The sound was clear through the open oval window.

Nir whipped around and lunged back into the room where he had fallen. The near window was almost entirely sealed as the door had sealed, but the far window was just beginning to grow smaller. Nir got to it as quickly as he could without slipping in the two pools of water. It was half closed now, but left him enough room to squeeze through, head first. There was no time for grace. He hung from one hand to right himself, and the window was about to close around his hand when he let go and dropped down the outside wall of the temple.

He hit the bed of icy gravel, rolled onto his side, and behind him heard a monstrous, deafening avalanche of sound as the Temple of Ugghiutu plunged over the rim of the Great Plateau.

But when Nir rose to his feet and followed the broad, deep path to the edge, he saw nothing but jagged rock below.

*

Only one of Nir's goats was found to have escaped before the temple's door sealed up. He kept it as his pet and closest friend. They had much in common. Both were legends for having been the only survivors, of their respective species, of those who had seen inside that forbidden structure.

And their experiences were not doubted. The gray fur of the goat had been bleached white as surely as Nir's hair had changed white from black.

Much mystery remained for the grim sermons of the priests, for the bedside story and fireside tale. But now, at least, one thing had been made clear about the Temple of Ugghiutu, thanks to the herdsman Nir. And that was this: there never had been a Temple of Ugghiutu.

There had only been . . . Ugghiutu.

Drawing No. 8

1

Maxim Komaroff only half remembered the dream, but its overall effect had been so profound that when he woke, he poured himself a cup of coffee and set to work sketching out what he remembered of it, perhaps in an effort to call more of the details to his waking mind.

In this dream he had been standing in a spacious room with a polished black floor and a single circular wall surrounding him, like the inside of a dome, also black and smooth as onyx. From the high concave ceiling, four young girls were hanging upside-down by their ankles. The cords that bound their ankles were smooth and black as well, more like rubbery tendrils than any kind of rope, and seemed to grow from the ceiling of stone itself.

All Maxim had for a studio was the living room of his small flat, in an apartment block in the colony-city known as Punktown, on the planet called Oasis. Seated at his drawing table, wearing only the boxers he'd slept in, Maxim portrayed in deft pencil strokes the four hanging girls as ballet dancers. He made them fresh young teenagers, virgins he felt, on the brink of womanhood. He couldn't remember them precisely from the dream, but somehow he had known they were dancers of some sort, though he couldn't recollect their costumes. Following his muse, or whatever other name he might ascribe to his artistic instincts, he pictured these four girls as wearing black leotards that left their slender arms and legs exposed, lacy black tulle skirts, and black ballet slippers. Their arms hung down limply, their fingertips just falling short of grazing the black floor. The skin of their limbs was not just pale, but ash gray.

If their fingertips fell short of touching the floor, their hair was so long it did reach that far. The hair of all four of the dancers was such a pure flat black that it ate the light like a black hole in space and didn't even shimmer, hanging so thickly it hid the girls' faces. But their slim necks were bared, and each throat gaped horribly where it had been slashed to the bone, half decapitating them.

The blood had run down into their hair, soaking it. Somehow the blood was black, not red.

In the dream, Maxim had been holding a long tube of rolled-up paper under his arm like a lance. He knelt down onto the floor below the quartet of dangling girls and unrolled the paper. It proved to be a large white disk. He stood again, approached one of the pretty corpses, and took her by the waist. Then, looking down at the disk, he moved the girl as she hung there like a pendulum.

Her soaked hair was a giant brush. It left swathes of black blood on the white paper.

After a time Maxim had moved on to the next dead girl and taken her slim waist in his hands as a male ballet partner might, to swing her carefully also and thus render another portion of the drawing that was forming on the circle of white paper.

On he went, from girl to girl, cautiously tiptoeing around the perimeter of the image so as not to tread on it.

Maxim left himself out of his pencil drawing, preferring to keep himself at a remove. After all, in the dream he had seen all this through the first-person perspective. But it wasn't just that. Though he found the vision of the suspended dancers itself compelling, he was uncomfortable with the memory of how he himself had manipulated the bodies in the dream. Funny, though . . . he didn't have the sense that he was the one who had cut the girls' throats. Still, by painting with their blood he was surely an accomplice to that inexplicable crime.

On his pad, though, Maxim did depict the same image that had finally taken shape on the circular sheet of paper in his nightmare.

The image was a round symbol resembling a black sun ringed by a corona of wavy tentacles, with a white spiral like a single hypnotic eye at its center.

2

Later that same day, Maxim's potential client—a Kalian man—asked him if he were familiar with the Alfreda Cubillos-Garavito Museum.

As an artist, Maxim was of course familiar with it, as he was with all the major museums in Punktown, and the many smaller and more obscure galleries throughout the city besides. In fact, if he had to choose, the Garavito Museum might be his favorite. Whereas a museum like the Hill Way Galleries neatly segregated its collection into categories based on time periods, distinct art movements, and types of media, and most especially the cornucopia of sentient races that had settled in this sprawling megalopolis, the Garavito Museum took a less orthodox approach.

Situated on the city's affluent Beaumonde Street, the museum had originally been the personal residence of powerful industrialist Rafael Garavito and his wife, Alfreda Cubillos-Garavito. To please his famously beautiful wife, formerly a fashion model, Rafael had filled their unusual home with art treasures from all across the worlds of the Colonial Network, and then some. After his death, his wife had relocated from Oasis to Earth, opening their former home to the public as a museum. This was why the pieces of artwork were distributed throughout the museum in such a seemingly disorganized, yet aesthetically appealing, way. Even the building's lavish furnishings were as they had been during the occupancy of the Garavitos. Maxim figured the widowed Alfreda, probably in her seventies now, was living in a house every bit as impressive on Earth.

Maxim and the Kalian, who had only given the name Nhil, had met at a nondescript little cafe, seated near the front window with a view of the street, which glistened with reflected neon and holographic light following a pummeling rainstorm, black clouds breaking open to let patches of sulfurous yellow sky glow through. Hovercars hissed past just above the pavement, trailing plumes of wet mist, while higher up helicars streamed along unseen navigation beams. Punktown's massed towers, of every architectural style and substance, looked like a titanic wall that endeavored to hold back that dramatic broken sky, or whatever might emerge through it.

The Kalian wore a traditional blue turban, and tunic and pants made from a metallic gold material. Maxim judged him to be in his early thirties, like himself. Nhil was handsome and clean-shaven, with the glossy gray skin and entirely black eyes that marked his race, which was otherwise very close to Maxim's own. This couldn't be said of most of the races that had immigrated to the city of Paxton, which was Punktown's official name, only utilized in an official context.

While Maxim sipped the coffee the Kalian had bought for him, Nhil said, "If you are familiar with the Garavito Museum, then you will know of the structure's so-called Nautilus Chamber."

"Of course," Maxim said. "I like it very much. The Garavitos had the building custom-designed for them. The Nautilus Chamber was one of Alfreda's ideas. Well, almost everything that has to do with that place was her idea. Rafael was so smitten with her, he gave her carte blanche."

"He was a foolish old man," Nhil said by way of agreement. "Like too many men, he allowed a woman to drag him around by the dick."

Maxim sipped his coffee again so he wouldn't have to agree or disagree. He was well aware of the intensely patriarchal attitudes of the Kalian majority.

"However," Nhil continued, "in this case the man was a dull pig who couldn't see beyond the money signs on his computer screen, while his wife was very much attuned—either through her artistic education or through her own sensitive intuition—with matters that extend beyond this physical realm of dust and blood. Matters of the cosmos."

"She was very interested in the artistic representation of religious thought," Maxim conceded, if this was indeed what Nhil was referring to, "especially the spiritual beliefs of non-Earth races."

"Yes, Mr. Komaroff, her collection reflects this. I am particularly impressed with some of her artifacts related to obscure Tikkihotto cults, and the ancient machine-sculptures of the Coleopteroids. But I am most interested, of course, in a series of drawings that are displayed in the spiral courtyard she dubbed the Nautilus Chamber."

"Ah, yes," Maxim said, and he could envision this exhibit in a general way, though he had forgotten the exact details of the series of framed ink drawings. "One of them was destroyed a few months ago. There should be nine."

"Eight," Nhil corrected, "and yes, one of the drawings was ruined by a madwoman."

Maxim recalled that recent incident. A Kalian woman, apparently a member of a group of young radicals who were at odds with their world's puritanical and oppressive attitudes, had snatched one of the drawings off the wall, torn the parchment out of its frame, and set it on fire right there on the steps that corkscrewed up the circular interior wall of the building's central courtyard. In the process of this act of protest—having either spilled the accelerant on herself accidentally or in a conscious act of self-immolation—the radical had set herself on fire as well, and died before she reached a hospital.

"They're very old, I take it," Maxim said, again not recalling the particulars.

"Yes, over three hundred years old, and immensely valuable to my people historically. The series is called *The Summoning of the Outsider*, by an artist named Narik Guul, who illustrated many of our people's most important texts, including an edition of the *Fizala*. It is scandalous that they were ever sold in the first place, to say nothing of the added ignominy of having ended up ultimately in the possession of a non-Kalian. Mrs. Garavito had exceptional taste, if little respect. If she had, she would have donated the drawings back to my people. In any case, at least by displaying the series publicly she kept the drawings accessible to any of my kind who cared to view and meditate upon them. *Commune* with them. To study them intently in sequence, giving a specific amount of time to each illustration in turn, all the while praying to oneself from the *Fizala* and ascending the spiral stairs just as one would a spiral chamber in one of our own temples on Kali—which I'm certain was the inspiration for Mrs. Garavito's design—is a potent experience that can put us in touch with the dreaming mind of our deity."

"Ugghiutu," Maxim said. He knew that much.

"Yes—the Outsider," Nhil said, as if reluctant to speak their mysterious demon-god's actual name aloud. "He who seeded the superior, human races such as mine and yours throughout the worlds. He who created all souls, consumes all souls, and gives rebirth to those souls to consume them again, in the spiral without end." Nhil's obsidian eyes, like the wet street, glittered with reflected multicolored light.

"It's a terrible loss," Maxim said, waiting to see how he himself factored into all this, and sensing that explanation was finally near.

"Have you been to the exhibit since this great misfortune?"

"Ah, no, I haven't."

"Currently where the picture in question was mounted, there is only a photographic representation and a notice that explains what occurred. But a copy of the original cannot truly replace what was created by hand, pen stroke by pen stroke, by a true artist. An impersonal, unfeeling machine cannot capture the life force that was imparted to that image. Only another artist could attempt to restore such life force."

"Are you suggesting . . . ?"

"Mr. Komaroff, my associates and I researched extensively until we found the artist we felt was best suited to create a reproduction of the destroyed artwork by hand, in the same medium and manner in which the original was created. We saw that you pride yourself on utilizing paint, charcoal, and the like—eschewing all the various technology-based techniques that the majority of contemporary artists favor. We were particularly struck by the intricacy of your pen and ink drawings."

"Well, I certainly do prefer the old methods. I like to get my hands dirty, so to speak. But I have to tell you, I have a very personal artistic vision. I've never copied another artist's work before."

"What we're asking is not for you to commit a forgery. Everyone knows the fate of the original. My associates and I have already contacted the museum and offered them a handcrafted original. They were intrigued and are willing to accept your piece if it proves to be as exceptional in quality as we promise. When it takes the place of the current reproduction, a new notice will accompany the drawing. It will clearly explain that you are the artist responsible for the reproduction."

Without willing it, Maxim raised his eyebrows. One of his artworks showcased in the Alfreda Cubillos-Garavito Museum? No new artwork had been added to the Garavito collection since Alfreda had lived in the former mansion herself. He found it hard to believe the museum could be convinced to accept a new piece, even to fill in for a ruined work. But then he realized that, with the photograph currently mounted, they had already done so. He wondered if Mrs. Garavito herself had given the final consent to this proposal.

"You speak of associates," he said.

"We are a group, dwelling in this city, devoted to preserving the integrity of our faith."

"I see." Fundamentalists, Maxim thought; but weren't most Kalians? The key word being "most," for were there no exceptions they wouldn't be having this conversation. Being an atheist, Maxim rather sympathized with the reformed Kalians who sought to throw off the yoke of religion, but he wasn't about to express his personal opinions with this man.

Not that he feared violence from the Kalian; what he feared was alienating him and missing out on an extraordinary opportunity to have his artwork recognized—even if it would be in imitation of another man's artwork. Since graduating from art school over a decade ago he had barely scratched out a living as an artist, and even then not from the sale of his own work but from designing company logos and restaurant menus, shop signs and labels for microbrews. All his high talk of "personal vision" aside, his work mostly languished in his humble apartment. He exhibited infrequently, sold his drawings and paintings rarely. He was lucky enough that this man and his friends had even managed to stumble upon examples of his work on the net. What doors this opportunity might open for him! But aside from his raised eyebrows, Maxim maintained a calm exterior, lest the Kalian take his excitement for desperation and offer him less compensation than he might otherwise.

And that was indeed the next point in the conversation. Nhil informed him, "As we can well imagine the amount of labor that will be necessary to re-create the intricate detail of the original, we are prepared to offer you a fee of forty thousand munits for the drawing. Twenty thousand up front—right at this meeting of ours, in fact—as a show of good faith."

Forty thousand munits? It was more than he currently made in a year, by about ten thousand. Maxim stared at the man's inky eyes, slack-faced, unable to speak for several beats, until finally he managed, "That's quite acceptable."

"Very good, Mr. Komaroff; I am pleased, as will be my associates. Then there is only one further detail, which I don't think will impede you in any way. Besides the fact that we need you to draw with a dip pen—"

"Of course," Maxim interrupted, "that's what I use in my pen and ink work. Real nib pens."

"Wonderful. In addition to that, as I say, we would require you to use a certain type of ink that we will supply you. It is the very same formula that Narik Guul himself would have used when creating *The Summoning of the Outsider.*"

Maxim spread his hands. "Certainly. If you can get that for me, that's what I'll work with."

"Wonderful," Nhil repeated. "Then that shall be arranged. We will be eternally grateful to you, sir. For now, all that remains is the matter of the advance payment I mentioned."

"Very well then," Maxim Komaroff said with false composure, as he avidly watched the Kalian shift aside the hem of his tunic and reach into the pouch he wore at his waist.

3

At seven the following morning, Maxim was woken by his apartment door being buzzed. How had his caller bypassed the building's front door without being screened? Cursing under his breath, he slipped out of bed and checked the viewscreen to one side of the door. Out in the hallway stood a shortish, stocky Kalian man in a blue turban and metallic gold outfit, carrying a package in both hands. Maxim touched a key and his door slid open.

Without a word, the Kalian smiled up at Maxim and extended the wrapped package.

"Thank you," the artist said, receiving it. He turned to place it on the end of his kitchenette's counter. When he turned back to the doorway, he saw that the Kalian was already moving off down the hallway toward the elevators.

Maxim tapped a key to get his morning coffee brewing, then took down a utility knife with a cutter beam from a kitchen cabinet and went about opening the package.

In a nest of crumpled hardcopy newspapers was a small glass jar filled with ink as black as the distilled essence of space itself.

4

An underground parking area had been created to accommodate visitors to the former home of the Garavitos. While a mechanical arm on an overhead track took hold of Maxim's vehicle and lifted it into an available slot, he strolled toward the elevators.

As many times as he had visited this museum—and he knew all its pieces because the contents were never altered—he had to resist the urge to stop and admire this painting hanging above an opulent red velvet sofa, or that sculpture resting atop an antique Choom table, on his way to the central courtyard . . . or the Nautilus Chamber, as Alfreda had named it.

Just before the entrance to the courtyard Maxim passed the museum's gift shop, and he noticed that the man tending the counter was a Kalian, wearing that familiar blue head-wrapping best labeled a turban. He didn't recall ever seeing a Kalian working in the museum previously. The young man met Maxim's gaze and gave a small nod, almost like a secret gesture of acknowledgment. Perhaps it was only politeness, but Maxim had the odd sense that the man had been expecting him. He nodded back and kept on walking.

The eight drawings that constituted *The Summoning of the Outsider* were just beyond. Of course, he could simply study the images on the net to get a feel for them—most especially the missing drawing—and he would indeed do that. But before he began, he felt he needed to see them in person again, *in situ,* to get himself in the proper mindset.

The courtyard was enclosed within a large dome, rising above the rest of the building's flat upper surfaces. From the outside the dome was an enamel white, with brown tiger stripes. The interior surface, however, was as glossy and iridescent as mother-of-pearl. At the center of the floor was a miniature tropical garden with a burbling fountain, surrounded by benches, at this early hour only occupied by one romantically whispering couple. A staircase spiraled around and around the dome's inside wall, ever tighter, right on up to the very apex. As it coiled, the staircase grew narrower, its steps smaller, so that not even a child would be able to climb the last of them to the very top. This odd effect gave the illusion that the dome was vaster than it was. Maxim tilted his head back, staring up. The spiral seemed to turn, like the lazy outer edge of a whirlpool. A wave of vertigo, bordering on nausea, suddenly flushed through him, and he almost rocked back on his heels. This feeling had never come over him during previous visits. The sensation was that in the next moment he would fall upwards, plummet into the eye churning at the center of that spiral.

"*Spira Mirabilis,*" said a voice just behind him.

In whirling toward the voice, startled, Maxim nearly lost his balance. The man who had spoken appeared not to notice, as he pointed casually toward the concave ceiling. He was a tall, lean Kalian wearing a metallic blue turban, but instead of the common golden outfit he wore the severe black business suit of a museum security guard. Here, the guards doubled as knowledgeable guides. "Excuse me?" Maxim said.

"The logarithmic spiral. One sees it in the shell of the chambered nautilus, of course, but also in the vortex of a hurricane, the swirl of a galaxy. Even the double helix of our DNA is a spiral. It is the ultimate organizing model of the universe, isn't it, Mr. Komaroff? The essence of infinity."

"You know me?"

At last the man lowered his head to face Maxim directly. "We were told to expect you, so that we wouldn't grow alarmed at the attention you'll be devoting to the drawings displayed above."

"I see. Did, ah, the museum hire you specifically to better watch over such an important Kalian exhibit?"

The guard only smiled and extended an inviting arm toward the foot of the looping staircase. The motion caused the flap of his jacket to open enough to reveal the pistol worn in a holster against his side. "Take your time, Mr. Komaroff. Against general museum rules, you may even record images on any device you might have brought, if you wish. No one will disturb you, but I am here for you if you have any questions."

"Thank you," Maxim muttered, turning away. He still felt unsettled, but now he didn't know whether it was due to his bout with dizziness or to this sudden preponderance of Kalians.

He mounted the first step, taking hold of the railing that thankfully ran along the outside of the staircase.

Niches were spaced along the curving wall, containing sculptures both naturalistic and abstract, glazed vases, strange fossils, deformed or bejeweled animal skulls, other artifacts and natural curiosities. Between these narrow hollows were mounted in simple black frames, under sheets of glass, the eight pen-and-ink drawings by Narik Guul that in their entirety were called *The Summoning of the Outsider*. Only a few steps up the staircase, Maxim came to the first in the series. It was surprisingly small, at a distance unassuming; merely nine-by-twelve inches.

He had numerous times admired and been inspired by this drawing's dense, obsessive detail, rendered entirely in black ink by the scratchy point of a dip pen. It portrayed a quartet of Kalian women, their long black hair shockingly unbound, not covered by turbans, wearing low-slung white skirts and white blouses that bared their midriffs. They were obviously dancing sinuously, sensually. This particular drawing, labeled No. 1, was entitled *The Dance of Ugghiutu.*

Hanging in the sky above the dancers was a black disk like an eclipsed sun. A fringe of wavy rays like the multiple arms of a starfish ringed it, and at its center was a white spiral.

"My God," Maxim said under his breath, snapping his head around to look further up the wall toward the next in the spiraling arrangement of framed drawings. *Of course.* He recalled, because he had viewed these illustrations before, that the Kalians often represented their demon-god Ugghiutu—the great creator/destroyer—as a boiling black orb with a single red eye or a spiral, red or white, as its nucleus.

He quickened his ascent to the next ink drawing.

The subject of drawing No. 2 was again the four women, but this time they were not dancing. Instead, they were hanging by their necks, dead. The drop from the ropes had severed their spinal cords, but in addition their femoral arteries had been slashed. Black serpents of blood coiled down their legs, dripping into a crater-like pool directly beneath them.

Maxim read the title of this piece. It was *The Sacrifice of the Maidens.*

"I dreamed this," he murmured.

Well, why shouldn't he dream about a series of technically brilliant drawings with such disturbing subject matter? But the question was, why would he dream of these pictures the night *before* Nhil had told him what his commission was to be? Yes, he had known he would be meeting with a Kalian the next day, but he hadn't known that these drawings would be in any way involved. A coincidence, then? Given that he was an artist, was this half-remembered artwork simply what his subconscious had called up by way of association with the Kalians?

He lowered his gaze to the card that accompanied drawing No. 2. It was a translation of Narik Guul's own intended caption. It read: *"Having aroused the notice of Ugghiutu, yet without fully waking Him from the slumber that binds the Dreaming One, the maidens are then willingly sacrificed to gather their nourishing blood."*

On then to drawing No. 3, and here was that circular pool again into which the virgins' blood had been drained. The four corpses were gone, but a smooth humped shape was rising up from the inky fluid, like the top of a huge skull slimed in gore. The title: *The Emergence of the Seed.*

Maxim's footfalls up the next steps were like the heavy tramping of his heart.

Drawing No. 4: *The Removal of the Seed.* Here, four males in the conical turbans of high holy men encircled the pool, each helping support what appeared to be a large black pod, egg-shaped but tapering to a blunt point at both ends.

Next, drawing No. 5: *The Planting of the Seed.* The holy men were seen standing the cocoon-like pod on one end in a little depression in the ground, outside the high stone wall of a city. Arrows and lances were flying down at them from warriors atop the wall, but the holy men carried on despite being multiply pierced.

"A god as a weapon," Maxim said. As familiar as these pictures were, somehow it was as though he were seeing them through new eyes, in some truer or fuller context. Maybe he had only concentrated on them individually before, and only as *art,* instead of absorbing the story they told.

He ascended further. The tropical garden looked much smaller already, a tiny oasis. The two lovers had gone. The gurgling fountain sounded like mocking chuckles from someone hiding among the fronds.

No. 6 was *The Temple Is Born.* It might seem like a strange title to one who had never seen the next two images or knew nothing of the lore of Ugghiutu. The four holy men lay slain, their bodies and heads bristling with arrows. Rooted at the center of their circle of dead bodies, the pod had risen into the air on a black stalk or trunk like a smooth column, looking like the glans of a giant phallus or the club-shaped cap of certain mushrooms.

Maxim was nearing the top of the dome's interior. The steps were not as wide as they had been. The wall curving lower over his head and the steps becoming narrower made him feel as though he were growing larger himself, like Alice. Wet with perspiration, his palm slid along the railing.

No. 7: *The Temple of Ugghiutu.* Now the earlier reference to a temple was made clearer. Somehow, since the developments detailed in illustration No. 6 that black pillar had become a great tower, with the former pod bulging like an onion dome at its summit. Furthermore, the black substance from which this structure had grown had spread out to either side of the central tower, having risen into smooth black walls perforated by circular windows without glass, which had the organic shape and puckered rims of orifices in a living body. It was as though a new city—as black as the icy void between stars—was growing just outside the wall of the stone city.

This, Maxim knew, was the classical form Ugghiutu took in numerous ancient myths and in relatively more modern folktales. From the deep sleep in which he was said to have been imprisoned by a race of enemy gods, the dreaming Ugghiutu would transmit (was that the right word?) this corporeal avatar or aspect of himself, masquerading as one of the countless temples that had been erected across Kali by his faithful. Either tricked into entering this living temple or perhaps even giving themselves over to it as willing sacrifices, Kalians would venture inside such an edifice only to be consumed. Their life force would feed Ugghiutu himself, in whatever unknowable dimension he resided. Later, such a mock temple would dissolve or vanish somehow, as mysteriously as it had appeared.

Maxim read the caption to No. 7. It simply stated: *"The Temple blooms outside the stronghold of the faithless enemies of His worshippers."*

He climbed toward the final piece in the display. One could proceed up the narrowing staircase no further than that. His scuffing footfalls echoed back from the great bowl just over his head.

Only one more drawing in the series remained, and it had been destroyed by fire. But in its place hung a scan or photographic replica in the original frame, with an accompanying notice describing succinctly what had transpired. Yet Maxim studied this image as closely as the others; *more* closely, since this was the drawing he had already been paid twenty thousand munits to re-create, with another twenty thousand promised upon delivery.

Drawing No. 8 had been named *The Outsider Triumphant*.

The black temple had indeed grown fully to the size of a city. Ebony towers of various sizes and shapes soared into the sky, with that central tower seeming to disappear into the clouds like a pillar upholding the heavens. The temple's swollen bulk had pushed against the stone wall of the conquered city, toppling it and crushing the buildings the wall had formerly protected. Furthermore, root-like growths, tentacles perhaps, had sprouted from the base of the temple, and many of these had snaked up over the broken wall, spreading throughout the decimated city beyond, branching off into innumerable smaller tendrils. Some of these had coiled around survivors, holding their squirming bodies aloft in the air. This black web had spread over the faces of buildings, over statues, across squares and rooftops, looking like dense parasitic vines that ultimately threatened to overrun every surface of the enemy city . . . cover every last block and brick . . . so as to smother and replace it utterly.

In every one of the illustrations, that same black orb hung in the same spot in the sky. But with each successive picture, the writhing limbs that formed its halo grew longer, more sinuous, beginning to coil. The spiral at the center expanded and expanded, until in the last drawing—its reproduction, at least—the whorl extended to the disk's outer edge.

Slowly leaning back from the drawing—he hadn't realized how close he had brought his face to the glass—Maxim felt exhausted, overwhelmed, as if he'd just woken from an unsettling nightmare that had had him tossing and turning. His heart still thudded. He supposed that was from climbing these steps and the excitement of the commission, comingled with the strange coincidence of his seemingly prescient dream.

"I guess that just means this was all meant to be," he said aloud.

"Sir?"

Maxim hadn't realized that the Kalian guard stood just a few steps below him. How long had he been there? Had he been shadowing him all this time, while he had lost himself in these artworks?

Well, as long as the Kalian was right here, Maxim decided to utilize him. He asked, "The man who hired me for this job, Mr. Nhil, said the interior of Kalian temples to Ugghiutu are configured a lot like this Nautilus Chamber here, correct? And Mrs. Garavito took her inspiration partially from that, so she could display these drawings in the way the artist intended."

"That was part of Mrs. Garavito's inspiration for this design, yes, but not all chambers in a Kalian temple are circular such as this."

"No? I've never been in a Kalian temple."

The guard's smile was a bit forced. "Nor would you—forgive me for saying so, sir—be permitted to do so. Only worshippers of Ugghiutu are granted entrance to one of our temples. But to return to your question: no, different chambers are configured differently depending on their usage. When Ugghiutu is to be consulted or communed with in his dreams—as one would be doing if one were to view these drawings in sequence while reciting, inwardly or outwardly, certain prayers—it might be best to do so in a circular chamber, because Ugghiutu and his brethren Outsiders move more easily through angles than through curves."

Maxim's brow rumpled. "I'm afraid you've lost me. If the Outsiders move best through angles, and you want to commune with them, wouldn't it be better to summon them in a room with corners? Wouldn't summoning them in a curved room be more difficult?"

"Precisely, Mr. Komaroff. You see, I didn't lose you. One must be careful, when communing with Ugghiutu, to arouse his dreaming mind only enough to interact with him, without fully awakening him . . . and hence calling forth a material manifestation one does not truly desire."

"Why wouldn't you desire that?"

The guard smiled again, with serene patience, as if explaining a commonsense notion to a child. "We worship the unimaginable power, the force of creation and destruction, that is Ugghiutu, who in his unthinkable superiority is an embodiment of the cold and infinite universe. The universe does not love us, any more than Ugghiutu loves his faithful. We do not expect it of him. He finds us useful, as you and I find yeast useful in the making of leavened bread. When we tear bread with our teeth and consume it to nourish ourselves, we may at best be grateful to yeast in some distant, unconscious way. But we do not love yeast. Do you understand this?"

Maxim nodded. "So . . . you keep Ugghiutu at arm's length. You're very afraid of him."

"Shouldn't we be afraid of a god, Mr. Komaroff?"

"So if one were to believe in all this stuff—uh, that is to say . . ." Maxim flushed red, afraid to insult the man's beliefs.

"Go on, please."

"Well, it sounds to me as if your people would actually be grateful that other gods imprisoned Ugghiutu and the rest of the Outsiders. And keep them that way."

"It would be blasphemous for us to be *pleased* that Ugghiutu is imprisoned," the man said very slowly, obviously choosing his words with care. "But the conflict that resulted in his imprisonment is beyond us . . . outside our humble human scope and experience. We cannot truly understand it nor judge it. Things are as they are. And as they are, Ugghiutu resides in a tomb of sleep from which it would be unwise for humans to wake him completely."

"But . . . physical extensions of him are believed to be conjured up sometimes," Maxim said, waving his arm toward drawing No. 8. "Either by himself—those simulated temples that pop up—or by his followers. As weapons, for example, like in these illustrations."

"Yes. Avatars of varying material presence, and hence potency, can be summoned by holy men of the highest order. But it is not done lightly. And even then, it would most likely be desirable to undertake such a conjuring in a circular chamber such as this, to ensure that only the required avatar is summoned . . . and not something very much more powerful, and impossible to control."

"So," Maxim summarized, his head feeling swollen with all it was absorbing, "the bottom line is, it's better to worship Ugghiutu than to liberate him."

"To use another analogy, sir, a person might worship the sun for its greatness . . . without wanting that sun to descend upon his world and burn it all to ash."

Maxim nodded again. That analogy was easily enough digested.

"Well," he said, "Mrs. Garavito was obviously intrigued with your culture, but wanted to follow her own vision in the design of this courtyard, too. She must have been horrified when that young woman burned the original of this drawing."

"Yes, it was a terrible blow. Just because she left her Punktown collection behind doesn't mean that she didn't still hold it in her heart. It was almost a mercy that she didn't live much longer after the incident."

"Excuse me?" Maxim stammered. "Are you saying . . . has Mrs. Garavito passed away?"

"Oh, I'm sorry, Mr. Komaroff." The guard affected a pained expression, as if breaking the news to next of kin. "Only a few days after that precious drawing was vandalized, Mrs. Garavito was killed during a robbery attempt at her home on Earth."

"She was murdered?" Maxim said, astonished that he had missed hearing of this. But one could scarcely keep up with the overabundance of crime reports in Punktown, let alone those on Earth as well.

The Kalian guard nodded solemnly. "One might venture so far as to say it was divine punishment for having acquired these important artifacts that never should have come into her possession. That is to say, if one believes in such things." He smiled his polite smile again. "Which I know you do not."

5

At first Maxim had thought he might trace at least a basic outline, in pencil, from the original drawing (a copy he'd printed from the net), using his light table. Then he would ink in that tracing. He figured it was permissible, if his patrons wanted as exact a replica as possible. But ultimately he had felt that would still be a cheat—not to the Kalians and the museum, but to his own ability. So he rose fully to the challenge and started sketching out the framework of his construction purely by observing the original, taped alongside his sheet of nine-by-twelve-inch drawing paper.

There was much erasing of this pencil work with a kneaded eraser. Adjusting slight angles of line, sometimes only by a sixteenth of an inch, he felt like a necromancer toiling over the precise geometric design of a magic formula.

Occasionally he would sit back to observe his work in progress from a bit of distance, trying to imagine it through Mr. Nhil's midnight eyes, the heel of his right hand silvery-black from leaning against graphite. The color was almost the same as Nhil's skin.

It took him most of the first day to finish the pencil outline that would underlie the ink drawing. But by that night, when he poured himself a congratulatory glass of expensive whiskey purchased with his advance, he was quite satisfied with the results.

The glow of pride, and of whiskey, made him feel lustful. Filling his shot glass a second time, he thought of calling Famuu. She was a Choom, the indigenous people of Oasis, who like the Kalians were one of the few truly humanoid races in the Colonial Network. The only obvious feature that would distinguish Famuu's people from Maxim's was that her mouth was cut back to her cute little ears, her pugnacious lower jaw heavy with compound rows of molars. But with her broad, distinct cheekbones and wide-spaced, ice-gray eyes, the overall effect was very pleasing to Maxim's artistic sensibilities. She always wore neon-glowing red lipstick on those wraparound lips—even when she wore nothing else—and her hair, chopped short as a boy's, was usually dyed neon red to boot. The red glow had lit their lovemaking in her cave-dark basement apartment. Yes, Famuu's legs usually bristled unshaven, and her smell was a bit musky, but he had never really decided if those were drawbacks or excitements. She owned a tattoo parlor on Morpha Street and had bought rights to several of his drawings to use as designs. She had offered to tattoo his own artwork on him, for free, using perhaps ink that glowed like neon, too, but she had stopped seeing him before he could take her up on that. She had been seeing another, younger artist at the same time she was involved with him. It hadn't hurt Maxim so much that Famuu had stopped returning his calls, since he had never felt as engaged emotionally as he was physically, but the hurt came from knowing that the other man was an artist. As one will wonder if a replacement lover is better in bed, Maxim had tormented himself wondering if this younger man was the better artist.

He turned from his drawing table to sit at his little computer desk, gesturing in the air to call up several overlapping holographic screens. He scrolled through his address book in search of Famuu's forgotten number. When he tried to connect to it, though, he found it was no longer in service; it had been changed and the new number was unlisted. For a moment he took this development bitterly, as if she had changed her number specifically to elude him . . . though he knew that this was illogical. There had been no animosity between them, only a fundamental indifference. He did a search for the number of her tattoo parlor, though it was probably too late to catch her there still working.

It was. He got a recorded vid of Famuu smiling hugely back at him without seeing him, as she gave her establishment's hours of operation and seductively invited him to come by her place to be transformed into a walking work of art. Her own body was a miniature museum of her craft, though she herself favored only works in black ink—no color, no glowing, nothing animated or holographic. In the vid, her lips and hair were a luminous blue. New number, new hair, new lover. Maxim broke off before her message was finished.

No matter. Maxim sipped his whiskey. He felt majestic with patience, replacing the desperation that had been his roommate for much of this past decade. New lovers would come. New showings of his art in better venues, new and better commissions. With that hovering vid screen banished, he found himself staring at his blank, default search screen. Curiosity crept in, like the insinuating warmth of alcohol, and he decided to do a search on the obituary of Alfreda Cubillos-Garavito.

It was as the guard at Alfreda's museum had told him. Over two months ago, just shortly after the act of vandalism at her museum in Punktown (though that incident wasn't mentioned in the news story he found), Alfreda had been attacked in her expensive home on Earth, despite the mansion's security system. Various pieces of art had been stolen—some Coleopteroid mechanical sculptures several hundred years old, and rare carvings connected to an ancient Tikkihotto religious group—but apparently Mrs. Garavito had disturbed the burglars and they'd fled. But not before they had slashed her throat, half decapitating her.

"Worthless punks," Maxim muttered. He raised his shot glass in a toast to Alfreda.

Thoughts of the former fashion model turned patron of the arts led him to think of the destruction of the artwork that he was in the process of reproducing; specifically, to the woman who had committed that crime. He started a new net search, wanting to learn more about this person who was responsible for his turn of good fortune. He should be toasting her, too.

Her name, he learned, had been Kaleet Dukenna-Ir. There was a picture of her, a college ID photo: smiling whitely, her black eyes shimmering with intelligence. Almost as shocking as the fact that she didn't cover her head with a blue turban was that her hair was buzzed down to black stubble. She must have given traditional Kalians in Punktown fits just walking down the street. On Kali, she wouldn't have made two steps without being assaulted with acid or bricks.

The article reiterated most of what Maxim already knew. Kaleet had visited the Alfreda Cubillos-Garavito Museum alone that day, apparently, and had taken down from the wall of the Nautilus Chamber drawing No. 8 of Narik Guul's series *The Summoning of the Outsider,* thus setting off a security alarm. Before security guards could reach her on the staircase, she had sprayed an accelerant on the artwork—which she had removed from its frame—and set it, and herself, on fire.

Kaleet had been a member of a group of young Kalians, several of them students at Paxton University like herself, who had devoted themselves to challenging the patriarchal and oppressive traditions of their native culture. Kaleet had lived in a flat she shared with a number of these friends at a Punktown apartment complex called the Octoplex, which Maxim was superficially familiar with: it consisted of eight tower blocks forming a circle.

Her friends had denied any advance knowledge of Kaleet's intent to destroy Narik Guul's drawing. They hadn't been able to confirm one way or the other whether Kaleet had intended to burn herself along with the drawing.

Maxim did indeed raise his glass to her. "You were a brave woman, Kaleet. Pretty, too. Thanks for the forty thousand munits." But he regretted his frivolous tone, felt guilty, and banished the news story so Kaleet Dukenna-Ir no longer stared at him from his array of virtual screens.

He wondered what she had hoped to accomplish by destroying that one illustration. It seemed to him an odd gesture, especially if she had given her life purposely in order to make it. With her advanced attitudes and her rejection of the bonds of religion, could Kaleet really have believed that she was removing one vital gear from a kind of spiritual machine, such as Nhil and that guard had claimed *The Summoning of the Outsider* to be? Were the primitive superstitions she had been raised on still that much ingrained in her mind?

His gaze trailed idly to related results his computer had dredged up when he had been looking for the story on Kaleet, the key words being *Kalian woman.* One news headline caught his eye, and he opened up the full article. As he started reading it, he wondered how he had missed hearing about this crime, too—especially since it had taken place right here in Punktown.

Early last week, the bodies of four young Kalian women had been discovered by children playing in an abandoned factory on Warehouse Way. The women were found naked, but medical examination had determined that not only had they not been sexually assaulted, but all four of them were still virgins. As of the time of this article, the identities of the women—who had all died within seconds of each other, it had also been established—had not been determined. Scans of their faces didn't match up with the records of any legal Kalian immigrants, though they may have been born and raised in Punktown.

The women were found hanging from ropes, their necks broken, and the femoral artery on the inside of their thighs had been sliced . . . though only a minimum of blood had dripped on the floor of the factory beneath their dangling feet.

Maxim realized his drawing hand was quivering, and he set down his glass of celebratory whiskey.

6

When he began inking black flesh onto the bare skeleton of his pencil sketch, Maxim wore a pair of digital spectacles that permitted him to magnify his viewpoint. It wasn't that he felt he had to replicate every last pen stroke of the original artwork—he hardly believed the museum or even his Kalian clients expected that—but he wanted to achieve the same style as best he could, and the closer he saw the strokes used in the original the better he could plan his own strokes to capture a similar overall effect. Even had he not been using another artwork as his model, he preferred to wear these magnifying specs when working with extra-fine detail in a drawing or painting.

He started toward the top of the drawing, working down, so that he wouldn't be resting his hand on portions he had already inked. That meant the sky of strangely twisted and knotted black clouds, and the emblem-like representation of Ugghiutu that hovered over his earthly avatar, having taken the form of a black city . . . overrunning and assimilating the stone city of his vanquished faithless enemies. In Narik Guul's drawing, even the darkest areas were still composed of uncountable tiny marks of the pen rather than, say, having been solidly filled in black. The only exception was the disk that symbolized Ugghiutu, which aside from the white spiral was pure black. For this area, Maxim used a brush with a very fine tip instead of the scratchy nib of his dip pen.

At one point his brush betrayed him and he accidentally painted into the outline of the white spiral, breaking one of its coils. He didn't panic or curse himself. He had a pen-like device with a delicate beam, which could burn away the ink without affecting the paper. He directed the pen's beam carefully, erased the ink, and then went to work with the brush once again. This time he didn't intrude upon the white spiral.

As he gradually worked his way down over the next few days and began inking in the corporeal manifestation of Ugghiutu, through the enlarging lenses he wore he began noticing a very curious detail incorporated into Narik Guul's drawing, which would never have been visible to the naked eye of its viewers (except, Maxim considered, Tikkihottos with the sensitive ocular tendrils they had in place of eyes). Here and there, among the dense pen strokes that comprised the organic city's black body, Maxim discovered words written in Kalian characters. Of course he couldn't decipher them himself, but he at least recognized that was what they were. He was tempted to copy one of these hidden phrases onto another piece of paper, then scan it and submit it to the net to search out its meaning, but then he remembered some of the other features of his spectacles. He tapped a key on the frames of the specs, establishing a connection between them and his computer. Next he zoomed in on one line of Kalian text and brought that up on a virtual viewscreen, using an art program he utilized only for his commercial, not personal, projects. Therein he highlighted the characters and dropped out the background. Then, as he had planned, he submitted the text to the net with a request for translation.

It was nothing that surprised him, in context. The line read: *"Ugghiutu will expand His greatness to absorb and extinguish every last infidel."* Maxim simply thought it was intriguing that phrases or prayers such as this would be buried in the drawing—not, obviously, to be appreciated by those who viewed the piece but with the intention of imbuing the work with more potency.

Late the following night, after another arduous stretch of unbroken hours bent over his table—riding his creative momentum and eager to claim the second half of his payment—Maxim reached the bottom quarter of the drawing. Here, on one of the serpentine roots that spread from the base of the sentient black city, Maxim discovered the longest line of text yet, curving along the rubbery limb. As he had continued to do, he had his computer translate it, and found it possessed none of the previous pretense of eloquence. It only chanted deliriously: *"Ugghiutu swallows all Ugghiutu swallows all Ugghiutu swallows all Ugghiutu swallows all Ugghiutu swallows all Ugghiutu swallows all Ugghiutu swallows all Ugghiutu swallows all."*

As Maxim inked in these words himself, meticulously replicating every nuance of every character lest he get one wrong and disappoint his patrons (assuming they were even aware of Narik Guul's little trick), he found himself counting how many times he wrote the same phrase.

One . . . two . . . three . . . four . . .

Ah, of course.

Five . . . six . . . seven . . .eight.

Having at last completed the wavy line of text, Maxim sat back from his artwork and pushed the magnifying specs up onto his forehead. He realized he had a spiking headache, though he didn't know for how long it had been there.

He stared at the artwork through naked eyes, no longer enlarged. After these many hours in which he had all but dwelt within the scene, it looked so small. He tried to imagine how it would look on the curved wall of the Nautilus Chamber.

He predicted he'd be able to finish it tomorrow. Right now, spent, he longed for his bed.

His eyes shifted from the paper to the little pot of ink that had been delivered to him. It was getting low, maybe three-quarters finished. The same concoction Narik Guul himself had utilized, Nhil had said. Maxim wouldn't dare switch to a store-bought brand if he ended up running short. If that happened, he'd have to ask Nhil for more. But he was certain Nhil had sent him just the right amount.

Without asking himself why he did so, Maxim reached out, picked up the glass jar, and brought it level with his face. He leaned his nose in over its open mouth and sniffed warily.

He flinched back sharply, though he couldn't say why. The ink smelled like ink. Only like ink. It didn't have the coppery, raw-meat smell he somehow thought it would. But the smell had nonetheless caused his headache to flare. He set the jar down and pressed the heels of his hands into his eyes.

After taking a pain pill, he stripped down to his boxers for bed. He switched off his drawing table's lamp, leaving the ink to dry in the dark.

Since taking the commission, he had had no further dreams that he recollected the next morning . . . but tomorrow he would recall tonight's dream, with the sharpness of a steel engraving.

He was wandering in some murky underground place, a series of rooms with low ceilings and damp-smelling walls—maybe tunnels connecting the basements of several abandoned industrial complexes, such as those found in Warehouse Way. He smelled incense ahead and crept more stealthily. Following the smell, he poked his head around the edge of a doorway and found himself looking into a room with water-stained walls and a blistering ceiling, which nevertheless served as a nursery. In a row of old plastic crates stuffed with blankets, four Kalian babies lay sleeping. Joss sticks had been jammed into cracks in the walls, smoking. Fluorescent bars in the ceiling fluttered wanly.

Maxim continued exploring, feeling his way through stretches of corridor that were pitch black, then coming upon other areas that were at least dimly lit. He followed that incense smell again and peeked into another room in which joss sticks burned and sickly greenish fluorescents flickered. Here were four cots, in which four adolescent Kalian girls lay sleeping, their beautiful profiles cushioned on their own silken black hair.

Onward . . . more incense beckoning him, guiding him, through more labyrinthine dark tunnels. In the next room, in four more cots, slept four Kalian teenagers on the cusp of adulthood. Maxim stared at them as they breathed slowly, evenly, dreaming within his dream. And somehow, even in his dream, Maxim felt as though he himself were merely a figment moving through the dreams of a mind outside his own—a vast, alien, slumbering mind. Russian nesting dolls of dream.

Maxim realized he'd been hearing a distant dripping sound, and assumed it was water leaking from one of the exposed pipes that ran along some of the ceilings down here. Still, the niggling sound diverted his attention, and he turned away from the sleeping girls to follow it to its source.

He came to a cylindrical shaft, containing an ascending spiral staircase. The dripping sound came from up there, resonating down through the shaft. He mounted the corroded metal steps, which rang with his footfalls, turning tightly around and around as he climbed. At the top of the shaft he entered a short, especially narrow corridor. At the end of this passage was an arched doorway, and he stopped in its threshold to look into the chamber beyond.

It was a spacious room with a single circular wall, like the inside of a dome. From the high concave ceiling, at the ends of black ropes, four young women had been hung by their necks. The dead women wore low-slung white skirts and white blouses that had long sleeves and high collars but were cut short to leave their smooth gray midriffs bare.

Their white skirts were heavily stained in blood. Kalian blood was red, but in the dream the blood was black as ink. Though Maxim couldn't see the women's upper legs through the folds of their skirts, he knew that their femoral arteries had been cut. The dripping sound he had heard was their black blood draining into a circular, recessed area in the floor directly below their bare feet.

There was one window in this circular chamber, on the opposite side from the doorway Maxim stood in. Lurid red light issued through it. He timidly stepped into the room and made his way around its perimeter toward the window, keeping clear of the edge of the crater-like pool that collected the life fluid of the dead women. Suspiciously, he watched their slack faces with their grotesquely distended tongues, as if suddenly their obsidian eyes might snap open and fix on this intruder accusingly.

He reached the window, which was circular and without any glass. Gripping its curved lower edge, he looked out upon a landscape that was both intimately familiar and nightmarishly transfigured.

It was the skyline of Punktown, silhouetted black against a ruby red sky that churned restlessly like an inverted ocean of blood, glowing radioactively. But the fact that it was silhouetted didn't entirely account for the megacity's utter blackness. Maxim realized the edges of office towers and apartment blocks were ever-so-subtly pulsing, as if life fluids were being pumped through the walls of these buildings, or as if the looming structures were breathing deeply in slumber. Probes that extended from the summits or jutted from the sides of some of these buildings, either gathering information from the ether or transmitting it, rippled slightly as if they had gone rubbery. And no light glowed in any window. The edges of every window, in fact, had a puckered look, as if these innumerable windows were all orifices in one impossibly gigantic living body.

Something had overtaken the colony-city called Punktown. Consumed it. Replaced it.

No neons glowed, no holographic advertisements lent color to the air. No hovercars could be seen gliding close to the streets, no helicars floated like swarms of dragonflies through the air. For all its organic aspects, this was a city of the dead.

The city was no longer Punktown. The city had a new name.

Ugghiutu.

In the foreground of this scene, eight towers were arranged in a circle. Maxim recognized them—despite their black-sheathed, undulating surfaces—as the apartment complex called the Octoplex. This was where Kaleet Dukenna-Ir had lived. This was where her friends and fellow radicals continued to live.

In the small park at the center of the Octoplex, its grass now paved over with a thick black membrane, a large red spiral floated a few feet off the ground horizontally. It glowed laser red, and it spun around and around like a vortex.

It reminded Maxim of a target.

A liquid sound behind him caused Maxim to turn away from the window. Four Kalian males had encircled the pool the dead women were suspended above. They wore golden robes, and the elongated conical turbans of high holy men. Maxim recognized their faces. They were Nhil . . . and the guard/guide from the Alfreda Cubillos-Garavito Museum . . . and the young gift shop worker from the museum . . . and the short, stocky Kalian who had delivered the special ink to Maxim's door.

They were bent forward and lifting an object from the inky pool. They raised this object reverently, cautiously, as if it were a bomb that might go off if handled carelessly. Streaming viscous blood, the black object did somewhat resemble a bomb, though it was actually something more like a giant pod or cocoon, tapered to a dull point at both ends.

Nhil looked directly up into Maxim's eyes and smiled. He said, "Thank you, Mr. Komaroff. None of this would have been possible without you."

7

Maxim purposely arrived about a half hour ahead of Nhil, at the same little unremarkable cafe. He wondered sourly why Nhil had chosen this particular place for their meetings. Because it was so anonymous? It would have been a nice clandestine environment for the sale of illegal drugs, perhaps, but a piece of art destined for an esteemed museum? The drawing rested on the sticky bench cushion beside him, sandwiched between two sturdy sheets of plastic and packaged inside a padded envelope. What if he had been mugged leaving his vehicle and the package stolen? Nhil probably wouldn't have believed Maxim, but it would have served him right for choosing such a location.

With the steam from his coffee rising aromatically into his face, Maxim stared out the cafe's front window at the street beyond. Immense skyscrapers all but blocked out the sky, with smaller buildings of every stripe huddled around their ankles. Pedestrians—human and otherwise—bustled along the sidewalk in an almost solid mass, some of them glancing in at him as they passed. Honeycombs of windows glowed against today's overcast grayness, fluidly twisted neons gave off fuzzy pastel auras, and holographic advertisements hovered in place or else floated past or even walked along with the pedestrians like ghosts. Vibrantly alive, the city appeared secure, strong. And yet to Maxim, all this now seemed like a fragile veneer—a thin translucent skin that could be roughly torn away in one motion, leaving only the cold bones beneath. There were forces that dwarfed even this great city. He believed that now. He always had, deep down on some primal level, but had never wanted to confront such intuitions.

Of course, he had always been conscious of the fact that, rather than fostering the organic, the universe was hostile toward living things. Life was just a byproduct of other processes that slipped past the universe's notice. All this he had accepted, certainly. But he had never consciously wanted to admit that some of the forces that composed the universe, while not life in the sense he understood it, might nevertheless hold sentience.

As he had finished the drawing that now rested beside him, so small and innocuous, he had considered secreting text of his own within it. Maybe a near-microscopic line that read: *"Ugghiutu is not coming."* Or: *"An infidel drew this picture."* A kind of vandalism of his own work, to defuse the drawing's imagined power. He had been quite tempted to do this, in fact, but in the end had been too afraid. What if the Kalians were aware of Narik Guul's subliminal technique and looked closely to see if he had incorporated it? They'd be furious.

And what if Ugghiutu *himself* realized what he had done? What if Ugghiutu became furious at him? Such a notion no longer seemed irrational to him. Not after his dreams—the way they had resonated in him. Continued to resonate in him, like a nauseating vibration in his nerves, his guts . . . in his soul.

But ultimately, maybe the main reason he had not hidden irreverent text in his drawing was pride. Because he had done such an impeccable job of replicating the artwork, he had not wanted to deface it at the last moment.

He saw Nhil out there on the street, among the other pressing bodies. The Kalian smiled through the glass at Maxim. A moment later, he was inside and approaching the table.

"Ah, you have it!" Nhil exclaimed, taking the opposite seat, as Maxim lifted the padded envelope and placed it on the table between them. "May I?"

"Of course," Maxim said, watching as the Kalian slipped the double sheets of plastic out of the envelope and lifted the top sheet away.

"Magnificent." Nhil wagged his head as if in awe. "Our faith in you was not ill founded." He reached into the little pouch he wore at his waist. Maxim's heart jolted, as he expected another wad of twenty thousand munits to be lifted into view. Instead, it was a folded pair of spectacles. Nhil put them on, tapped a key on their frames, and leaned in to examine the drawing again.

Maxim's intestines knotted tight. He held his breath. It was as though he feared he had unconsciously buried some message of his own inside the artwork after all.

Nhil shook his head again, then sat up straighter, removed his digital specs, and grinned. "Perfection."

"It's gratifying that you like it," Maxim said.

"You did not fail us." Nhil replaced the specs in his pouch, and this time he did withdraw a tightly bound stack of munits that he slid across the table. Maxim pocketed the bundle quickly, lest someone at another table witness the transaction and decide to mug him on his way back to his vehicle. "You earned every munit, Mr. Komaroff. Narik Guul's treasure is lost to us forever, but you have still done more than you know to undo the damage caused by that deluded young girl.

Once again, the unique cycle of prayer *The Summoning of the Outsider* provides is accessible to us."

"Aren't you afraid her friends there in the Octoplex might try to do the same thing?"

Nhil narrowed his eyes slightly. "So you know those lunatics live at the Octoplex?"

"I read about Kaleet a little," Maxim admitted. He badly wanted to swallow, so he took a sip of his cooling coffee.

"Someday, I assure you, blasphemers like those wretched children—whose minds have been polluted by exposure to outside cultures—will cease to be a threat to our faith."

"Would you be willing to destroy a whole city to eliminate one tiny group of radicals?" Maxim asked. "As collateral damage? Or would destroying an entire city of the unfaithful even be a desirable bonus?"

Nhil leaned against the backrest of his bench and smiled at Maxim in a whole new way, though the expression was a subtle one. "What a curious thing to say, Mr. Komaroff. Please tell me . . . what is it exactly you're thinking?"

"Nothing," Maxim mumbled, breaking his gaze. He gulped down the rest of his coffee, then rose from the table. "I'd best make a trip to my bank. Thank your associates for me, please, Mr. Nhil." He extended his hand out of mechanical politeness.

Nhil took his hand and squeezed it in a strong grip. "I trust you will attend the official reception, when the piece is revealed to the public. I'll contact you with details."

"Are you sure the museum will accept my work?"

"Oh, I have no doubt of it. So you must attend, of course. This is quite a coup for you; the pinnacle of your career, I should think."

"I'll be there," Maxim said, slipping his hand free and heading for the door.

8

The turnout at the Alfreda Cubillos-Garavito Museum for the unveiling of Maxim's drawing was impressive and looked like a miniature cross-section of the city's sentient races. Kalians dominated, but that was no surprise to him. Several journalists were present, and Maxim's picture was taken as the museum's director shook his drawing hand.

The director was an Earther like himself, though at this point Maxim had expected this man to be a Kalian, too.

Coffee, tea, wine, pastries and cheese—all of it expensive and exquisite. Maxim had worn his best suit, which to his eyes still looked shabby alongside the attire of the other attendees.

Maxim noted that no Kalian women had attended. Traditional Kalian women were not even permitted to speak outside their homes.

He should have been drunk with pleasure at all this—the realization of his loftiest fantasies. Especially when a beautiful blue-skinned Sinanese woman began flirting with him, touching his arm for emphasis as she spoke. But he knew that the smile he wore on his face tonight was like a dying animal doggedly dragging itself along. His heart, buried inside him like a secret line of text even he couldn't read, felt much the same. *What are you celebrating?* he wanted to ask these pretty, fragile people. *The end of this city? The end of your lives?* He wanted to ask the Sinanese woman, her petite slender body sheathed in a form-fitting green silk gown, if she would like to go to bed with him, where they could lie together and look out the windows of his apartment as a cold, pure blackness spread its ravenous bulk through every street of Punktown.

As he listened to the Sinanese woman, grinning rigidly and nodding, he nervously fingered an object in the right-hand pocket of his suit jacket. It was his erasing pen, which projected a delicate beam that could burn away dried ink without damaging the paper beneath. He knew its beam was still effective when penetrating glass, because he had experimented with this earlier today at home.

Several times already he had ascended the coiling staircase to stand beside his mounted drawing, to have his picture taken and to explain his approach to various fascinated museum patrons and fellow artists. But now, with a vague excuse, he extricated himself from the Sinanese beauty and started up the stairs on his own, hoping that none of the other attendees intercepted him on his way. His heart shouted at him with every upward step he took, past Narik Guul's drawings numbered 1 . . . 2 . . . 3 . . . 4 . . .

His heart blurted: *"Don't do this now, in front of so many witnesses!"* And with the next step: *"Come back another time, when no one else is in the Nautilus Chamber!"* But his mind retorted: *"It could be too late by then. Too late for those Kalians at the Octoplex. Maybe even too late for Punktown."*

5 . . . 6 . . . 7 . . .

His heart cried: *"Come here in disguise to do it! Then run, and use your money to escape to Miniosis, or the Outback Colony, or even to Earth!"*

His mind said: *"They got Alfreda on Earth."*

8.

He stood before his drawing, and for the first time he gazed on it without pride . . . only poisonous contempt. He felt tricked, exploited. Today he was a cherished fool. His hand closed around the little wand-like device in his pocket, squeezing it like the handle of a knife. Right now he wished it *was* a knife, to slash right through the paper itself. But the museum's new security scan, in the foyer, would have detected such a crude implement. The wand was the tool of an artist, and it was the artist's prerogative to unmake his work.

He started withdrawing his hand from his pocket. His heart throbbed: *"No-no! No-no! No-no! No-no!"*

A hand closed on his right wrist, so gently that at first he thought the Sinanese woman had crept up after him, but when he looked around he saw it was the tall Kalian guard in his sharply cut black suit. In reaching for Maxim's arm, his jacket had opened enough for the artist to see again the gun strapped to the man's ribs. Leaning in close to Maxim's ear, the guard said quietly, "Perhaps you've had too much wine, Mr. Komaroff. Perhaps you should go home and rest."

Maxim met the man's eyes, and after a second or two of paralysis that seemed to last much longer, he finally nodded his head and murmured, "Yes. Yes . . . I was going to do that."

And he turned away from his artwork, titled *The Outsider Triumphant,* brushed past the perplexed Sinanese woman as she was climbing the stairs toward him, and started for the exit from the Nautilus Chamber. He passed Nhil on his way. The Kalian was beaming tonight, as if he were the artist of Drawing No. 8 himself.

He smiled—knowingly, Maxim felt, so knowingly—and said, "Good night, Mr. Komaroff."

Maxim ignored him and wandered out into the museum in a shuffling kind of daze, as if he actually *had* imbibed too much wine tonight. He hadn't, but he planned to when he got back to his apartment. Not wine, though; he had that bottle of expensive whiskey. That was his only plan now. At this moment he could not wrap his mind around a return to the Nautilus Chamber on a quieter day, or in disguise, or any other scenario. There was only that bottle of golden oblivion.

Oblivion. It was life's lone certainty, life's lone destiny. Whether humankind lived for another millennium, another year, another day—and in the vastness of time, those increments were much the same thing—in the end there was no escape from mortality. In the full scope of things, Maxim told himself, it didn't really matter in the end whether a person was a hero or a coward, strong or weak. How could it? What difference could he hope to make, this puny creature wielding his little pen like a child's toy sword against a real dragon?

And yet, he answered himself back, though he didn't know if it was his mind countering his heart or his heart countering his mind, *wasn't it you who gave that dragon the means to rise up, by wielding your little pen?*

He recognized that he was trying to convince himself not to fight—that he *wanted* to be impotent.

Whiskey. He craved it more than forty thousand munits. More than a harem of Sinanese women.

In the museum's underground garage, he fidgeted restlessly while he waited for the mechanical arm to hunt out his vehicle, retrieve it from its slot, and deliver it to him. It was after regular visiting hours, and his reception went on without him, so he was currently the only person in the garage. He glanced around nervously at the shadowy tiers of stacked vehicles. The shadows seemed to throb. He imagined they were rubbery and cold to the touch.

The arm whispered along its track, mindlessly taking its time. Maxim kept glancing toward the elevator he had emerged from, expecting to see its doors open any time now and that soft-spoken guard emerge, holding out a pistol with an internal silencing feature.

His hovercar was set down delicately at his feet, and he hurried to lock himself inside, for the flimsy security the familiar little compartment afforded him. The car levitated a bit above the garage floor, and he pointed its nose toward the exit to the street.

Outside, Punktown loomed both black and bright around him, as if to reassure him with its lurid bravado. The gargantuan city almost convinced him that it was too vile a creature, itself, to allow any other vileness to overtake it. *Almost* convinced him.

He reached his apartment. He reached for his whiskey.

Having lost count of how many times he filled his shot glass, and spilling the last shot when he tried to set the glass down on a window-sill and missed, he tottered to his bed, fell upon it, and plunged imme-diately into sleep. Immediately into dream.

He stood in a spacious room with a polished black floor and a sin-gle circular wall surrounding him, like the inside of a dome, also black and smooth as onyx. From the high concave ceiling, four young girls on the brink of womanhood were hanging upside-down by their an-kles. The cords that bound their ankles were smooth and black as well, more like rubbery tendrils than any kind of rope, and seemed to grow from the ceiling of stone itself. These four girls wore black leotards that left their slender arms and legs exposed, lacy black tulle skirts, and black ballet slippers. Their arms hung down limply, their fingertips just falling short of grazing the black floor. The skin of their limbs was not just pale, but ash gray.

Maxim looked down at himself and saw that in his left hand he held a small empty glass jar. In his right hand he held the utility knife with a cutter beam that he kept in his kitchen cabinet.

Looking up at the nearest of the suspended girls, Maxim said, "I'm sorry . . . I need this."

She wasn't dead yet. Her eyes were open, black as space, and gaz-ing at him passively. She knew this was her fate; she had been raised for it like a veal calf.

He took several steps closer to her, ready with the jar to catch the stream of blood he knew would be black instead of red, and he flicked on the knife's soundless beam. He brought the beam so close to the girl's taut, smooth throat that the red glow was reflected on her skin.

Just before the beam could burn through her delicate flesh, Maxim was awakened by the sensation of two people seizing hold of both his arms and pinning them down to the mattress.

Enough hours had passed while he slept, and enough adrenaline surged through his body, that Maxim snapped awake sober. Glancing right and left, wide-eyed, he saw that it was two Kalian men who had gripped his arms. They didn't wear clothing of metallic gold material. They didn't wear blue head wrappings.

A young woman climbed onto the bed, swinging a leg over him and sitting atop his thighs like a lover. She too was a Kalian. She too was without a blue turban. Her hair was exposed, unthinkably, but chopped short and spiky. She held a knife with a curved single-edged blade, which she put to Maxim's throat. He stopped jerking his head from side to side to look at the two young men.

Leaning over him, her features fierce and contemptuous, the woman said, "You painted magic for them, in the blood of innocents. You opened a door for them—a door our sister died to close. Now they will attack us for revenge, and we will be lucky if we can stop them."

Maxim stared up at her, as if listening to the accusations of a judge before sentencing.

The woman straddling him continued, "If we'd known about you earlier, and what you were going to do for them, we'd have already killed you."

"I wish you had," Maxim whispered.

The woman said nothing for a second, as if absorbing Maxim's words and the look in his eyes. Perhaps in that second she almost reconsidered. But then she pressed the knife's razor-keen blade down against his throat and drew it across. Maxim's blood splashed free and spread quickly across his pillow and sheets like paint upon a blank canvas.

Redemption Express

One of the people who had been sheltering on the grounds of the unfinished construction project was an elderly man—an indigenous Choom like Posy herself—whose name she didn't know. One day he was rummaging through large plastic garbage cans outside a little Thai restaurant, across an alley at the rear of the construction site, when an automated trash zapper came gliding around the corner. Startled, as if afraid he'd get in trouble, the old man had tried to make a dash, but in so doing collided with a trash can, overturning and falling atop it. He and the garbage can were crushed between the bottom of the hovering zapper and the curb. Posy saw his upper body extending from under the trash zapper, rolling beneath it with arms flopping as the machine slowly came to a halt. When at last he was uncovered, he'd been torn in half, leaving a long smear of blood and wilted lettuce on the sidewalk. He was still alive, however, with one arm covering his eyes and his head moving from side to side. Posy stepped from the shadows and ventured toward him, though Aargh and Welder had tried to catch hold of her. She was slippery that way. Once, the wide-brimmed white bride's hat someone had discarded and which she always wore, so big on her ten-year-old head, had been covered in a profusion of synthetic flowers. Now there were only a few left. She plucked one flower from her hat and knelt down to place it in the man's hand. He clenched his fist around it without removing his other arm from his eyes, holding onto the flower as if she had tossed him a lifeline. His head stopped moving from side to side a few minutes later. Posy stood over him until, almost an hour later, a vehicle finally came to take the old man's remains away, like so much trash himself.

*

Posy didn't know what this building's purpose was to have been before its construction was halted, or even why construction had never been completed. She had heard conflicting explanations, probably just theories, from others who sheltered here. An office block for a company that had run out of funds with the latest dip in the economy. An apartment complex that had been found to be in violation of health codes. A syndy casino that the authorities had shut down for lack of sufficient bribes.

Four levels, including the ground floor, had been sketched out in lines of girder and beam. Would there have been more levels later? There was a basement, too, but members of an Asian gang called the Snakeheads had claimed that. Posy had never seen it, though once she had almost been brought down there against her will. Anyway, she knew the rest of the skeletal building well. Some sections of the floors on the upper levels were more or less finished. There were even portions of wall, seemingly laid in arbitrarily. Mostly the walls were open, though sometimes great sheets of clear plastic or blue tarps had been stretched taut or draped loosely to shield against the elements. There were some roughed-in staircases. Work lights were strung throughout, here and there, tied into thick bundles of cables laid onto ceiling supports that looked like ladders or inverted train tracks. Fat silvery ducting hoses snaked in and out of the exposed ceiling beams like maggots fattened on the great carcass. Graffiti abounded. Graffiti seemed to bind the whole house of cards together. One squatter, a soft-spoken middle-aged addict, remarking on the seeming chaos of it all, had told Posy, "I think it wasn't supposed to be a building. It's an artwork. And it isn't unfinished. This is the way the artist wanted it."

Posy had only listened and digested the possibility, but drew no conclusions of her own. Whatever it *had been* meant to be, this place *was,* very simply, her home. Just as whatever life she *might have had* was irrelevant to her. It was beyond her imagining, or at least her desire to imagine. There was only *this* life. That way of thinking, she'd found in the two long years she had lived on her own, was the only way to stay alive.

*

"Can you give me a munit to ride the shunt?" Posy asked one woman walking along the sidewalk in front of the construction site. "I missed my school bus." But the woman kept her eyes forward, her businesswoman's high heels clicking sharply as if to drown out Posy's voice. Posy quickly turned the other way, looked up at a muscular young man as he came striding along. At least he took a moment to glance down at her, but he also took a moment to spit in her face. His phlegm ran down her forehead, and a drop fell on her lips. She brushed it away with her sleeve, biting back the urge to shout a curse after the man. She wished Aargh was with her just then, instead of foraging for food elsewhere on the site's periphery, but then again she was glad he wasn't. She wouldn't want him arrested for dismembering somebody in plain view.

When she had only been sheltering on the site for a few days, almost two years ago now, three of the Snakehead gang had approached her, had begun talking in a friendly way, and offered to take her to the basement where it was warmer and there was food. But another squatter had already warned her that the gang sold runaway young girls and foggy-headed junkies to low-level street pimps. Posy had not said a word to the chatty trio, had tried to turn and walk away. That was when they made a grab for her.

And a second later, one of the youths was yanked backwards as if he had been snatched out of existence. With two boys holding her, Posy had looked over her shoulder to see Aargh there (though of course he didn't have that name back then), looming behind her, hugging the Snakehead to his chest. The boy's spiky-haired head was turned completely backwards. One of the pair holding Posy let go of her to pull out a little pistol, but the seven-foot KeeZee was already there and grabbing onto his arm with one hand (the crack of bone still echoed in Posy's mind to this day), punching him in the face with the other hand. The boy's face was pushed in like a doll Posy had once owned that a neighbor kid had stomped with his heel. The third Snakehead boy managed to run off, to hide away in that cozy basement kingdom of his.

The Snakeheads had never bothered her since, even when the KeeZee hadn't been at her side. Anyway, that was how they'd met, she and Aargh, and more often than not he'd been by her side ever since.

As she'd turned to glare at the receding figure of the man who'd spit on her, Posy noticed something she had somehow missed before. With her familiarity of the grounds, she was surprised it hadn't jumped out at her. Maybe she'd seen it peripherally but mistaken it for a bill-board announcing some product or movie.

Affixed to the fence that separated the construction site from the sidewalk was a huge sign that showed a building or series of conjoined buildings in a kind of whimsical fantasyscape. It was the uniform pink color of the building(s) that lent that fantastical air. Above this mystical vista, this mirage, loomed the words COMING SOON. Just under that, in a different font: *Funtown*. At first she had thought it said Punk-town. That was what they called this megalopolis that soared up all around her, built by Earth colonists upon the much humbler city of her own native ancestors. But no . . . the sign said *Funtown*.

"Huh," said Posy. "Funtown." Even though she had no conception of the sign's significance, she said the word with a suspicious tone, as if it were some kind of bitter medicine in the thinnest of candy shells.

*

They regrouped at noon. Posy had made three munits begging for change to ride the shunt line, and Aargh had rounded up a fair amount of recyclable beer and soda cans with a deposit refund. There was a grimy little supermarket nearby with an automated system for deposit-ing these and collecting the refund. The separate chamber in which one did this was titled REDEMPTION CENTER.

In the market they bought a few snacks with the money they made and ate them on the walk home to the site. As they neared it, Posy re-membered the new sign she had seen that morning and took Aargh by the hand to show him. She ignored the looks thrown their way, the lit-tle girl with the ear-to-ear Choom smile hand-in-hand with the seven-foot-tall KeeZee, all dressed in black as KeeZee usually were, his strangely flattened head like a pipe wrench thinly covered in translu-cent gray skin, into which were set three small eyes like black pearls, and his hair in dreadlocks that Posy had braided for him. He walked with a strong limp, because he had one prosthetic leg, and by prosthet-ic leg that meant he had fashioned it himself from a length of black metal pipe. KeeZee often found jobs as bouncers, guards, strong-arms, but Posy was sure his missing limb, and maybe some defeat or disgrace that went along with it, was the reason why he had taken to living on the construction site. She couldn't ask him because his kind couldn't articulate human language. That was why, for lack of knowing his true name, she had given him the name Aargh.

"See?" she said, pointing toward the new sign affixed to the outside of the surrounding security fence. "Funtown. Just like I said." She added, "Coming soon."

She looked way up at him and he wagged his head, but whether that meant he didn't comprehend or didn't like what he comprehended, she couldn't know.

*

Evening fell, and they retired to the spot they had claimed as their own: a far corner on the second floor, where there was a cement floor upon which they could unroll their sleeping bags. Aargh had surprised her with the padded sleeping bags about a year ago; he couldn't tell her if he'd saved up for them or stolen them from a store or even from other squatters. Aargh had made walls for their little corner, using sheets of corrugated metal tied in place with metal wire.

After Aargh had erected these walls, through pantomime he had demonstrated what she took to be a safety measure, a means of quick escape from a dangerous gang or a snipe on the hunt if the need arose. He showed her that if they used his pair of cutters to snip the wire where it held the upper portion of the rear metal sheet in place, it could be pushed outward, where it would bang onto the edge of a tall concrete wall that reared close to this flank of the unfinished building. Instant bridge. The neighboring wall was actually the base of a shunt platform, though no shunt had ever stopped there for passengers. Perhaps one would have, if the construction project had been completed; a service stop for the building's tenants, workers, or shoppers, depending on what its purpose was to have been.

But shunts did frequently shoot past in either direction on the two cables strung above that platform, occasionally raining a drizzle of bright sparks in their wake, which fizzled out as they struck the top of that close wall. Sometimes a spark even struck the floor near their feet. A passing shunt would send a wave of air washing down over them. Once a wave of warm air had flashed a memory into Posy's mind— riding in a hovercar with her father, the passenger window down and summer air blowing in across her face—but that memory was quickly gone like the fleeting shunt, either because the memory was too untenable to hold on to or too painful. A firefly memory, like the spilling sparks that dazzled and faded.

There was one shunt that stopped nearby, however, one evening every week, and here it came now like clockwork. As Aargh and Posy sat on the edge of the cement floor, dangling their legs over the side of the building and finishing the last of the day's hard-earned sustenance, they saw the shunt shoot right past their shelter—vibrating the metal sheets a bit—but gradually slow to a stop over the roof of the supermarket they had visited earlier today. A panel in the market's roof slid back, and a ribbed tube extended from the bottom of the shunt like an insect's proboscis dipping into a flower. The fat tube squirmed and rattled as it sucked up the cans crushed in the automated refund machines of the market's redemption center. The shunt must make similar stops all over Punktown, because the words in red on its silver flank were: *Redemption Express.*

Once, Posy had asked their old friend Welder, "What does 're-demption' mean?"

Welder had thought for a moment, and then replied, "Repurchasing ... redeeming ... atonement. Deliverance, rescue, salvation." Welder was a robot.

"Rescue," Posy echoed. "Salvation." She had looked wistfully toward the same shunt line they sat watching now, and had said to Welder, "Someday I'm going to run down the platform when I know that shunt is coming soon, and wait until it stops to suck up those cans. Then I'm going to climb up on its back and ride right on out of here."

"Ride where?" Welder asked her.

"To where you said. Deliverance."

"You will only ride to the next supermarket or liquor store where that car collects its load," Welder had said.

"You're such a killjoy," she'd told him sulkily—and he could be—but how she missed him.

She and Aargh watched the *Redemption Express* glide back into movement along its elevated cable. It sprinkled a phosphorescent spray behind it. "See you next week," Posy muttered.

She held a last bit of spongy cream-filled cake in her hand. She knew Aargh wouldn't be happy about it, would prefer she eat the cake herself, but before she turned in for the night she'd want to set the cake out for the snipe.

*

Aargh came with her, of course, because he wouldn't let her out of his sight at night, but he knew better by now than to try to hold her back. So he followed her downstairs, to an area toward the rear of the ground floor where heaps of trash had accumulated, discarded by tenants and blown in by the winds. Piles of busted garbage bags, mattresses too vile for even the most desperate junkie. Here, atop an altar of moldering wooden shipping pallets, Posy set down the piece of cake.

She and Aargh withdrew to a safe distance to watch. Posy was always afraid someone else would steal the food. She had seen a shambling, badly deformed mutant do that once, and Aargh had started forward to dissuade him, but she had stopped her friend.

A few minutes later it slunk out of the darkness: a single snipe. They often hunted in packs, but this one was missing an eye and moved with a limp like Aargh himself. An old, wounded rogue. Damaged and on its own—just like them. It was a pale ghostly blue, so skeletal its skin was an afterthought; something between a greyhound and a demon. As they watched, it rose onto its hind legs so it could pluck up the cake and stuff it between its fanged jaws. As it chewed, it turned its head and looked directly back at them with its remaining eye. Then it swallowed, dropped back to four legs, and silently plunged back into the dark.

"You're welcome," Posy whispered, smiling but shuddering at the same time.

*

She always remembered Welder advising her not to put food out for the snipe, the first time he'd seen her doing it. "They're wild things . . . scary things," he had warned. "You can't tame this creature."

"I'm not trying to tame it," she'd told him. "But it's like us. It's got nowhere else. Anyway, if we feed it, maybe it won't try to eat anybody."

"Dubious logic," Welder replied. "They follow their nature. Their nature is to kill."

Posy had bugged her eyes under the brim of her floppy hat, made claws of her dirty hands, and said, "I hear they like to eat rusty old robots best of all . . . arooooo!"

She had nicknamed Welder, too. He was a blocky automaton of peeling bright yellow paint, whose creators had given no thought to making him look anthropomorphic. When she first met him—when he had wandered onto the grounds to escape a dense blizzard—and found the machine could talk, she asked him if he were one of robots that had been displaced during the violent worker riots of the Union War and gone underground. No, Welder explained, he hadn't existed back then; he had been slated for junk when the factory where he'd been working as a welding automaton had shut down. Posy had then told Welder about her father, who had lost his job when *his* company closed up. Her father had later left her and her mother to fend for themselves. She even told Welder how she and her mother, who was a drug addict, ended up homeless, living on the streets. On a snowy night just like this they had sheltered on the floor of a warm ATM booth. But when pretty pink dawn had come, sparkling drifts sloping up against the sides of the ATM kiosk, Posy had found her mother slumped dead beside her.

"I'm sorry," Welder had said. He had sounded sincere about it, too. So Posy had liked him right away.

He became the third member of their little group. She loved Aargh, but their conversations were one-sided. Aargh didn't seem perturbed by Welder's inclusion, or worried for Posy's safety around him, as the robot could take no undue interest in her. They were a family of three. They were as much a family as Posy had ever known.

But after only a few months, Welder's power source had run down without warning one night when they were rushing across a section of the building where there was no finished floor above them, just bare girders against a sudden onslaught of rain. Posy had seen that Welder was no longer hovering along beside her and the loping Aargh. She had looked back to see him resting on his base in a growing puddle. When she called to him he didn't come, and she and Aargh had no idea how to reactivate him no matter how soaked they became peering inside those service panels of his they could open. He stood in the same spot in the brightness of the following day.

Posy didn't want gang kids breaking him up for fun or spraying graffiti on him, so she directed Aargh to lift him up and lug him to a dark corner of the grounds—not far from where she fed the snipe—where there squatted a large, inactive trash zapper. They secreted him in the narrow space between the back of the zapper and the wall, lying on his back. Posy tugged a flower free from her bridal hat and placed it in one of his claw hands. "You just rest here for a while, Welder," Posy had croaked, throat raw from crying. "We'll get you a new power cell someday, okay? We'll do our best. And then we'll come back here for you."

*

Posy watched Aargh through the whole operation as he dragged down a loop of insulated cable from a bundle overhead, using a board with a nail at the end to hook it. Then, using his wire cutters, he chewed away the rubbery insulation to expose the copper veins within. "Are you sure that's safe?" Posy asked, but of course he didn't answer. Still, she commented, "Don't take too much of that or we won't have lights around here anymore."

Aargh was wrenching out more and more of the copper wire, wrapping it around his hand, when a voice behind them called, "Hello there!" Posy spun around, startled. Aargh's movements were slower, but she knew he would be ready for trouble.

Three people were walking toward them, distinctly odd figures Posy knew she'd never seen on the construction site before, though it was a variegated bunch that was dispersed throughout the building and the squatters came and went. Aargh quickly snipped free the ends of the wire coiled around his hand, his fist now doubly huge and metallic. He put his other hand on Posy's shoulder, urging her to get moving. Perhaps noticing this, from a distance the central approaching figure raised an arm and called, "Don't be afraid! Hold up, there!"

Posy was tensed to bolt like a startled antelope. She *wanted* to . . . but still she held off, curious.

"We don't mean you any harm," the man said as he drew closer. His cheery voice echoed off the cement ceiling. "We have gifts for you! We bring good news!"

The trio was near enough now that Posy could see that the man who had spoken wore an expensive business suit. Flanking him, though, were two fully armored soldiers carrying big two-handed guns. She was sorry now she hadn't fled. Were they forcers? But how could they be? The police force always wore black.

The two soldiers wore full-head helmets and body armor, all of it colored a light pink. Even the bulky guns they carried, which Posy didn't know were called assault engines, were the same hue. She thought their pink armor was very peculiar. Were there women inside? Their padded bodies didn't look female. She thought the color made them look less convincing than even toy soldiers.

The man in the suit had sandy hair, greased back but with a few strands drooping across his forehead, and a goatee sprinkled with crumbs of silver. His forehead was filmed in sweat; he looked hot in his five-piece suit, having loosened his shirt collar. The entire suit, except for the white shirt, was a pale candy pink, the same pink as the toy soldiers. Maybe they weren't women after all. When he spoke, the man in the suit had an accent like the boss bad guys in old VT movies Posy had seen. She didn't know the word "British."

"I've been talking with all you folks on the site today," the man said, still closing the space between them, "and you two appear to be the last!" When Aargh felt the trio had gotten close enough, he took a threatening step forward, metal fist bunched at his side. The newcomers stopped in their tracks. The man in the suit held up both hands and said, "Slow down, big fella. I'm your new best friend, trust me."

"He doesn't speak or understand English," Posy spoke up, her tone wary. "He doesn't have a translator chip or anything. I call him Aargh."

"Well, that's funny; 'aargh' is what I thought when I saw him." The stranger chuckled. "Just kidding. And what's your name, my lovely?"

"I'm called Posy."

"Oh, how fitting. Allow me to introduce myself. I'm Teddy Cannula—chief of security for an exciting new project I'm introducing to all of you on the site today."

"Who are they?" Posy interrupted, motioned toward the flanking soldiers.

"Two of my security team, dear, nothing to be alarmed about. As I was saying, there's a wonderful, fabulous new place coming soon to this very site—a place called Funtown. It's going to be a mall, but the word *mall* doesn't do it justice. You're too young to know what the

Canberra Mall was like back when it was the Canberra *Circus* Mall . . . how fun it was before it became all boring stores like any other shopping center. But Funtown is going to bring back the fun! It's going to be the bestest mall in the whole of Punktown!"

"You mean, they're going to finish this building?"

"Oh no, no. This building itself isn't big enough to house Funtown. They're going to tear down most of this whole block. Funtown's going to be *huge!*"

"The supermarket over there and everything?"

"Huh? Oh, that old supermarket, yes. But there'll be a new supermarket *within* Funtown. And so much more! Therefore, demolition of this old eyesore here is going to commence shortly, my pet—next week, in fact—so I'm afraid everybody who's been staying and playing in here is going to have to move it along very soon."

"Very soon?" she echoed, trying to absorb all this.

"Yes. But the Funtown bunch are concerned for your welfare, believe me, so they're going to help you all with the transition. See here." From a shopping bag he'd been carrying—with the same image of a fanciful pink city on it that Posy had seen on the sign affixed to the security fence—Cannula withdrew two folders with glossy pink covers and extended them to Posy. "For you and your friend, here. These booklets contain a whole slew of great vouchers for free food and clothing from a bunch of markets throughout the city. Plus—see inside, there."

Posy opened her folder. She had tried to hand Aargh his own folder, but he wouldn't touch it. From inside, she pulled out a white card with raised pink ink.

"That there," Cannula said magnanimously, "is an invitation for you to stay at any number of a dozen participating homeless shelters in the city, the city's *top* homeless shelters, for a whole month, all the associated expenses funded by the Funtown bunch. Until you folks can get your feet under you. They have programs to help you look for work, see, and find a permanent place to stay . . . so you don't have to live a sorry life like this anymore, Posy. Stealing," and here he nodded at Aargh's glinting fist, "to survive."

"But . . ." Posy began. She couldn't articulate her protest. After all, she didn't *want* to live in this shell of a building forever—did she? So she could only say again, "But . . ."

"Let me show you something, my little posy," Cannula purred, crouching down beside her now and pulling aside the flap of his pink jacket. A gun holster was strapped to his side, and he slipped out a pistol, holding it on the flat of his upturned palm.

Aargh raised his coppery fist above his head, like a hammer.

"*Whoa!* Tell your friend easy . . . easy," Cannula said, raising his free hand. "I only want to show you how beautiful a thing this is."

It *was* a beautiful thing, Posy had to admit. Oddly, though its outlines appeared modern, the gun was made almost entirely of wood, with only bits of trim in what appeared to be gold. The wood was a deep red, with swirls and whorls under its thick glossy finish.

"I take pride in the beautiful things I own," Cannula cooed, like a father giving her an important life lesson, "because I worked hard for them. *I earned* them. Wouldn't you like to have a whole bunch of nice things of your very own someday? Well, you never will unless you take the first bold steps to turn your life around, dear. And that's what Funtown is offering you. You can't put a price on that, can you?" He shifted the gun on his palm, so that light played across its varnish and gold hypnotically. "Things like this, and so many other beautiful things, will fill the shelves of Funtown, Posy. Thousands and thousands of beautiful things."

"A person needs money to buy beautiful things," Posy noted sourly.

"Ha! Of course they do! But Funtown is going to give jobs to tons of people—you see?" Cannula tucked his handgun away again, apparently content with whatever point he had intended to make. He rose to a standing position.

In a bold voice, still sounding dubious, Posy said, "Maybe we'll think about it . . . if you bring us some burgers."

Cannula stared down at her for several seconds, as if he simply couldn't translate her words. Then a grin cracked his face and he barked a laugh. "She wants burgers," he said to the security trooper on his right. "Gerry, go fetch the princess and her friendly ogre some burgers."

"You want me to go alone?" the man named Gerry said via his helmet mic.

"Precisely, yes, I want you to go alone. Go get her some burgers right *now.*"

"Will you be waiting here for me?" Gerry asked, with an unmistakable touch of nervousness.

Cannula turned to face the man directly, his eyes gone wide. "No, I will not be *waiting* here for you. Lon and I are going back to the car. These two will be waiting here for you to return." He grinned down at Posy again. She saw a twitch in one corner of his grin. "Won't you, my little beauty? But I suggest you do more than 'think about' my offer. It's a one-time offer. One time means there won't be a second time."

Cannula started to turn away but gave Posy another look, and on a whim stepped nearer to her and snapped free one of the last remaining synthetic flowers on her hat. He tucked it into the buttonhole of his breast pocket like a groom's boutonnière. "Adieu, princess," he said with an exaggerated, sweeping bow.

*

Gerry came back within the half hour—rushing, perhaps, in the hope of still rejoining Cannula and the other trooper—and gave Posy a bag of BurgerZone burgers (one for her and three for Aargh), cups of soda, and bags of fried dilkies. Posy wondered if he'd been wearing his helmet and even carrying his gun when he ordered the food.

When he'd trotted away, Posy held her hand out, wiggling her fingers, for one of Aargh's three burgers.

That night, huddled within their corner shelter, burning some flammable oil in a metal can for a measure of heat and light, Posy fretted aloud to Aargh, "What if the homeless shelter we go to tries to send me to some kind of foster home? Or a school? Someplace you and me can't be together?" She wagged her head. "Where will the snipe go if they tear this place down? If they see it, they'll kill it. And what about Welder? When they find him behind the zapper, they'll scrap him." She looked up from the flames at Aargh, and he seemed to be listening to her thoughtfully with the firelight flickering in his three black pearl eyes. She was sure he understood her sentiments, if not her words. She told him, "This is my *home*."

Before they turned in for the night, they ventured back down to the ground floor, and Posy placed the burger she had taken from Aargh on the stack of wooden pallets for the snipe.

*

Over the following days, it was easy to fall into denial about the changes the man named Cannula had described to Posy. Nothing seemed changed; every day unfolded the same as ever. Maybe he had been lying, to frighten them all off the property. Maybe these vouchers and the invitation to a homeless shelter weren't worth the paper they were printed on. She hadn't tried redeeming any of the vouchers herself yet, and Aargh still hadn't wanted to touch his folder. So, paralyzed by uncertainty and disbelief—and the naturally helpless state of being a child—Posy did nothing but go along with her usual routine. If it really came time for change, then fate would push her where it would . . . as it always had.

Today they brought bags of cans with deposits to the redemption center at the grubby little supermarket, and now Posy was nostalgic in advance, thinking how Cannula had said the poor old market would be torn down, too. Was it true? If so, the *Redemption Express* would never stop here again. Thinking of the shunt car bearing that name made Posy count off days in her mind, and she knew it would be making its collection this very evening. As she always did when thinking of the shunt, she recalled her dream of scampering onto the top of the cable car and riding it to some brighter destination. Was she to be denied even the comfort of that fantasy?

When they returned from their excursion to the supermarket, they were met by a trio of mutants on their way out into the sunshine from the murk of the incomplete building. The mutants carried bed rolls and plastic bags of their meager belongings. One mutant with growths like the squirming tails of huge larvae growing out of his forehead and cheeks, whom Posy knew as Nester, said, "Good luck to you, child. We're heading out now. That man Cannula came around again and said today is our last chance to leave. He said something about turning over the rock now, so all the bugs underneath will have to run away."

"Where are you going?"

"To a shelter on Forma Street. It's one of the places on the invitation."

"Do you know if anyone else is leaving, too?" Posy glanced over Nester's shoulder, into the cavernous interior of the construction site.

"Some have, some haven't. But—"

Nester's words were cut off, as from deeper within the building came the clatter of automatic gunfire. At the sound, Nester and his two companions scurried away toward the street. Posy and Aargh, however, turned toward the sound. They looked to each other . . . and then moved stealthily into the gloomy depths of the construction site, to investigate.

From behind a riveted metal support column the two of them peeked toward a number of idling vehicles that had obviously driven onto the site in their absence. Two of them, bright yellow in color as Welder must have once been—and maybe they were even robots themselves—were plainly construction vehicles, with the formidable hulking shapes of demolition machines. A third vehicle, painted red, was apparently a mobile trash zapper. The trash zapper was close to one of the entrances to the basement, where the gang called the Snakeheads made their home.

Posy flinched at another burst of gunfire. It was strangely muffled. *Underground,* she realized.

Several moments later, two men in pink armor emerged from the basement, their assault engines slung over their backs, carrying something in a black plastic bag. They brought it to the lip of the trash zapper's open maw and together swung it inside. Then they returned to the basement. Shortly thereafter, they reappeared carrying a second zippered black bag.

Posy and Aargh watched the pink troopers toss six of these bags into the back of the trash zapper, before they withdrew into the shadows which were all they clung to now . . . had ever really clung to.

*

Aargh took Posy's hand and with long strides dragged her to another spot on the ground floor: the inoperative trash zapper behind which they had stashed Welder. Posy felt a pang when she saw the flower still clutched in his insect-like hand. Standing near his hover base, she watched confused as Aargh awkwardly wedged himself between the zapper and the wall, hunkered over Welder, took hold of his head, and strained with all his strength.

"What are you doing to him?" Posy whined, feeling more overwhelmed than ever by this seeming act of violence against their absent comrade, but then she understood. "We're going, aren't we? And we're taking his head. His brain." Suddenly, her forlornness turned to a kind of excitement. Dare she even call it hope? They were going *onwards*, and right now *where* didn't matter. Yes, they would lose this home . . . but she had lost homes before. Home could be a warm ATM booth in a winter storm. You carried home with you.

Aargh twisted this way and that, loosened the head from its socket, then used his trusty clippers to disconnect some bright veins of colored cables. Then, with the head under his arm like a ball, he rose up and stepped out from the cramped space behind the zapper.

"Ah!" Posy heard a voice with a familiar accent exclaim, though from her point of view at the other end of the zapper she couldn't see the speaker. "The scavenging ogre. Drop what you have there, ugly, and move along. You won't be stealing from this site anymore."

Posy peeked around the corner of the graffiti-smeared zapper to see three pink-armored security troopers and the pink-suited security chief who had introduced himself to her last week as Teddy Cannula. She saw that one of the troopers was moving in toward Aargh, whom they had backed against the side of the zapper, holding out his hand and commanding over his helmet mic, "You heard the man: let's have whatever it is you've got there."

Posy wanted to cry out then, to either the troopers or to Aargh, to stop, *stop*, because she knew Aargh, but it was too late, he was already in motion.

He swung Welder's head in a wide fast arc against the trooper's pink helmet, with such force that Welder's head dented and the security man's helmet split down the side. As the man fell away, unconscious, Aargh dropped Welder's head, turned toward the next trooper, stepped in, and took hold of him. He lifted the soldier off his feet, spun around, and slammed him against the flank of the zapper. When he let go of the trooper, he had finished by twisting the man's helmet around to face backwards, much more easily than he had wrenched Welder's head off.

But by this time the third trooper had leveled his assault engine, and Cannula had pulled his beautiful pistol of glossy red wood and gold trim from its holster, and when Aargh had released the dead trooper they both opened fire. Aargh rushed toward them silently, big as a toppling tree, even as automatic gunfire opened a strip of holes across his chest.

Cannula was batted aside, thudding onto his back with the wind slammed out of him. Aargh slapped the soldier's big gun aside, got his hands on the man's helmet, and tore it off. Posy had begun screaming when ragged exit holes appeared in Aargh's back, but now she was screaming at what Aargh was doing with both hands to the trooper's face.

Aargh let this man drop, too, and turned toward Posy with jerky movements. He reached into a pocket of his black clothing, pulled something out, and extended it to her in a hand gloved in blood. It was his pair of clippers.

Looking up into his three unblinking eyes, Posy took the clippers with understanding and sobbed, "I love you."

Aargh fell to one knee, his only knee. And when Posy saw Teddy Cannula getting back to his feet, she darted to Welder's head and gathered it up in both arms, cradling it to her chest. It was heavy with all the thoughts and memories she hoped still waited inside to be restored. She saw Cannula kick Aargh's metal leg out from under him, saw Aargh fall onto his chest, and as she ducked behind the trash zapper again she heard three thundering shots that reverberated off the partial walls and ceilings of the unfinished building, like a furious ghost roaring away into an endless labyrinth.

She crouched low to the ground, weeping soundlessly, still hugging Welder against her chest. His headless body lay at her feet, an empty suit of armor without a knight to occupy it.

That familiar voice came to her from the other side of the zapper. "All right, then . . . where did you go? Hm?" Cannula's voice drew nearer. "I can smell you, my little unwashed beauty. You smell like the whore you'll grow up to be. If you aren't one already." Now here he was, moving into view at one end of the slim channel between the zapper and the wall. He hunched down low, on her level, like a gentle father appealing to a distraught daughter. He was grinning, but his grin twitched at one corner. She saw that he still wore the flower he had stolen from her hat in the buttonhole of his breast pocket. "Don't be afraid, Posy." He held out one hand, wiggling his fingers, though in his other hand he still gripped his expensive pistol.

"Remember I told you? I'm your new best friend."

Posy whimpered, inching backwards.

"Come *on*," Cannula sang, like a lullaby, reaching his arm out further. Blood oozed from a gash at his hairline. "Come on, you little bitch."

And then Cannula was jerked backwards, jerked mostly out of view again. Only his legs showed around the edge of the trash zapper, and they kicked madly. There was a chaotic flurry of movement just out of sight—luckily out of sight—but Posy could hear the terrible snarling and the terrible gurgling.

She turned toward the other end of the zapper and lunged out from behind it. She started running toward the nearest set of steps that would take her up to her shelter on the second floor. But she paused briefly to glance back at Cannula, and saw that his legs barely stirred now.

The snipe raised its head, jaws drooling blood, and regarded her with its single remaining eye for a moment before it lowered its head again and resumed feeding.

*

After setting Welder's head down on her unfurled sleeping bag, Posy climbed the studded rivets in a vertical girder to reach high enough to clip the wire that secured the top of one of the corrugated metal panels Aargh had installed to shield them. Hinged by more wire at its bottom, the sheet fell away from her when Posy pushed at it. Its top clanged against the edge of the concrete wall facing this side of the building. Instant bridge.

Posy rolled her child's sleeping bag up again, with Welder's head secured inside it. She pocketed Aargh's clippers. Then, after hoisting the sleeping bag onto her back with a grunt, she crossed the warbling, bowing metal sheet to the shunt platform and emerged squinting into the blaze of the golden sun as it lowered behind the silhouetted skyline of Punktown.

Posy started down the platform, already seeing in the distance the roof of the dirty and doomed little supermarket, where she would stand and wait for the imminent arrival and departure of the *Redemption Express*.

Story Notes

I thought I'd briefly discuss the stories in this collection, to give them a little context, or perhaps to enhance the reader's experience with them after the fact.

Carrion

I recognize that there is a lot of similarity between the stories "Carrion" and "The Left-Hand Pool." These two stories were written shortly after I had moved to a new town, after having lived all but a fraction of my life in another Massachusetts town, which was less rural. Though I welcomed the change, change of any type can be disorienting, throw us off center, and that seems to be reflected in these stories as I analyze them myself. And I say analyze them myself, because—while much of what I write is plotted in my mind or in notes before I set out, carefully weighed and considered—there is usually a large component to my writing that comes freely from the subconscious, often surprising me, and leaving my work open to interpretation even by myself.

These two stories also address alienation—as do others in the collection, centering on characters who are divorced or fear losing their loved ones, or who have never known love at all. I wouldn't want to reveal overmuch about my personal life here, except to say these are feelings I've known myself, as have too many of us.

I feel stories should be about *transition* of some kind. The transition can be toward growth or decline. A static story is not a story. The transitions in some of the stories in this book mirror aspects of my own life, chiefly from the recent period in which they were written, when I was experiencing a sense of diminishment, which included an increased awareness of aging. Even the fact that a number of these stories focus on driving somewhere in a car, or fleeing in a car, or being forced to halt a car at a toll station, surely must relate to my having obtained a driver's license and purchased my first car only a few years ago. (Till then, I had been too intimidated to drive, owing partly to the blindness of my left eye.) I should point out that now I love to drive; I cherish the freedom of it after years of dependence on others and severely limited horizons. This sense of moving myself to new/other places, literally and figuratively, I see unconsciously and repeatedly translated into this body of work.

Getting back to the similarities between "Carrion" and "The Left-Hand Pool" . . . well, I'm a writer who likes to revisit a concept or location or what have you if there is something different to extract from it. As I like to say, Monet didn't only create one image of water lilies; he produced 250 paintings of them, over a thirty-year period. Water lilies and the pools they float upon can present different effects in varying light, and from varying angles. No one artwork can capture their entire essence.

And now that I've given a rough overview of the collection, and whatever general tone or unpremeditated themes might loosely unite it, I'll continue with the other stories.

Spider Gates

My son Colin—twenty-four years old as I write this—is autistic, and several events from his own life contributed to my inspirations for this story. Odd events, which seem to suggest that on at least a few occasions he has seen beyond the barriers . . . and not just in the sense of fantasizing play. But I'll let you decide how to interpret these occurrences.

When Colin was about fourteen, we were walking into town together—perhaps on a library excursion—and for some reason I had the song "This Is Halloween" from the movie *The Nightmare Before Christmas* running through my head, but I hadn't sung it aloud. Nevertheless, Colin suddenly turned to me, exasperated, and said, "It isn't Halloween!"

On another occasion around that same time, while waiting for the special needs van to drop Colin off from school, I sat at my computer looking at a rather alluring photo of my future wife, Hong. Hearing

Colin at the front door, I minimized the window before he could see the image. He entered the house, came into the room with me, and exclaimed, "Put some clothes on, you crazy bitch!"

I laughed in shock at his words, but at the same time I marveled and asked him, "Colin, who are you talking about?"

"Hong!" he said.

There was no way that he might have seen the photo on my monitor.

My father passed away in 1999 when Colin was only seven. A year later, on the very day my dad had died, I sat at my computer with Colin standing at my side. At no time had I mentioned that this was the anniversary of his grandfather's death, nor had I mentioned it to anyone else in his presence. Suddenly Colin looked past me into a darkened bedroom close beside us and exclaimed in a tone of surprise and recognition, "Grampa!"

I snapped around to look into the darkened bedroom myself—but I saw no one there.

Feeding Oblivion

This story was very much inspired by my mother, who was alive at its writing but passed away in a nursing home before the book in its entirety was completed.

Mr. Faun

In 2013, a painting by Barnett Newman sold for $44,000,000. It's a large blue canvas with a white stripe down its center. Ah, but such a white stripe!

I'll let this observation serve to explain the kind of thing that was on my mind, and that I sought to express, when I wrote "Mr. Faun."

A lot of modern horror fiction revolves around dissolving marriages, disharmonious relationships, dysfunctional families. I'm not excluding my own work here. It can get to feel like a trope. In this story, however, I wanted to portray a good relationship between the protagonist and her husband.

The Left-Hand Pool

See my discussion of "Carrion," above.

The specific jumping point for this story, though, was a divided body of water just as I describe it in the story—presenting two very different moods—that I still pass every day on my way to and from my day job. No monsters sighted yet, however, to alleviate that monotonous drive.

riaH gnoL

Like "The Green Hands," "riaH gnoL" found its initial inspiration in a painting by artist Kim Bo Yung, this one created with my fiction in mind. (There's a nice Ouroboros for you.) I decided to approach that image, of a two-headed woman with three breasts, metaphorically. Another inspiration came from a conversation I had with a young woman who told me she was attending bartending school, and that she is schizophrenic. I was moved when she thanked me and shook my hand for having talked with her. I feel a little bad about using her in some small way in my story, but then people talk to a writer at their own peril.

The Toll

My favorite television program of all time, I'd say—beating out even the original *Star Trek* and *Twin Peaks*—is the original black and white *Outer Limits*, which was no doubt influential in the blending of horror and science fiction in much of my body of work. I approached "The Toll" as if I were scripting a story for that chilling, atmospheric, and thought-provoking* series.

(*Oh, and such monsters it had!)

Saigon Dep Lam

As of this writing I've been to Vietnam nine times. (My ex-wife Hong is Vietnamese, and we have a daughter, who at the age of seven has already visited Vietnam four times herself.) Most of the damaged people who assemble at the end of this story, the man of mixed race included, are based on real people I've observed, primarily in the city of Bien Hoa. When I saw him, I wondered what that angry-looking man's story was, just as Lan does.